By J.L. O'Faolain

THE SECTION 13 CASE FILES
The Thirteenth Child
The Thirteenth Pillar
The Thirteenth Sigil
The Thirteenth Shard

NO MORE HEROES
Push Comes to Shove
Scratch & Sniff

Published by DREAMSPINNER PRESS
http://www.dreamspinnerpress.com

The Thirteenth Shard

J.L. O'Faolain

SECTION Case Files

Dreamspinner Press

Published by
Dreamspinner Press
5032 Capital Circle SW
Ste 2, PMB# 279
Tallahassee, FL 32305-7886
USA
http://www.dreamspinnerpress.com/

The Thirteenth Shard
Copyright © 2013 by J.L. O'Faolain

Cover Art by Paul Richmond
http://www.paulrichmondstudio.com

Cover content is being used for illustrative purposes only
and any person depicted on the cover is a model.

ISBN: 978-1-62380-633-0
Digital ISBN: 978-1-62380-634-7

Printed in the United States of America
First Edition
June 2013

To Curt.
Thank you, Lover. For everything.

RAIN.

The snowstorms which had blanketed New York, along with half the country, were finally gone. Ordinarily, Cole wasn't one to complain about the weather. The snow and cold reminded him of his father's kingdom, and while that salty old wound tended to act up whenever flakes dusted the dirty streets, he nevertheless found it oddly comforting. No matter how much time Cole spent in the mortal plane, his heart considered Faerie home. It was ironic considering what all had happened to him there, including the loss of his ancestral land and later banishment by Oberon. Even considering all of that, Cole thought of snow as a blessing, unlike the rest of New York's population.

Of course, his attitude toward it had shifted somewhat in the last several months. Since becoming a cop, a special detective for the NYPD's Section Thirteen, Cole spent a great deal more time driving through traffic. Cole had always hated driving. Sharing the roadways with humans and their highly combustible death traps of metal and glass wasn't worth the time it took getting from point A to point B faster. When one added slick roads and impatient drivers to the equation, snow lost some of its distinct flavor.

Fortunately, April had come, bringing with it the great thaw of spring and an abundance of rainfall and flooding. Several areas were under warnings, and while the president of Manhattan hadn't summoned the ark just yet, more than a few locals were ready to batten down the hatches.

Being a novice at police work, Cole was unused to how it sometimes interfered with the job. Only a short human year ago, he had been a gun-for-hire, willing to take jobs from the fey hiding amongst humans in exchange for gold or the occasional favor. The closest he'd come to working with cops was his side job as a police consultant. Cole had worked to help solve supernatural crimes in the past when conventional forensics had failed to provide an explanation for the nonbelievers.

Several months prior, a rash of murders had forced the city's higher-ups to conclude that the situation was getting worse, not better. Inspector Joss Vallimun had proposed the reformation of Section Thirteen, a clandestine division of cops that had solved occult crimes through the fifties, sixties, and seventies. Cole had been brought into the group along with his former police friend, James Corhagen. As a one-time enforcer for the Irish Mafia, becoming a cop had felt odd, but Joss had sweetened the pot by offering Cole something more under the table.

Namely, becoming his lover.

Since then, the two had discreetly shared a bed while they chased down those that threatened to spill New York City's oldest, and sometimes worst-kept, secret.

Currently, he and his partner, in and out of work, were driving through the backstreets of Chinatown while rain pelted them relentlessly.

"I am going to murder Rainette and Marcel for phoning in sick," Joss grumbled over the sound of the rain pelting hard against the roof of Cole's car. "Twenty-four-hour cold, my ass."

Cole held the steering wheel in a loose grip as they rounded a sharp corner. "I doubt their night consists of what you're implying," he said, bringing the car to a stop in front of a nondescript building. "Marcel and Rainette still haven't consummated their relationship."

Joss climbed out of the passenger side while Cole put the car in park and killed the engine. "You know I don't pay attention to precinct gossip," Joss replied once Cole had gotten out.

"That's because it's generally about us," the sidhe pointed out, and he and Joss stood side by side in the rain. "Or what we're working on."

Directly in front of them stood a decrepit building with no signs giving away its purpose and no lights shining behind the windows. Cole jerked his head to his left, motioning for his partner to follow. Joss kept in step as Cole led him down an alley that was barely visible in the pouring rain. Keeping close to the building's side, Cole felt along until his hand brushed against the slickness of solid wood. Joss kept several steps back as Cole had instructed before they had arrived, waiting for the signal.

A moment later, a slot on the door opened at eye level. A pair of eyes belonging to what Joss guessed was a man glared out through the rain at them.

"*P'taitus an'klusta m'yika tu as ipu*," Cole whispered in his native language.

The man on the other side nodded, closing the slot before opening the door to allow them passage. Cole gave the human-looking man with the long beard a nod in return as he passed. Joss kept his eyes on his lover and hurried to catch up, paying the stranger no mind.

"What was he?" he asked, following Cole down a flight of stairs directly to their left.

"Human," Cole answered, maintaining a slight lead ahead of his man. "A practitioner of the Craft, as they say. I believe his ranking is that of sage, or maybe wizard. With men, it generally depends on the beard."

The stairwell was long and narrow, barely enough room for the two of them. Joss let out a chuckle as they reached the landing. Light was spilling around the edges of a thick curtain, the only visible exit in sight.

"Even with magic users," Joss said, snickering the whole time, "it all comes down to size."

Cole smiled wryly in response. "I think it has something to do with the fact that they're human," he said. "Then again, the sidhe were known for their gigantic towers, so perhaps not."

Reaching out, Cole parted the curtain to allow his lover to pass. Joss seemed taken aback by this but smiled after a moment's hesitation and entered first. Cole let the curtain fall back into place as he stepped through, feeling a slight chill roll over his skin as he passed safely through the ward.

Joss shivered, reacting to its presence as well, and looked at him. "What was that?" he asked over the sudden din coming from all around them.

Cole registered the look of alarm on Joss's face and moved closer to reassure him. "It was just a ward," he explained, bringing Joss's head down so he could hear better. "This building has been mystically shielded."

"From what?" Joss asked, looking into Cole's face now.

"Cops," Cole replied, smiling slightly. "Or curious humans who lack the necessary magical talent. One must either have a certain amount of power in one's blood or be other than human to pass through. If you had met neither of those requirements, the spell on the building would have knocked you out cold for several hours. Anything you might have glimpsed in your last few seconds of consciousness would have been chalked up to bad dreams." Cole's smile became a smirk. "It's just to keep out snoopers."

Joss frowned. "Thorough," he commented. "Are you sure either of us should be here, then? In case you'd forgotten, you're on the right side of the law now."

Cole gave his man a peck on the cheek. "It's just a security precaution," he insisted, taking Joss by the hand. "The fey in Manhattan have learned to be properly paranoid. Neither one of us qualify as a threat because we're not on duty. Relax and try to have a little fun tonight."

"I'll try," Joss replied stiffly. "But I'm not making any promises yet. Do I want to know where I would have ended up had the spell knocked me out?"

"Without me here?" Cole asked for clarification, to which Joss nodded. "Probably in an alley nearby, if you were very, very lucky."

Joss gave Cole's hand a squeeze and allowed himself to be led through the cavalcade of surreal weirdness that was the fey bar. Tables and chairs far too large to house humans covered most of the center of the room. The further out one went, the smaller things got. Shelves holding miniature versions of the same setup adorned the walls for pixies and nixies, who giggled and whispered among themselves at what was going on below them.

Joss did a quick scan of the more visible residents and spotted several ogres sharing a table with what looked like two hags. Several members of what Joss recognized as the sluagh were hissing to one another over in a corner by themselves. Joss remembered too late the effects that the Wild Hunt had on mortals but, by that point, had been staring for several seconds with no ill effects. Jolted by this, he almost didn't notice when Cole stopped in front of the bar, where a rather full-figured woman with pointed ears was serving up a barrel-sized mug of mead to a lone hobgoblin.

"Be right with you, sirs," she said as Cole took a seat.

Cole motioned for Joss to do the same, and he quickly climbed onto the stool next to him. "I feel a little out of place," he muttered, getting comfortable on the surprisingly plush stool.

"If you were human, anyone in here would have smelled it by now," Cole explained, taking Joss's hand again once his lover got situated. "Typically, this place isn't very friendly toward even the higher-level spell casters."

Joss frowned, now that he had time to think on it. "I made it through the wards," he said, more to himself than Cole.

Cole went rigid for a second as he watched Joss closely. "We've been wondering for a while now how much the transfiguration changed you," he began, keeping eerily still. "You are not wise in the ways of human magic, yet the wards did little more than give you a creeping chill."

"That was normal, incidentally," Cole added when Joss remained silent.

"Oh well," Joss said finally, as the barmaid approached. "Life's full of surprises."

Cole watched Joss closely as he looked up at the barmaid. "Something I can get for you gentlemen?" she asked, her eyes drifting back and forth between the two of them.

"Mead," Cole said when Joss gave him a quizzical look. "Old oak, if you've got it."

"Coming right up," the barmaid said, nodding.

Joss shot Cole a cockeyed glance as the woman walked off to fetch their drinks. "Mead?" he asked, smirking.

"It's basically honey beer," Cole explained.

"I know what it is," Joss cut back playfully. "I was in a fraternity at one point. I'm just surprised this place has something like that."

Joss paused as the words left his mouth. "I probably shouldn't be, though," he admitted, before the barmaid plunked two tall glasses in front of them.

Cole passed a handful of gold coins to the woman in exchange. "Keep them coming," he instructed. "We've got a long night of drinking ahead of us."

Noting the surprised look on his lover's face, Cole seized his glass and took a long draw from it. Joss did the same, setting his back down with a nod of approval at the same time that Cole did.

"Not bad," he said. "A little sweet for me, but I think I could get used to it. Do places like this always take gold coins?"

"It was leftover gold from before I moved into the sithen," Cole told him. "Places like this typically keep things in the old ways, but it's getting to where cash or credit will spend just as fast. I prefer to avoid credit cards, though."

"Can't say I blame you."

Cole watched Joss for a moment more, looking for some sort of sign. "You took the news that you were no longer human very well," he said at last. "I was expecting more of a reaction from you. Is this your way of being in denial?"

Joss frowned. "I thought we'd already assumed that," he replied. "I mean…."

Joss held up his right arm in front of Cole. Nothing happened, but Cole didn't require a demonstration to understand his lover's meaning. Several months prior, Joss had been attacked by an ogre named Marcel. Marcel had been under the influence of a fey-enslaving device called a black ring. These days, he was repaying his debt to society by working for Section Thirteen.

However, before joining the so-called white hats, Marcel had torn Joss's right arm out of the socket and destroyed one eye. Cole had bargained with the Goddess to regrow Joss's missing parts. She had yet to inform Cole of what he would be asked to pay in exchange, something that constantly gnawed at the back of his mind. Meanwhile, the process had turned Joss into something other than human.

Cole had been worried about how his lover would take to the change. Thus far, Joss was responding to his newfound lack of mortality a little too well. Cole had never changed a mortal before, save one instance where misfired glamour inside a hospital refused to wear off. In his experience, though, it was not in a human being's nature to take to such a transition without recriminations of some kind.

Joss was lowering his arm now and looking at Cole worriedly.

"Are you angry with me?" Cole asked boldly, deciding to skip beating around the bush, as humans called it. "Or were you ever angry to begin with?"

Joss laughed a little, then stared off into the distance, where two wood nymphs were dueling playfully.

"I don't know how to put it," he tried, struggling over his words. "It feels right, for right now. I keep thinking that the shock will wear off, or maybe kick in, but I feel fine. Actually, I feel the best I've ever been. It feels like a weight's been lifted off me, only I never knew it was there."

Joss reached over and squeezed Cole's hand. "I'm not mad," he stated, giving the sidhe a warm smile that heated Cole's insides better than any mead could. "I was surprised at first. Maybe a little overwhelmed by everything, especially when we couldn't be around one another afterward, but you were the one who healed me. I couldn't hate you for that."

Cole smiled back, though his face betrayed the unease squirming around inside him. Silently, he cursed his weakness. He'd once been able to maintain an utterly straight face with almost no effort at all. One had to learn such things in order to survive the Faerie courts.

And especially Oberon.

"I don't know how I'll feel later on," Joss finished. He took another sip of his mead and smiled at the sweet taste. "I might not care for another ten years, or twenty. I wish I could answer you better, but I just don't know."

Cole returned Joss's smile with one of his own before taking a long draft from his glass. "If that is the truth," he said, "then I can't ask for anything more."

"You worry too much," Joss teased, turning around to wave the barmaid over so she could give him a refill. "I thought fairy-kind were supposed to be all frolic-y and whatnot."

"It's a common misconception," Cole fired back dryly.

Joss thanked the barmaid as she topped off his glass. "I guess, if I'm going to be dating and living with one, I need to know more about you."

"Isn't that why we're here?" Cole asked, polishing off his own glass. "You wanted to see more of Faerie life here in Manhattan, outside of work."

A loud crash resounded through the room. Both Cole and Joss turned toward it, Cole much more slowly. The two wood nymphs were wrestling with one another now, pulling at each other's hair as they shrieked curses in their native tongue. The other bar patrons merely glanced at their antics as though it were no big deal.

"Is someone going to stop them?" Joss wondered.

"I wouldn't," Cole advised seriously, not thanking the barmaid as she topped off his own glass. "If this keeps up, people will start placing bets. You don't want to rob someone here of the chance to make a little extra gold."

Joss continued to stare openly as the two nymphs struggled on the floor. "So this is a typical thing, then?"

Cole looked at Joss. "This is one of the very few places inside the city where we can truly be ourselves," he said, explaining. "You are new at this, and I understand that, but one thing you have to realize right now is that we are wild things, as untamed as nature."

Joss divided his attention between the fight and Cole's words, looking toward his lover more and more as Cole went on.

"We got here fairly early," Cole was saying now, as both wood nymphs got to their feet, drawing weapons. "Later on, things will get much more exciting. Because there is no one here to judge us, we don't have to pretend to live by humanity's rules. We don't have to fear breaking anything softer than ourselves."

"So I see," Joss said grimly as one wood nymph sliced a deep cut on the arm of her opponent.

Sensing Joss's unease, Cole finished off his glass of mead, then hopped down off the stool so he could move in closer.

"There is another way of looking at it," he said, leaning in to whisper in Joss's ear. "There's no need for us to fear being judged in this place. I've told you this before, but the fey do not frown on what you call same-sex relationships."

Joss turned sharply to look Cole directly in the face. "What we're doing right now is no more a crime than if we were alone in the sithen," he whispered, bringing their faces closer together. "No one here sees anything wrong with this."

Turning, Cole gestured toward the crowd. "Look," he said encouragingly. "See for yourself. No one here is paying us any mind. The fight going on right now is more engaging than us, as far as they're concerned."

Joss looked around, and, sure enough, the patrons seemed more interested in the fight than the two of them. Furthermore, it looked as though they'd been ignoring him and Cole whispering intimately with one another for some time now.

Cole reached down and brushed a hand along Joss's leg, caressing the outside of his thigh through his jeans. Joss jumped, reacting to the touch, but then relaxed and even laughed softly at himself. Cole smiled back but didn't stop as the fight raged on. Joss reached down, clasped his hand over Cole's, and held on, not stopping his touch. Rather, Joss pressed Cole's hand harder against him.

Cole began moving both his hand and Joss's farther down toward the knee, then back up along the inseam of Joss's jeans. Just before he reached Joss's groin, Cole pulled away. Joss looked up, a little confused by this, but then glanced around, as though remembering where they were. Cole, however, was not fazed at all and jumped up into Joss's lap, straddling his legs. Facing him, Cole leaned forward to kiss Joss firmly on the lips before he could pull away.

"Shh," Cole whispered, pressing their foreheads together. "No one cares."

Joss stared up at him warily, gripping Cole's hips in his hands, as if preparing to shove the sidhe off him at any second. The combined weight of the two men caused the stool to rock backward slightly. Joss started to flail, thinking they were both going to end up on the floor. As his back connected with the bar, he relaxed yet again.

"Shhh," Cole repeated, louder this time, before kissing Joss harder. "Don't worry. We could have sex right here on the floor by the bar and no one would care."

Joss felt his whole body tense at this. "Cole," he managed to mumble out.

Their mouths were connected again. Cole's hands had begun exploring Joss's upper half. Fingers danced roughly over the surface of his clothing, feeling through the woven fabric to the hard muscle trapped underneath.

"Cole," Joss forced out as his sidhe lover rained kisses down along his jawbone and up to his ear.

"Stop fighting it," Cole hissed out, before seizing Joss's ear between his teeth in a playful bite. "Give in to it. You'd be surprised at how amazing it can feel."

"People are watching."

The words flew out of Joss's mouth. He knew at once that they wouldn't deter Cole for a second. What shocked the NYPD inspector more, though, was how little he cared. The bar's patrons watched them grasping at each other's rock-hard bodies, more from the shelves on the walls than out on the main floor, but a handful were drawn away from the fight. Joss gasped as he felt Cole's hand wrap around his girth. At some point, when he wasn't paying attention, Cole had freed Joss's bull-sized cock.

Now, the sidhe was stroking it roughly, using the same hard touch as before. Joss stared up into Cole's eyes, somewhere between arousal and fury. He was pissed, but more than that, he wanted to take his anger out on Cole's asshole.

And if the look Cole gave him was any indication, this was exactly what the sidhe expected him to do.

With an easy movement, Cole swung himself backward off the stool, taking Joss with him. The two men landed on the dirty floor, Joss crushing Cole under his weight, which the silver-haired man tolerated easily. Leaning down, Joss kissed Cole roughly on the mouth, forcing his tongue deep into Cole's throat. The sidhe suckled it like a baby calf at its mother's tit.

Somewhere, off in the distance, Joss was aware that the fight had died down. Other fey gathered around them in a semicircle, staring as both men shucked their clothes. A cheer went up as Joss rammed his dick into Cole's ass, spearing the sidhe on his thick cudgel.

Cole howled.

He didn't scream. The sidhe actually howled, baying like a wolf might as the tube of flesh carved a path through his insides. Joss hadn't thought to use lubricant, but the look in his love's eyes told him everything was fine. A sidhe had far greater tolerance for pain than humans typically did, and Cole had been bred to serve as a warrior for the Queen of All Faerie herself. Something as simple as this wouldn't break him. A second later, Cole's face changed, and Joss knew he was ready for more.

More cheering followed as Joss picked up his tempo, thrusting into Cole's ass like a racehorse making a mad dash for the finish line. Even the barmaid had stopped working to get in on the fun. Patrons of the bar were calling out to one another, taking bets.

Joss tuned every last one of them out, throwing his concern and reservations to the wind as Cole's eyes locked with his. Warmth spread through them, rising from the fire in each man's loins. They rode the heat like a wave. The faces of the fey watching went slack as the warmth spread through the air and into them.

A few minutes later, it had become a very different sort of party.

AN HOUR had passed, and the party inside the fey speakeasy was still going strong.

Cole felt a grin tug at his mouth as Joss let out a long, satisfied sigh. The two of them were back on their stools, resting leisurely against the bar while the barmaid ran her fingers through Joss's hair. Joss had given Cole a nervous look when the woman began touching him, but Cole had merely smiled and nodded his consent.

"He likes it when you start off at the roots," Cole had said, raising one of the fresh glasses of free mead she'd provided for them. "It tickles ever so slightly."

All around them, fey of every shape and size were rolling back and forth in an orgy of sexual release. The brawl from earlier now felt more like a friendly arm-wrestling match. Pieces of wooden furniture lay broken on the ground, the result of not being able to hold so much weight at one time. Pixies danced with one another, caressing and rolling through the air, moving from partner to partner in a strange sort of aerial square dance.

Following their romp, Joss and Cole had tried cuddling on the floor, but it became painfully clear that they couldn't stay there without being stepped on. Joss had half dressed, tugging his pants up without zipping them and leaving his shirt opened all the way. Cole hadn't bothered, preferring to go casually nude. Now, as the barmaid continued her playful teasing through his love's hair, he reached over with the glass and let a trickle from it splash down the treasure trail to Joss's groin.

Joss rolled his eyes and gave him a look as Cole leaned over to lick up the golden fluid. "You're nothing but trouble. You know that?" Joss muttered between soft groans.

Cole ran his tongue all the way down to the hairs fanning out below Joss's waistline, lapping there for a moment like a canine in heat, before moving back up. Cole paused, nibbling at his lover's nipple for a moment, then continued upward, kissing a trail along the underside of his jaw.

"You love it," he growled low, moving down to Joss's neck.

Bringing his glass forward again, Cole tipped it toward Joss's mouth. Joss drank from it graciously, enjoying the taste. Once Joss had his fill, Cole took a mouthful of his own but did not swallow. Leaning forward, he pressed his mouth against Joss's, letting the rich liquid pass from his body to that of his love. Joss drank slowly from him while the barmaid watched, mesmerized.

"Drink from me, my love," Cole whispered as the last of the mead passed Joss's lips.

A few drops landed in the fur on Joss's chest, sinking in there along with the sweat built up from earlier. Joss raised up, inadvertently jerking his hair loose from the barmaid's fingers, and kissed Cole hard on the mouth. Their tongues danced together for a moment, licking playfully while the orgy continued all around them.

Joss smiled as he and Cole leaned back in their seats. The barmaid had moved over behind Cole now and was reaching to brush his hair with her fingers.

"I wasn't expecting this wild of a night," Joss mused, looking out at the crowd. "I don't think I saw anything this exciting when I was a college boy."

Cole smiled to himself as he watched the crowd. "The Goddess has moved among them this night," he said. "They all felt the presence of Danu and the Horned One, her Consort. Something like this has not happened for many years."

Joss seemed interested by this. "How come?"

Cole sighed. "Everyone you see here tonight is living in exile," he explained. "They came to the mortal plane because there was nowhere else for them to live. It was believed for many years that Danu and Consort both had forsaken us all."

Joss took a moment to digest this bit of information. "What about the sithen, though?" he asked, before drinking from his own glass of mead, which had been resting behind him on the bar. "I mean, there's the chamber you took me to."

Cole gave Joss a warning look but then relaxed when the barmaid moved away to see to a quartet of drunk, nude ogres that had stumbled up to the bar on the other end.

"The sithen is something of an enigma," Cole admitted, grateful for the distraction. "In the old days, before I was exiled, there were stories of the Tuatha De Danann. They settled in what you call Ireland after driving out the then-current residents."

Joss waited as Cole paused. "What happened?"

"I don't know everything," Cole said, "but the stories of their exploits reached Faerie and became what you might call folktales. The Tuatha De Danann were a band of anarchists who protested Oberon's right to rule after he ascended to power in Faerie. Many of them were from very old clans and dangerous, so Oberon decided to banish them to the plane of mortals rather than risk having their extended families turn on him."

Cole paused for a second and looked thoughtfully out into the crowd. "I suspect that might have been Titania's doing," he added. "The better ideas always came from her."

Joss chuckled at hearing this.

"At any rate," Cole continued, "the Tuatha De Danann settled in Ireland but were forced to retreat into hollow hills after the Milesians invaded. Thus, this is how the modern sithens originated."

Cole paused again. "Though there are people who insist the sithens existed in some way before the Tuatha De Danann were forced into them. In any case, what one is doing beneath Bowling Green Park is still a mystery to me."

Joss nodded, then thought for a moment. "Doesn't Mal know?" he asked. "He is a part of the sithen, I thought, so couldn't he tell you?"

"I've asked," Cole replied. "Many times, but Mal claims the information is 'encrypted'."

Joss gave Cole a blank look.

"In computer terms," Cole tried. "The information is sealed. He can tell where it is but can't access it. Or won't. Either way, I haven't pressed him about it that much. Given that the chamber beneath the sithen is a temple devoted to Danu and Consort, I don't think we'll have to wait forever to find answers."

Joss opened his mouth to speak, but a loud crash echoed through the room, cutting him off. Another table had collapsed under the weight of several hags, who were all trying to swarm on top of a troll.

Joss averted his eyes, then looked back at Cole. "You're worried," he said, noticing the look on Cole's face. "Is it still because of…?"

Their eyes met, and Cole nodded. "Yes," he said. "I fear what the Goddess may ask of me in exchange for healing you."

Joss's face grew taut as his breath grew quicker. "That one from the tulpa's hideout," he said. "What was his name? Ashwyn?"

Cole nodded.

"He said that you'd elevated me," Joss said. "If that's true, then she did more than heal me."

"Either way," Cole said, taking Joss's free hand, "it doesn't really matter."

Joss looked confused by Cole's sudden change in mood. "How come?" he wondered. "I thought you were expecting something bad to happen."

"I am," Cole said, lacing their fingers together. "But I would do it all over again in a heartbeat if it meant getting to sit here with you."

Cole slid off his stool, his movements like a predator stalking its prey. Joss watched and waited as Cole crawled up his body to plant a quick kiss on his lips before slinking back down.

"I want you again," Cole declared while he wrapped one hand around Joss's growing cock.

"You just wanna fuck some more," Joss teased, though he did nothing to stop Cole this time.

Cole ran his tongue over the head, licking it playfully, before pulling back. "If I just wanted to fuck," he countered, "I could join the crowd behind me. What I want is you!"

Joss grunted as Cole buried the tip of his tongue in the slit, where precum had begun oozing out like a leaky faucet. As Cole began to work on the thick shaft, something rumbled near him, in the leg of Joss's pants.

Joss reached down to pull out his cell phone, but Cole grabbed his hand before he could draw it all the way out, intent on stopping him.

"Let it go," he said insistently, giving Joss's cock a squeeze with his other hand for good measure.

"It could be important," Joss countered, fighting against Cole's grip.

"It's always important," Cole pointed out. "Tonight was supposed to be our night off."

Joss yanked the cell phone free and checked the screen. "It's Rainette," he said as Cole went back to licking the head of his shaft.

"Yeah?" Joss answered in a somewhat strained voice.

Taking this as a challenge, Cole sucked on the head, making sure to work his tongue in circles around it. Joss gasped and immediately seized the back of Cole's head to pull him off. Cole, however, was not about to be denied.

"Yeah," Joss repeated, still struggling with Cole. "I'm fine. What is it?"

Cole sucked more of the thick cudgel down his throat, using the muscles there to milk the thick precum out of the head so that it lubricated the passage all the way down.

"What?" Joss gasped. "Yes! Yes, I can be there. Give me the address."

Cole took several inches down his throat in protest.

"I'm good," Joss said. "No, it's nothing. We'll get there as soon as we can."

Cole growled, letting the sound massage Joss's cock.

"Bye!" Joss said quickly, hanging up. "That was Rainette," he spat down at Cole. "And would you stop, already?"

Reluctantly, Cole looked up, letting the cock pop out of his mouth. "You don't like what I'm doing?" he asked.

"Rainette just got off the phone with a friend of hers," Joss said, ignoring the question. "Someone from her coven. She was trying to get a recipe for homemade chicken soup when there was a disturbance in the background. She's already called 911 but wants us to go over there."

Cole groaned, not letting go of Joss's cock, which had yet to go down. "Okay," he said, getting up slowly. "Let's go."

Joss began collecting his clothes, but Cole beat him by snatching his roughly off the floor and marching toward the exit.

"Come on," he insisted. "The sooner we get this over with, the sooner I can go back to what I was doing before she called."

Joss followed Cole out through the curtain and back up the stairs. "Put your pants on before we get out into the street, at least," Joss insisted, sighing.

Cole stopped dead in his tracks, shot Joss a look back over his shoulder, then proceeded to dress himself there on the stairwell. Joss took the time to finish making himself presentable for humans and was done just as Cole pulled his shirt down over his head.

"Satisfied?" Cole asked, heading up the stairs before Joss could answer.

Joss gave the bouncer a nod before exiting through the open door after Cole. "What is wrong with you?" Joss asked as they spilled out onto the rainy Chinatown sidewalk together. "You're acting like a…."

Joss hesitated for a moment. "Well, this isn't like you," he settled on. "What's the matter?"

Cole didn't stop until they reached his SEMA. The vehicle was, in actuality, a member of the old Wild Hunts, and had taken the form of a modified Camaro to blend in. The doors on either side sprung open automatically as they approached.

"Get in," Cole said, closing the door after he climbed in.

Joss followed suit, getting more frustrated by the second. Cole started the car and pulled out into the street. Rainwater had saturated the surface, giving it the appearance of a dark stream. Cole reached underneath the wheel and hit the strobe lights, a new feature the car had recently manifested on its own.

"This was our night off," Cole stated, still fuming. "Rainette knew that."

Joss looked at Cole for a moment as the sidhe spun the wheel into a sharp turn, making the tires scream for purchase. "She wouldn't have called if it wasn't important," Joss said, forcing himself to sound calm. "Cole, her friend might have been attacked."

"I know," Cole said through his teeth after a moment. Then, more calmly, he added, "I know that. I just…. We've been chasing Naryssa's ghost all over Manhattan for a month now, ever since she sent that flame golem to the Beckrindle place. This was our night off, and I wanted to show you a good time."

Cole's mouth turned upward in a sour scowl. "I wanted to show you some of my world and how great it can be," he said more quietly. "I was going to show you what it could be like outside of work, outside of chasing down trolls and coming up with excuses for the brass. We weren't supposed to answer any calls tonight."

Joss reached over until he touched Cole's right hand, which was gripping the steering wheel tightly. Reluctantly, Cole let go and allowed Joss to grasp his hand between the warmth of his own.

"I was having a good time," Joss told him. "It was… different, to say the least, but that didn't make it bad. I wasn't sure what to expect before we got there, but everything turned out okay."

Cole glanced toward him. "You weren't upset?"

"Nope," Joss answered. "Why would I have been?"

Cole shifted in his seat. "I've learned not to question human sensibilities," he said flatly. "You were raised in the human world, to be a human. Tonight was your first look at what a different culture is."

"And you thought it might not sit well with me?"

Cole shrugged at the slight edge in Joss's voice. "It was a concern of mine," he admitted ruefully.

The address Rainette had given Joss took them far outside of Chinatown, into the region parallel with Hudson Street. From there, locating the apartment proved easier than they would have liked. Outside the apartment building, several police cars had gathered. It didn't look as though the officers on the scene had been there for very long. Despite this, Cole gave a scowl as he brought his car to a stop on the opposite side of the road.

"How did they beat us here?" he wondered, climbing out.

"They didn't have to come all the way from Chinatown," Joss replied, wearing a knowing smirk as he got out on the other side. "Let's see what happened and hope that this is all one huge coincidence."

"I don't believe in coincidences," Cole said flatly as they crossed the street together.

"And I don't relish telling Rainette what happened to her coven member," the inspector countered.

Cole was quiet for a moment as they reached the cluster of squad cars. The strobe lights cast oddly-shaped shadows on the building's surface. There was no sign of an ambulance or anyone standing guard outside. The cars appeared to have been left unattended.

"Shouldn't someone be here?" Cole asked.

Joss nodded. "Let's go upstairs," he said, already heading toward the door. "I've got a real bad feeling about this."

Cole kept his senses on alert as they passed over the threshold of the building. Joss gave a shudder at the sensation and hesitated a moment while Cole caught up to him.

"Threshold," Cole explained, knowing what the look on Joss's face was for. "This building is very old. Hudson Street has been around since before there was a United States of America, if I recall correctly. This place has had more than enough time to develop a life of its own."

Joss looked blankly at Cole.

"You're becoming more in tune with these kinds of things," Cole told him. "That's what the sensation was. You sensed this building's threshold."

"Oh," was all Joss said.

He and Cole made tracks for the elevator. "Rainette said it was the fourth floor," Joss said, once they were inside.

Cole pushed the appropriate button and waited as the doors closed. "I am sorry for my behavior earlier," he said stiffly. "I shouldn't have gotten upset."

Hearing this, Joss eased his body closer to Cole's as the machinery above them ground and groaned in its struggle to heft them up to their destination. Joss brushed his hand tenderly over Cole's knuckles, giving each of them a soft stroke before pulling back.

"You're tired," he surmised. "We've been on the beat almost nonstop. That would wear anyone down, even someone who doesn't age."

Cole scowled but didn't protest. "There was a time when I never felt fatigued," he said quietly.

"I mean emotionally," Joss clarified as the elevator came to a rough halt and the doors squeaked open. "You're wrung out on the inside. It happens to all of us at some point. We all need downtime, but as it stands right now, that isn't likely to happen."

Cole thought this through as they stepped out onto the floor. "Even so," he said at last, "I should not have been so angry."

"Forget it," Joss told him. "You didn't hurt anything, and I really did have a great time with you tonight."

Cole stopped suddenly, forcing Joss to do the same. "Really?" the sidhe asked, the uncertainty evident in his voice.

"Yes," Joss said, laughing now. "Were you really that worried?"

To Joss's surprise, Cole looked away in embarrassment. "I haven't dated much over the years," he said, looking for all purposes like a bashful child at that moment. "Courtship rituals change so much that it's hard to keep track."

"So you've told me," Joss quipped playfully.

"Forgive me," Cole said, looking up to meet his eyes. "I am still getting used to this, to us, being together."

Joss waited a moment, then jerked his head toward the end of the hallway. "Come on," he said, wearing a full-blown smile now. "Let's see if there's anything we can do here. If it's nothing serious, we'll go back to our date."

Cole brushed his arm against Joss's in reply as he moved along beside the inspector. The end of the hallway veered sharply to the right. Around the L-turn were two uniformed officers standing watch in front of an open door. From inside the apartment, a foul, familiar stench wavered out into the hall.

"We're not going to finish our date," Cole said flatly as both uniformed cops turned to stare at them. "Not tonight, anyway."

BOTH officers were built like tanks. They reminded Cole of the sort of hired muscle he'd been paid to herd around back when he was a mob enforcer. One stood well over six feet tall, with skin almost the color of coal and short, thick hair cropped close to the sides of his head. The other was bald, a few inches shorter, with skin that looked sunburned.

"Inspector Vallimun and Special Detective MacColewyn," Joss said as he and Cole raised their badges for the officers to see.

"Officer Tate," the dark-skinned one said after staring at their badges for a moment.

"O'Riley," the other replied, staring hard at Vallimun. "What brings the monster hunters down here?"

Cole blinked. "What do you mean?" he asked evasively.

Tate sneered. "You two are with Section Thirteen," he said plainly. "Vallimun is the inspector in charge of the whole outfit. They say an albino is his right hand, or some shit. I'm guessing that means you."

Cole cocked an eyebrow at the albino comment.

"Who said anything to you about Section Thirteen?" Joss asked, curious.

O'Riley rolled his eyes. "Most precincts know about you guys," he said. "They say that if Section Thirteen gets put on a case, you can bet it will go straight to hell in five seconds flat."

Joss didn't appear to know what to say to that.

"I'd argue against it," Cole replied calmly on his lover's behalf. "But chances are, it wouldn't matter. I'm sure you two have heard more than enough about us, since you know who we are."

"There aren't any ghosts here for you two to chase down," O'Riley all but spat out. "The victim's head hasn't spun around on her shoulders, as far as we've seen, and no one's found a trace of pea soup."

Tate snickered. "Right," he added. "So what brings you down here?"

"Someone was on the phone with the woman who lives in this apartment," Joss explained, maintaining his professional demeanor. "They heard a disturbance, called 911, then phoned me, asking if I would look in to make sure everything was okay. We haven't been officially assigned here, but I was hoping we could get some info. Some good news, if there is any."

Tate and O'Riley glanced at each other, a silent conversation passing between the two men in seconds.

"Go on in," Tate said, motioning them past. "Ask for Detective Carroll. She was called in the minute the crew saw the body."

"I'd love to know how all of them beat us here," Cole muttered as soon as they had crossed into the apartment.

There was no question that a fight had broken out in the room. While Cole had seen worse, the evidence of a struggle was unmistakable. Furthermore, he detected trace remains of magic in the air. Spells had been cast in the room, and recently. The witch that once lived here had not gone gentle into the night, not without putting up a fight first. Cole paused as he remembered his former loft mate, Katalina. Finding her dead on the floor in her bedroom was a memory he would not likely shed for a while.

"They didn't have to drive all the way here from Chinatown," Joss pointed out, "again," which interrupted Cole's morose train of thought. Joss stopped beside a table someone had righted and retrieved a pair of latex gloves from a box for himself and Cole.

"We were riding in a carriage of the Wild Hunt," Cole reminded him, looking at the gloves disdainfully. "And must I wear these?"

"You know the drill," Joss said, forcing the gloves into Cole's hands. "Why are you always such a baby about these things?"

Cole scowled as he reluctantly slipped the gloves over his hands. "It's a man-made material," he said. "All processed and factory-made. There's nothing natural inside these things."

"So?"

"For fey, even the sidhe, these kinds of products are dangerous, poison even," Cole reminded him, already scratching at the skin on his hands. "The material affects us the way some people react to wool or any other skin allergy."

"You're saying you have a latex allergy?" Joss asked, watching him closely now.

"If you want to sum it up like that, yes," Cole said. "Corhagen used to provide me with latex-free alternatives when I was a consultant, or let me pass gloves-free if no one else was watching."

Cole paused and shot Joss a look. "We've been working together for months now, and you mean to tell me you still hadn't figured that out?"

Joss glanced away, embarrassed. "Well, it certainly explains your stance on condoms."

Cole stripped the gloves off and examined his reddened hands. "The sidhe do not transmit pathogens the same way that humans do," he reminded him. "We are immune to sexually-transmitted diseases. You have been safe with me this whole time, or else I would have suggested alternative means of intimacy."

"I know," Joss said, laughing at Cole's bluntness. "And I was just teasing you. Go wait outside so that you don't contaminate the crime scene. I'll see if I can convince this Detective Carroll to speak with us out in the hallway."

"Don't do anything with her that I wouldn't," Cole quipped, before heading back through the foyer. "At least, not without inviting me along first."

A few minutes later, Cole was waiting out in the hallway near O'Riley and Tate, who had remained dutifully behind to guard the door.

Both officers kept shooting him looks out of the corners of their eyes every few minutes.

Finally, after a moment more of this, Cole turned toward them and leaned his left shoulder into the wall. "What?" he asked, point-blank.

Both officers stared straight ahead, as though neither had heard him. Cole held his ground, however, keeping his eyes fixed on the two. Slowly, Tate's gaze drifted toward Cole again. O'Riley shifted uncomfortably, his legs jerking ever so slightly from being held in such a rigid pose for so long.

Still, Cole waited.

"They say a lot of strange stuff about you." Tate spoke at last, still not making direct eye contact with Cole.

"I'm used to it," Cole said coolly. "I doubt there's ever been a point in my life here where someone wasn't saying something about me."

"Is that really your hair color?" O'Riley said very quickly, as though afraid. "They say you're part of some weird underground movement, kind of like goths, but more extreme."

"I don't consider myself part of any movement," Cole told him. "Unless you count police work. And I'm only underground for part of the day. The rest of the time, I'm usually at work."

Both officers look at him, bewildered by this statement. Cole remained relaxed, tucking one hand into his pants pocket.

"Are you as good as people say?" Tate asked.

Cole smiled. "I'm good at most things," he said. "Typically, anyway. It all depends on what you want done and who you want it done to."

Tate frowned, and a bead of sweat ran down the side of his face, showing his discomfort. Seeing this, Cole smiled even more.

"You'll have to ask whether I can do it to you, though," he finished, earning him a blanched look from both men.

Before either officer could respond, a rather peeved-looking woman with rust-colored hair came storming out of the door they were guarding, followed by Joss. Cole righted himself, knowing this must be the mysterious Detective Carroll they'd heard about.

The female detective in question stopped short at the sight of Cole and scowled. "You didn't tell me he was here," she shot at Joss.

"He's my partner," Joss explained.

"Yeah, I heard," Carroll replied. At once, Cole did not like her tone. "I'll make this quick, then," Carroll continued, blithely ignoring the look Cole was giving her. "I don't want either of you here. Section Thirteen has no business sticking its nose in my investigation."

"We're not here to stick our noses into anything," Joss explained, holding on to his calm face, though Cole thought he looked a bit strained. From the way Joss was holding himself, Cole guessed he'd been verbally wrestling with the detective this whole time.

"You're here," she fired back sharply. "Therefore, you're both trampling all over my turf. I want you and the freak show gone, now."

Joss looked past Detective Carroll at Cole.

"Might the freak show speak freely for a moment?" Cole asked icily.

"No," Carroll said, turning to glare at the sidhe. "What part of 'get the fuck out of my investigation' were the two of you unclear on?"

"You have a burned body somewhere in the back part of the apartment," Cole stated, taking several steps toward her. "A witch, most likely. Someone broke into the woman's home and set fire to her. Am I right?"

Carroll's forehead wrinkled in confusion. "How did you know that?" she demanded, glancing back at Joss. "He said you were waiting outside."

"I have been," Cole told her. "I can smell the corpse from here. Since the body hasn't been taken to a hospital, it's safe to say the resident of this place is dead. Our friend who called us said she heard a struggle over the phone. I saw enough of the apartment to know a fight broke out in there."

Detective Carroll frowned thoughtfully as Cole continued. "Whoever did this broke into the woman's home, subdued her, then lit the body on fire. That should have taken a while, yet I'm guessing the assailants were long gone by the time the first officers arrived on the scene. Since the 911 call most likely came through right after the attack occurred, there shouldn't have been that much time for the attackers to escape."

"You keep referring to 'attackers'," Detective Carroll pointed out as she folded her arms in front of her. "What do you know about any of this?"

"The victim was Alice Tweedle," Cole replied calmly. "A witch and member of the Shadewater coven. I have a difficult time believing a single person, no matter how experienced at this sort of thing, could disable a spell caster so fast."

Detective Carroll snorted. "So you guys really do buy into that whole voodoo hoodoo bullshit?"

Joss and Cole exchanged looks. "Five minutes," Cole said to the detective. "I'm in a generous mood tonight, thanks to someone else, so I'll offer you five minutes of my time. Chances are, I can find something that will help you."

"And if I refuse?"

Cole shook his head, letting the curtain of silvery hair fall around his face. "Then we both leave, and good luck to you in finding out who did this while we explain the situation to our friend. She's most likely going to need our support once she finds out."

Carroll took a moment to think this over. "Is your friend a cop?" she asked, pulling both arms tighter to her body.

"Yes." Joss answered instead. "She's a member of the Section."

"And a witch herself," Cole added.

The detective took several moments more to digest all of this. "Three minutes," she told Cole, letting both arms fall to her side. "Then you both get the fuck out, and I never want to see either of you anywhere near an investigation of mine again."

Cole marched past Detective Carroll without a word. Neither Tate nor O'Riley tried to prevent him from reentering the apartment. Once inside, Cole headed straight for the back, where the foul odor was emanating from strongest. The interior of the bedroom had a rustic feel to it, like the house of someone who was better suited for the outdoors but lived in the city for pragmatic reasons. This room, more than the kitchen and living area, felt like home. It carried a personal touch and flavor far stronger than the others, though there were smaller traces of it there as well.

In a corner near the broken window was the burned body of the apartment's former tenant. It looked as though the body had been arranged there after death. At this early stage, there was no way his Hand of Power would be able to raise her for questioning.

As Cole stared, he noticed something lying around the body. Before he could investigate, though, Detective Carroll entered in front of Joss. Seeing his lover, Cole gestured toward the bathroom door, which was in the wall opposite the broken window.

"Gloves," he said, indicating the latex ones Joss was still wearing. "I don't wish to contaminate a crime scene."

Detective Carroll watched as Joss opened the door for him. "Is he being serious?" she asked, glaring hard at Joss's face. "Or just trying to get under my skin?"

"Both," Joss explained, stepping back out of Cole's way. "But you sort of get used to it after a while."

"What do you need to do in there?" the detective asked quickly as Cole began closing the bathroom door behind him.

"I'm just going to retrieve our police dog," he said, before sending a look past her at Joss. "It won't take but a moment."

Detective Carroll's eyes doubled in size. "Say what?"

"Our police dog," Cole repeated, holding the door open a crack. "He'll sniff around the apartment and see what's what."

Detective Carroll planted a hand firmly on the door, preventing Cole from closing it all the way. "You think this is some kind of joke?" she demanded, furious.

"Not at all," Cole said, "but if I told you the real reason why I'm going in here, you wouldn't believe me. It's just easier to say we have a police dog that comes out of nowhere to sniff around for clues."

Rearing back, the detective stuck her foot out and kicked the door in. The wood panel stopped short upon coming in contact with Cole, but the intent was clear all the same.

"Get out here," she ordered, pointing at the space beside the bed. "Whatever the hell it is you're doing in there, you can do it just as well in front of me."

Joss hesitated a moment before nodding at Cole, who stepped back out into the bedroom.

"I had this same conversation with another woman back during the fifties," Cole said to himself while nudging the door closed with his foot. "Both times, the women in question had the wrong idea about what I was doing."

Joss shot Cole a look, warning him to be serious, as Cole began stripping out of his clothes. Detective Carroll's eyes widened as Cole folded his shirt neatly and dropped it onto a clear spot on the carpet.

"Why is he taking his clothes off?" she asked Joss leerily.

"It's much easier to do it now than afterward," Cole told her as he slid out of his boots. "You'll see in a moment."

"See what?"

No one bothered answering her. A moment later, Cole was fully nude. "All right, gentlemen," Carroll said, looking thoroughly pissed now. "You've had your fun. I'd like for both of you to leave now."

"This isn't a joke," Cole said, before melting into his wolf form.

Detective Carroll had opened her mouth, intending to retort. Instead, it fell all the way open in shock as Cole stared irritably up at her in his wolf guise. When the woman said nothing, he slunk around her legs and headed for the living room, passing the forensics team, who were busy searching the kitchen for clues.

In his wolf form, Cole stretched for a moment, adjusting to the difference of being in such a contrasting state. It had been a little while since he had used this body. Thus, he took a moment to sniff around and grow re-accustomed to his surroundings. From this perspective, everything was different. Scents had masks concealing them and layer upon layer to differentiate from one another. He could hear sounds radiating through the walls, ceiling, and floor of the room.

Cole gathered himself and made a quick sweep of the area, careful to stick his nose anywhere that smelled suspicious. Feeling a pair of eyes on him, he glanced back toward the kitchen and noticed one of the forensic analysis team members watching him closely. Ignoring her, Cole nosed around for a bit longer, then nudged past her, back to the bedroom.

After closing the bedroom door with a kick from his rear foot, Cole then shifted back to his sidhe body. Detective Carroll hadn't moved from the spot where she'd been standing when he left. Her mouth was still hanging wide open. The sound of the door closing caused the woman to jump, and her eyes tripled in size at the sight of Cole standing before her in the nude once more.

"No applause," he told her wryly. "Or screaming. It causes problems if you scream."

The blood left the detective's face. "It's true, then?" she said, her voice hardly a whisper. "All of it is true, isn't it?"

Cole ignored her and looked at Joss. "There were two intruders," he said. "A man and a woman. Both adults and probably in their early or midthirties. Something about them smelled familiar, but I haven't put my finger on why yet. Each one was armed, though I didn't smell any gunpowder from a shot being fired. It looks like they pulled this off some other way, maybe through magical means, but I won't be certain unless I do a more thorough sweep."

"How do you know about the guns?" Joss asked.

"Gun oil," Cole answered, tapping his nose. "I could smell small traces of it around the room. Their guns must have been cleaned recently, and then brushed up against some of the furniture."

Cole turned toward the body again. "What is that stuff spread around the corpse?" he asked, speaking directly to Detective Carroll now. "It smells like croutons."

Detective Carroll blinked several times, shook her head as if coming out of a trance, and coughed. "What?" she asked, noticing Cole was pointing at the body. "Oh, it's bread crumbs. Just like the report said."

Cole and Joss each reacted to this bit of news, but Detective Carroll appeared not to notice or care. If she realized her slip of the tongue, her face gave no indication.

"So, two assailants," Joss surmised, "broke into a witch's apartment, murdered her, set fire to the body, and spread bread crumbs all around the corpse before vanishing."

Detective Carroll faced Cole properly then, suddenly all business and not fazed in the slightest bit by his lack of clothing.

"Two days ago," she said crisply, "a file landed on my desk. It was a report from the FBI, warning us to be on the lookout for a serial killer duo. They'd heard a report that the two might be headed for Manhattan. If a body turned up fitting their modus operandi, the case would be assigned to me. I was told I had until the FBI got wind of the situation and showed up on our doorstep to solve it."

Detective Carroll fell silent, allowing the noise of traffic coming through the broken window to fill the room as she watched both men carefully.

"Cole," Joss said, shattering the moment.

"Hm?" the sidhe asked. "What?"

"Pants."

Cole looked down at his unclothed state, shrugged, then marched past the detective without a word. Cole retrieved his clothes and dressed quickly while Joss approached Carroll, who was still watching Cole closely.

"So we have two serial killers running around New York?" he asked.

Detective Carroll looked around Joss at the body, avoiding his eyes entirely. Joss noticed how her eyes darted back toward Cole every few seconds, and scowled.

"It looks that way," Carroll said, before Joss could open his mouth. "According to the FBI file, these guys are pros. Their work is closer to that of professional killers rather than serial murderers. They typically target anyone connected with the occult, especially women. Occasionally, they've been tied to religious extremist groups, like those nutters down in Topeka, Kansas. Nothing was ever proven on that front, though."

Joss looked the body over for a moment, thinking hard. "You said that both scents were familiar," he said to Cole, who was slipping his boots back on. "Does that mean you can locate them?"

"Maybe," Cole said, grunting as the boot slid into place. "I can't promise anything, though."

"Why not?" Joss wondered as Cole stood. "I've seen you track someone all the way through Manhattan up into the Bronx before."

"Yes," Cole replied. "But I was tracking someone who had a very distinct scent at the time. As near as my nose can tell, the two perps that were here are human. You are talking about tracking down two specific humans in a whole city of them. This is the proverbial needle in a haystack scenario. I'll need a little bit more to go on."

Cole looked past Joss at the detective for a moment before meeting his lover's eyes. "Does this really concern us, though?" he wondered. "The case wasn't assigned to us, and Detective Carroll here was kind enough to remind us several times to stay out of it. Also, I'm pretty sure our three minutes ran out long ago."

Joss considered this. "Good point," he said, offering his hand to Carroll, who stood there as though she were a bump on a log. "It was nice meeting you, Detective. We have to go inform our friend of her loss. I'm sure she'll appreciate the time you've given us."

Cole followed in Joss's footsteps as the inspector left the room. The whole time, he could feel Detective Carroll's eyes watching him like a hawk.

"BITCH!" Rainette spat out, before launching into a coughing fit.

Joss and Cole waited until her hacking subsided. "I hate being sick," Rainette muttered. "Stupid twenty-four-hour flu is supposed to be gone after twenty-four hours."

"In theory," Joss said, passing a glass of water to Rainette, who was stretched out underneath the covers of her bed, looking thoroughly miserable. "You may have more than a twenty-four-hour bug on your hands."

Rainette accepted the glass and almost spilled its contents all over herself as her whole body spasmed from a very loud sneeze.

"Marcel called before you got here," she told them, taking a tentative sip. "He's even worse off than I am. Shit, it's bad enough that the coven's tattoo artist had to get called away because of a death in his immediate family. This is really going to shift things out of synch."

"What do you mean?" Cole asked, sitting down on the foot of the bed.

Rainette took another sip of water and sniffed. "I'm supposed to be ordained," she said. "The coven nominated me as the new sword maiden."

Rainette was a witch, the only one to be officially deputized into the Section. Her coven, the Shadewater, occasionally helped out on consulting jobs when the Section required the expertise of people knowledgeable about human magic, something Cole was hardly familiar with. Following an incident last month, the coven had awarded Rainette DuBois the title so that she could better serve both her sisters and Section Thirteen. The Shadewater witches saw it as killing two birds with one stone. As a member of the Section and a police officer, Rainette was charged with protecting and serving the fey and other mystical members of New York's underworld.

Cole was not intimately familiar with what all this entailed, but Rainette had made it sound like a very big deal.

Rainette, meanwhile, had set the glass of water back down on the nightstand next to her bed and was shifting to a more comfortable position. As she propped her back up against her pillows, the covers fell off slightly, exposing some of the tattoo work. Cole studied them for a moment as Rainette pummeled the pillows into a shape suitable for her comfort.

"Oh," she said, upon seeing Cole staring at her upper leg, which was poking out from the bathrobe she wore. "Right. I forgot to mention that part. Apparently, part of the ritual involves me looking like a mechanic's pinup girl."

"They're very nice," Joss commented innocently.

Rainette glared at this, then moved the sheet to where it blocked most of his view. "They're holy symbols," she said. "Belonging to the

Shadewater coven. I have to be inscribed with them, then submerged in water under the light of a full moon."

"Sounds reasonable," Cole said. "Your ancestors already paved the way for you being held underwater against your will. Now, you'll be doing it of your own volition."

Rainette shot Cole a very unfriendly glare as her nose twitched. "Unfortunately," she began, "Richardo, the tattoo artist the clan keeps on retainer, had to go to a funeral down in Transylvania."

Neither man blinked as Rainette let out another sneeze. "Louisiana," she added, wiping her nose with a tissue. "Apparently, there really is a Transylvania down in the swamplands. I was as surprised as you.

"So, with him being out of town and me having a cold, it looks like the ceremony is going to be postponed until next month, at least."

"Just get better," Joss said. "Someone is already on the case."

"Who?" Rainette wondered, her eyes going wide. "Wait, are you saying the Section isn't being assigned to this?"

"The FBI sent word to a detective at a different precinct," Cole said, looking unhappy all of a sudden. "She was told to find the killers before they could show up and take over the investigation. Personally, with what she has, I doubt very much that will happen."

"Same here," Joss agreed. "The killers have eluded capture this long. Finding them in such a short space of time is asking a lot."

Rainette looked angry. "That still doesn't explain why we weren't given the case," she insisted. "This sort of thing is our territory."

"Detective Carroll was given the assignment before the murder occurred," Joss told her. "She showed up on the scene after the crime was reported."

None of this seemed to matter to Rainette. "And this is irrelevant," Cole said to her, "because your coven sister was killed, and you feel responsible."

Rainette looked down at her lap. "I was talking to her when it happened," she said quietly. "The line was cut, so I dialed 911 and then phoned you guys."

"It's best if you leave it alone," Joss advised gently, giving Rainette's shoulder a tender squeeze. "Take it from an old man whose been doing this for a while. Getting involved in a case you are emotionally connected to is a bad idea. Take the time to grieve, and let someone else handle this."

Rainette wiped something out of her eye, but Cole said nothing. She would never forgive him if he acknowledged seeing her cry.

"I'm sword maiden of the Shadewater coven," she insisted, her voice rough but steady. "Or I will be next month, if no other disasters get in the way. This is my responsibility."

"Not yet, it isn't," Joss said firmly. "Get some rest, and we'll keep you posted. There's nothing that says we can't keep you informed on the case's progress. Once the FBI get dragged in, that'll be a different story, but we'll try to keep you updated with anything we find."

Cole had a feeling Rainette wasn't about to back down, but relaxed some when she pulled the covers up over herself.

"How good is she?" Rainette asked, looking at Joss. "This Carroll woman, I mean. Can she find the two that did this?"

Joss looked unsettled by the question but answered anyway. "I don't know her," he stated. "But word around her precinct says she's very determined."

Joss looked over at Cole and spotted the curious look on his face. "I phoned a friend who works as a janitor there while you were in the shower this morning," he explained, before turning back to Rainette. "According to him, Carroll has eyes on becoming an inspector someday. I think she'll see this case as her big chance, so regardless of her motivations, she won't let the opportunity pass without a fight."

Rainette nodded. "Good," she said. "Put in a good word with the higher-ups on her if she manages to find them."

Joss laughed along with Cole. "I'll see what I can do," he said. "I'd feel better if the woman had more time, though. The FBI is sure to find out in the next couple of days. That's not much time to track two elusive killers."

Rainette let out a miserable-sounding sigh and blew her nose again. "Her name was Alice," she said sadly. "I wasn't sure whether you knew or not, but she was one of the ones who visited me when I was in the hospital last month."

The smile on Joss's face was a bitter one. "We'll remember," he said. "Now rest. We'll keep you and the rest of your coven posted."

Cole could hear Rainette sniffling as he closed her bedroom door. Joss was quiet as they made their way downstairs to where the SEMA was parked.

"What now?" he asked as droplets of rain struck the windshield.

"Back to work," said Joss as they ducked into the car to escape the fresh rainfall. "What else? We still have a devil godmother to hunt down."

"No rest for the wicked," Cole said, starting the vehicle. The roar of the engine was lost as the rain intensified, drowning out any chance of further conversation.

They were never able to finish their date. Joss had wanted to inform Rainette right away once they were done cleaning up in the sithen. Afterward, neither of them felt like celebrating, so it was back to the sithen, where they turned in for the night. Lately, that was what their routine consisted of.

A little over a month ago, they had stumbled upon their first real lead about finding Naryssa since the year started. Naryssa was a half-sidhe night hag and serial murderer. The Section, in a dark twist, had her to thank for being allowed to reform. Part of the upper echelons' conditions in giving the occult division to the NYPD was that they locate the missing children she'd abducted.

Years ago, Naryssa had begun a crusade of murdering the parents of half-fey children and stealing said children from their cribs. According to her, half-fey children had no place in human society and could only look forward to a life of mistreatment and rejection. Cole had a difficult time arguing her point but could not deny that what the woman did was psychotic at best. After their first encounter, Naryssa had escaped, leaving the Section behind to spend several frustrating months searching for her. Last month, Cole and another member of the Section named Staffelbach had stumbled upon Naryssa's handiwork moments before a flame golem incinerated any chance of locating her.

Since then, the Section had run into several brick walls trying to hunt Naryssa down. It was for this reason that Cole had suggested they go out and blow off some steam. Joss had been reluctant to go to a fey bar at first, especially without Rainette and Marcel accompanying them, but he assured Cole, once they got home, that he hadn't been lying about having a good time.

"Where are we going?" Joss asked as Cole made a right turn. "The precinct's back in the other direction."

"I know," Cole replied. "We're going to Central Park."

"Central Park?" Joss's frown made his forehead wrinkle. "Why would we be going there?"

"There's someone I wish to talk to," Cole said, holding the car steady as rainwater washed over the busy city street. "It's high time I check in with the goblins and see if they've heard anything yet."

"Ah," said Joss, understanding now. "I gotcha. Are we gonna stop for donuts first?"

"That's their preferred method of payment." Cole held the steering wheel tightly as they turned off onto a side street. "Why?"

"Nothing," Joss answered quickly. "I was in the mood for a bagel. Did you want one?"

Farther down, through the swishing of the windshield wipers, Cole spotted the sign for the bakery and pulled into a space not far from the canopied doors. Even this far away, he could smell the unmistakable scent of freshly baked bread.

"Get me one with cream cheese," he said as Joss got out.

"Right."

A little while later, Cole was pulling into a space near the south gates of Central Park. Joss was holding the box of homemade donuts while licking the last few bits of bagel from his fingertips. Cole had nibbled on his during the drive and wrapped what remained in the paper covering before tucking it down into the cup holder at his side.

"I really wish we could have done this when it was sunny," Joss grumbled, fighting a losing battle to keep the box of donuts dry under his coat as he exited the car.

"They won't care," Cole said, keeping in step beside his man. "If they complain, I'll just have to hurt them a little."

Joss glared at hearing this. "Am I going to have to remind you yet again that you are a cop now?"

"I wish I could remember to pack an umbrella," Cole muttered over the sound of the rain hitting the sidewalk. "It's going to take forever for my hair to dry."

The goblins that lived in Central Park were a mercurial lot that occasionally worked for Cole as informants, provided he paid them in donuts. Cole was hoping the homemade variety would encourage them to get a move on in locating Naryssa's hideout, or at least some idea of where she might strike next. Bugbear, his cousin, Boogaloo, and his younger brother, Bugaboo, shared a space underneath a bridge.

As they approached the bridge, a flash of lightning flickered overhead. Joss hesitated in midstep, but Cole kept going. The lightning flashed again, and this time, it illuminated the spot under the bridge where the goblins lived. Cole saw through the rain and the darkness into the space and broke into a run. Without asking why, Joss pulled his gun out and took off after him.

Down around the creek, the remains of the goblins' home lay broken and scattered. The nest where the goblins had settled had been torn to shreds. It looked like the work of a wild animal, but as Cole knelt down on the riverbank, his nose twitched.

"Spinner," he said.

The rain had almost washed the scent away, yet it was unmistakable. Spinner was one of Naryssa's adopted children, a shape-shifting spider goblin who believed in Naryssa's mission wholeheartedly. The last time they'd met had been when Joss, Cole, and Corhagen had driven Naryssa's whole family from the sithen that Cole now called home.

Thunder rumbled overhead. "Naryssa commands the Hand of Storms," Cole reminded Joss, who stood with his gun drawn next to him, keeping watch. "I'd wager this rain is her handiwork. It looks like she was trying to wash away Spinner's trail."

"What was Spinner doing here?" Joss asked, passing the box of donuts on to Cole so he could shift his eye patch over.

"Looking for the goblins," Cole said. "The question is, why?"

Joss raised his gun fast and pointed it toward a thicket of bushes not far away. "There's your answer," he said, before calling, "Come out slowly where I can see you."

Cole noticed Joss was looking through his mystical eye, the one that had been granted to him by Danu. The eye glowed softly now against the rain, and it was aimed at a short figure wearing a Mets jacket.

"You're getting better at that," Cole noted as the short goblin waddled toward them.

"I'm remembering to use the darn thing now."

Cole waited while Bugbear trudged up along the riverbed toward them. Once he was close enough, Cole set the box with the donuts down on the ground, placing his foot atop it.

"What's the story, Bugbear?" Joss asked. "Anything we should know about?"

"Yeah," Bugbear said, keeping both of his beady little eyes on Cole's foot, which was applying the barest amount of pressure to the box. "One 'er two things cum ta mind."

"Such as?" Cole pressed, pushing his foot down ever so slightly.

"Well, one," Bugbear said, scowling. "Some fuzzy dame named Spinner paid me 'n' my family a visit jus' before ya showed up. Said summin' 'bout me, and givin' info to you, 'n' maybe bad thing happenin'."

"I see," Cole said, not letting his foot up yet. "What else?"

"Jus' one other lil' tiny thing," Bugbear said. "I quit."

Cole stared down at Bugbear. Joss did not raise his gun away from the goblin. Cole had taught him not to trust the little fuckers for a moment.

"You what?" Cole demanded angrily.

"I quit," Bugbear repeated. "An' I'll take the donuts as back pay now, iffin ya don' mind, ya white-haired sissy sidhe faggot."

JOSS pointed his gun down between Bugbear's legs. "Say that again," he demanded. "A little louder this time, I think."

Bugbear didn't back down. "Ye wouldn'," he challenged bravely. "Yer a cop, an' ye don' have that sorta stuff inya."

Cole stepped forward slightly. "I would," he stated, pulling out Aed Deigh, the double-bladed sidhe weapon which held the powers of fire and ice. "And I am a cop, remember?"

For once, Joss didn't make Cole back down. "Plus," the inspector said, "we can always see that these donuts get put to good use afterward."

Cole smirked. "Exactly," he said. "Just because you quit doesn't mean we should assume the same is true for the rest of your family. They might feel differently, after all."

The scowl on Bugbear's face gave Joss an immense sense of satisfaction. "These are homemade, incidentally," Cole added. "Not the prepackaged kind."

Bugbear lunged toward the box, but Cole was ready. Bugbear's snout face wound up acquainted with the front of Cole's boot. The blow sent him tumbling backward into the stream. Cole waited patiently as the wood goblin struggled to regain his footing in the muck while simultaneously cussing up a storm.

"Now then, what's this about you quitting?" Cole said as the goblin shook himself off. "I assume it has to do with the current state of your home, but a few details would be welcome."

Bugbear bared his teeth at the sidhe, but seeing Cole brush his thumb over the surface of Aed Deigh's hilt made him rethink things.

"The bitch godmother," Bugbear spat. "Iffin' you two couldn't've guessed. Her flunkie came this way askin' questions 'bout whether I'd sold infermation ta either one a' yous, er anybody else from the Section. The little spider-cunt didn' give me a chance ta answer, either. She went ahead 'n' figured you two'd be along sooner or later, and was jus' gonna use me ta leave you a message."

"I see," Cole replied calmly. "Where is your brother?"

Bugbear actually looked flattered at Cole's concern, but it lasted only a second before the scowl returned.

"Wit' Boogaloo," the goblin said. "Those two thought they'd be safer with sum distant relatives a' ours. Bugaboo's the only reason a no-account sack a' goblin eunuch like that cuz a' mine coulda shown his face there."

"Then Naryssa most likely knows where they are," Joss told him. "That, or she will soon enough."

"An' it's all a' because I sank so low as ta help out the lot a' you!"

"You could have sent word to us," Joss pointed out, putting his gun away. "We'd have put you under police protection."

"As what?" Bugbear wondered, cocking an eyebrow at Joss. "Escapees from da city pound? 'Sides that, I'd sooner die than accept favors from a cop, much less a no-account sidhe cop!"

"Would you like for Bugaboo to share that same fate?" Cole asked.

Bugbear's eyes doubled in size at Cole's frankness.

"Find your cousins," Cole told him. "Gather together anyone Naryssa might try and use to get to us. We'll find a place to put you all until the heat dies down."

Bugbear didn't look convinced. "Where?"

"You let us worry about that," Cole said. "Go, and bring them here. I know you well enough that they can't be very far. You can make it there on foot and back here in a relatively short time."

Bugbear took an instinctive step away from them to do that, then hesitated, as though forcing himself to stop.

"What makes ya think that?" he asked, shooting Cole a suspicious look.

"You love your brother," Cole stated as though it were obvious. "Whatever else you might want people in the community to think, there is no doubt in my or anyone else's mind that you would give up your life to keep him safe."

Bugbear looked as if he wasn't sure what to make of this.

"Go," Cole ordered. "Bring them back here. We'll have made arrangements for your whole clan by the time you get back."

"On your word?" Bugbear demanded.

"On my word," Cole answered easily. "Now hurry."

Bugbear had taken all of two steps when Cole stopped him again. "One other thing," he said warningly, extending Aed Deigh's firebrand to where the tip was pointed at Bugbear's crotch. "If you ever make a statement such as the one earlier ever again, I will personally deliver you to Naryssa's front doorstep with a ribbon and bow tied around your neck. Is that clear?"

"Sheesh," Bugbear retorted, trying to make light of things. "Can' ya take a freakin' joke once inna while?"

"I can," Cole said, "if it were remotely funny. What you said was not only crass, but against everything the fey are. You reduced yourself to the standards of humans with that statement. How would the other goblins respond to something like this?"

Bugbear's face distorted into a scowl again, but Cole wasn't finished. "What would Bugaboo think?" he added, drawing the blade back.

Bugbear looked revolted by the idea but turned his face away before it betrayed anything else. As the wood goblin retreated to gather his relatives, Cole's nose detected a shift in Bugbear's scent, indicating the wood goblin was far less opposed to the idea than he'd let on.

"Not that I'm taking his side," Joss began, giving Cole a look as he put Aed Deigh away, "but he did bring up an interesting point. Where are we going to put all of them that won't cause a stir?"

"I was thinking about that," Cole said, steeling himself for Joss's response. "And there's always the sithen."

Cole waited, and when Joss didn't immediately protest, he met his lover's eyes. Joss was looking back as though he hadn't heard Cole right.

"They don't have to live next door to us," Cole insisted. "With the way the sithen works, the goblins could live miles away. Since they're all wood goblins, the natural environment for them is the forest, and Mal could set one up, far away from anyone else."

"Underground?" Joss asked in a neutral tone, as though his willing suspension of disbelief were being stretched thin.

"Of course," Cole replied.

"Still inside the sithen, though?" Joss pressed, skepticism still ringing in his voice.

"Right," Cole affirmed. "You've seen the sithen do stranger things than that. We have working indoor plumbing and high-speed Internet, after all. How is a forest that much more of a stretch for you?"

Joss stood by the stream, looking as though he would very much love to argue but couldn't come up with a plausible example. After a moment, he gave up.

"So Mal is just going to grow a forest inside our home, far enough away so the goblins don't cause any problems," he said, though it sounded more like a question.

"Exactly," answered Cole. "I've thought about this for a while, and I rather like the idea of keeping the goblins on hand in case something goes wrong."

"You have?"

Cole frowned at how upset Joss suddenly sounded. Thankfully, before he could speak again, the reason dawned on him.

"Not without discussing it with you first," he added, remembering the little quirk most humans today had concerning communication. "I did not think it would be that big of an issue for you so long as we keep them far enough away."

Joss gave Cole a puzzled look at this. "I wasn't worried about that," Joss said, his eyes narrowed slightly now. "I'd figured out that much. I was just wondering why you thought they needed to be so close. We haven't used them that much in the past few months."

"True," Cole admitted. "Part of that, I think, is because none of them are available at a moment's notice. But if the goblins are in need of protection from Naryssa, we could offer them sanctuary in return for them working for us on a full-time basis.

"Plus," he added, while Joss was thinking this over, "we wouldn't have to keep buying them donuts."

Joss didn't look happy. "This sounds a little bit like indentured servitude," he said grimly.

"How so?" Cole wondered. "We're giving them jobs in exchange for room and board. They'll serve as the Section's informants and spies."

Joss still looked reluctant. "True," he said at last. "But you're still taking advantage of their situation."

"They'd do the same if the situation were reversed," Cole pointed out, unfazed. "Besides, if they don't like it, there are other alternatives."

"None of which I'll like, I'm sure," Joss muttered, keeping an eye out for the goblins' return. Cole ignored the statement.

"It's just that the sithen is the safest place to hide if Naryssa shows up," Cole concluded.

"How do we know that?" Joss asked suddenly. "The sithen used to belong to Naryssa. She could have set up some way to get back into it without us knowing."

"The sithen didn't belong to her," Cole objected, as though the fact were obvious. "It allowed her to live there because she was a strong enough power to hold it and because it needed a host."

Joss didn't look convinced at all. "Meaning?"

"It didn't have any other options at the time," Cole said as the goblins appeared not far away. "Besides," he said in a less obvious tone, "that was before Mal bonded with it. Nothing happens in the sithen now without him knowing it."

"Don't remind me," Joss grumbled as Bugbear came into full view along the edge of the bridge with several other goblins in tow, none of whom looked happy to be there.

"A'right," Bugbear grumbled, his beady eyes drifting back and forth between Joss and Cole before settling on the sidhe. "We're all here. This issit."

Joss did a quick head count and came up with a total of nine goblins.

"You know Boogaloo and Bugaboo," Bugbear said by way of introduction, gesturing to his cousin and younger brother.

Bugaboo grinned, letting his enormous tongue hang out from between two rows of dangerously sharp teeth. Boogaloo nodded, which Joss and Cole returned in kind, causing Bugbear to pause.

"This 'ere's my other cousins, Barbossa 'n' Blackadder," he went on, pointing a claw at the two slightly larger goblins standing behind him. "Then there's Bitterbeer, Bumblebarb, Beauregard, 'n' Bimbo."

Cole noticed that Bitterbeer and Bumblebarb were the only females in the group.

"Beauregard izza transplant from way down south," Bugbear explained, covering part of his mouth as though whispering. "We try not ta hold that against 'em, though."

"I'll keep that in mind," Cole retorted.

"Bitterbeer, Bumblebarb, 'n' Bimbo originally came from the West Albany branch of the family," Bugbear went on. "Before immigratin' down thisaway."

"Fascinating," Joss threw in as one of the female goblins began sizing him up.

"We have a proposition for you," Cole said, getting their attention. "None of you are obligated to comply, of course, but the offer stands, given the recent troubles your family has had."

It didn't take long for Cole to pitch his offer. The whole time, Joss thought the goblins looked less than thrilled at the idea. Bugbear, though, watched Cole's face as if he were trying to solve some kind of intricate puzzle.

"Sounds fishy," Bitterbeer said once he finished speaking.

Barbossa agreed wholeheartedly. "Ain't no way eyez goin' ta werk for a no-account—"

"Done," Bugbear said above his cousin's shouts. "We're all in. Every last single one of us."

Seven pairs of goblin eyes stared daggers into Bugbear's head. Only the younger brother looked into his brother's face with something other than malice. Concern mapped Bugaboo's face as Bugbear faced Cole, ignoring the rest of his family.

"We come work for ya," Bugbear stated, "inna exchange for protection from the Naryssa cunt anna chance to live in da sithen, right?"

"Right," Cole said.

"Ya gonna just sell da whole clan out to a…," Barbossa began, but Bugbear silenced him with a paw swipe to the nose.

"For the chance ta live in a sithen," Bugbear repeated. "For that, I'd skin you here and now an' make ya into a decent pair a' shoes for the sidhe to wear. Izzat clear?"

Blackadder stared at his cousin with something that resembled respect for a moment. "Clear," he said finally. "We all swear fealty to the white sidhe, the forsaken son of the Seventh Frost King."

"Good," Cole said. "You are now under my protection, and seeing that Naryssa has already struck here once, I suggest we leave before any of her children decide to make a second pass on the place."

"How are we getting them there?" Joss asked. "The subway?"

"Ya kiddin' me?" Bumblebarb spoke up for the first time. "Ya want us ta get mugged?"

"They can ride in the back of the car," Cole said. "It won't be comfortable, but the trip shouldn't take long."

"How do you figure that?" Joss wondered as they made their way up the small incline away from the stream with the goblins in tow.

Cole paused. Thankfully, the goblins were keeping to the bushes and didn't walk headlong into the backs of his legs.

"I'm not sure," he said after a moment, moving forward again. "It's just a hunch I had."

Sure enough, the garage that served as the secondary entrance to the sithen turned out to be not far away. All nine of the wood goblins had managed to squeeze into the backseat, though, as Cole had predicted, not comfortably. As soon as the magical garage that disappeared and reappeared throughout Manhattan slammed shut, the goblins burst out of the car and onto the concrete.

Mal appeared in front of Cole as he was getting out and gave a repulsed look at their guests. "I didn't know we were expecting company," he said derisively.

"They're staying here from now on," Cole said, leaning on the side of the opened car door. "They need protection from Naryssa, so I offered them a place to live in exchange for their full-time services."

Mal's face distorted into a copy of an Edvard Munch painting. "*No!*" he shouted, the sound magnifying as it echoed off the garage walls.

"Can the histrionics," Cole snapped, in no mood for Mal's antics. "Make a place for them in the sithen's lower areas, far away from the kitchen and both Joss's and my chambers. They're wood goblins, so a forest should do."

"You want me to make a forest inside the sithen?" Mal wondered.

Cole scowled. "Just do it," he ordered, before getting back into the car. "There haven't been any new cases assigned to us, so we should be home tonight."

Joss hadn't bothered climbing out. "Do you really think this is such a good idea?" he asked as Cole waited for the garage to reopen.

"I didn't think you would approve of us leaving them to die by Naryssa's hands," he said, backing the car out into Ninth Street, a good chunk of distance from the Section's precinct. "Literally or otherwise," Cole added. "Besides, if this doesn't work out, we don't have to keep them any longer than it takes for us to track Naryssa down."

"That's another thing that's been bothering me," Joss said as Cole drove across the busy city street. "What do we do with Naryssa once we catch her?"

Cole didn't answer as fresh rainfall began splattering against the windshield yet again.

"Well," Joss pressed, unwilling to let the subject drop. "I was hoping you had an answer. Is there a way to keep her locked up to where she can't hurt anyone, because the only other option is something I was hoping to avoid."

"I don't know," Cole told him, feeling trapped by the conversation. "It wasn't something I wanted to think about. Given what happened last time, Naryssa may not give us a choice in the matter."

Joss's face went rigid as Cole maneuvered through a set of flooded lanes toward the turn he needed to take.

"True," the inspector said, though it felt more as though he were giving his consent to something. "Maybe we shouldn't worry about that until we have a solid lead on her."

"We're getting closer," Cole replied, his voice thick with gentle warning. "And we have to consider it sooner or later."

The drive to the precinct didn't take as long as Cole expected. Though traffic was rough, he managed to steer through it more easily than usual. The two continued to discuss what options they had regarding Naryssa and what would happen to her once she was captured. In the end, though, neither of them could come to a satisfying conclusion. It seemed to Cole that the best answer to the problem was the most obvious one.

Unfortunately, this was also the answer his love was doing everything to avoid thinking about. From where Cole sat, there was just no splitting hairs. It seemed best for everyone if Naryssa died, and as soon as possible.

COLE had not been looking forward to today. There was to be a meeting between the Section members to cover the mountain of paperwork they'd been buried under. This was due to Cole having shot a member of Internal Affairs last month. The Section had been sent in along with a squad of commandos under the flag of the Hermetic Order of the Golden Dawn. The Order, for short, was a group of upper-class spell casters that had a general dislike of the fey. They'd infiltrated the IA at some point with one or more of their numbers and assigned a member to be the Section's liaison.

The higher brass did not like the idea of Section Thirteen, period. In their minds, it was a waste of taxpayers' money. The truth was that none of them wanted to believe what the Section fought on a frequent basis was true, that the dark had never lost its fangs and claws as technology marched onward, and that they were no safer now than their ancestors had been during the more primitive times.

The long and short of it was that Cole had shot and killed the Order's man. It had occurred when none of the parties involved had been occupying Earth space, though, and Cole wasn't sure personally how human law fit into that kind of thing. A group of imaginary friends brought to life by errant magic had gone on a rampage inside a TV studio, and in the end it had resulted in their pocket dimension home collapsing. Internal Affairs had been forced to rule the loss of one of their own as an unfortunate casualty, since Cole had been deliberately vague on the circumstances.

Thus far, both the agents of Internal Affairs and the Order had given the Section, specifically Cole, a fair amount of breathing space. It would not last long. Every last one of them knew that, but the reprieve was to be savored while it lasted.

The meeting in question, on the other hand, had to do with how their superiors were handling the Section's continued existence. No one involved in the fiasco survived save for Cole and Joss, as well as Marcel and Rainette, their fellow Section members who had gone on the mission with them. Since there was no evidence of what went down one month ago, the brass had taken a different approach, bringing down the hammer of paperwork on the Section's collective heads instead. A backlog of cases from the past several years had arrived on their proverbial doorstep recently. Each one of them had gone through stack after stack of cold cases with the goal of determining whether or not the cases in question had involved the paranormal in any capacity. Ironically, this had actually helped the Section out a great deal. Recent events had made it clear to Cole that the Section was going to have to become more adept at using the unique skills that each one possessed in a more pragmatically combat-oriented way.

Thus far, they'd been unable to get a handle on this because of the fieldwork usually involved in their cases. However, with there only being six members and a truckload of files to go through, the team's time frame had to be measured. More time was now being spent sitting behind desks and wrapping up old cases, most of which hadn't involved anything supernatural in the slightest. This meant the team was spending more time together and were able to sneak away during periods when the precinct gym was not in use, for training.

Granted, there had been more than a few mishaps, such as the floor somehow gaining several smoldering holes in it and a vaulting horse getting bent in half. Marcel had apologized profusely afterward, but Cole had chalked it up as the typical bumps in the road when it came to giving an ogre a crash course in police training.

Another benefit of this was that, rather than being sent off to chase down every false lead the brass could send them on, the team was able to narrow down their search for Naryssa. The trail had grown cold several times, but just when it looked the bleakest, another of Naryssa's adopted children would make an appearance.

Cole had found these unsettling. The sightings were almost always random, yet there were tiny hints of a bigger pattern. In the end, he had agreed with Joss's conclusion: that either Naryssa was trying to get them to follow a wild goose chase, or something had happened that was forcing the children to take unnecessary risks.

Either way, the month of April had been anything but dull. The constant rain and flood warnings alone would have made many a native New Yorker think about looking for drier ground. Tracking down an immortal serial murderer and kidnapper in such conditions would have taxed anyone. These days, the only thing keeping Cole dry was the warmth from Joss's body when they were wrapped up in each other's arms.

Only Staffelbach and Corhagen would be at the meeting today, since Rainette and Marcel were out sick. Both should have been waiting for Cole and Joss to arrive in Joss's office. However, before the two were even halfway there, a shout echoed down the hall from back behind them.

"MacColewyn! Vallimun!"

Both turned to see a sergeant Cole didn't recognize marching down the corridor. "The captain wants to have a word with you," he said, moving briskly through the space between them.

"Oh good," Cole muttered. "I wonder what he wants."

"No telling," Joss said. "Let's go find out."

Captain Hawkins never looked happy to see Cole. As a rule, the captain didn't have much contact with the sidhe. This time was no different. The moment Cole set foot into Hawkins's office, the man's heart rate doubled. Anxiety rolled off his body in waves, so much that Cole could smell it. His eyes zeroed in on Cole and lingered there for several seconds before acknowledging Joss at all.

"Sit down," he ordered, gesturing to the chairs placed against the wall in front of his desk.

"I received a request this morning to allow two members of Section Thirteen a temporary transfer," Captain Hawkins said, once Cole and Joss were seated.

"Transfer," Cole wondered. "To where?"

"Precinct 1120," Hawkins answered, his eyes once again staring at Cole for longer than was considered polite in human circles. "A Detective Carroll called in a favor and requested two members to help with a serial killer case she'd been assigned."

Cole glanced at Joss at the mention of the name. "Officers DuBois and Marrowdrinker are out with the flu," Joss told the captain, who took a moment meeting Joss's gaze. "This puts us on short order until they get back."

"It isn't my call, Inspector," said the captain. "Detective Corhagen and Special Detective MacColewyn are to report to her within the hour to begin their new assignment."

Cole frowned. "Why myself?" he asked. "And why Corhagen?"

Joss gave Cole a quick look, advising him to remain silent. "She asked for the both of you specifically by name," Captain Hawkins said, folding his hands on his desk. "You can ask her when you see her. I need to have a word with you before you go, Inspector Vallimun, but you, MacColewyn, had better move your pasty white ass."

Cole took his leave reluctantly but waited down the hallway a ways for Joss to exit. A few minutes later, Joss ambled back toward Cole, looking less than pleased.

"I was just given a warning," Joss said quietly as Cole fell in step beside him.

"About what?"

Joss kept quiet as they passed through a crowd of officers relaxing around the watercooler. Almost every one of them watched the two closely. Cole overheard one snicker, and shot him a glare, silencing the man instantly and causing him to spill his water.

"There's been talk that someone from higher upstairs is planning to assign a new liaison between Internal Affairs and Section Thirteen," Joss continued, once the coast was clear.

Cole snorted. "I'm surprised anyone would accept the offer, considering what happened to the last one."

"Yes," Joss agreed as they rounded a corner in step with each other. "Well, I suspect that has something to do with why it's taking them so long. In any case, the good captain thought I ought to know. He didn't say who was coming down on him, but I think we can both guess."

"The Order," Cole said flatly.

"Right."

Nothing was said the rest of the way up to Joss's office. Discussing the Order in any capacity was risky, and Cole didn't feel like being overheard at the moment. Joss felt the same way, evidently, though the slightly strained look on his face never left as they rounded the corner to where Joss's office sat. The door was open, and Corhagen stood leaning against the frame slightly, with both hands in his pockets. Cole couldn't resist giving the mortal a glare as they approached.

"You've been reassigned temporarily," Joss said without preamble.

"I know," Corhagen replied, and it sounded to Cole like he wasn't thrilled with the idea. "Hawkins already filled me in. I got the word just as soon as I walked through the doors. Guess this means it's you and me again, like old times, huh?"

The last part was said to Cole, who didn't answer. "We have to be there in less than an hour," Cole said, specifically to Joss. "Will you be all right here with just Staffelbach?"

"I'll have to be," Joss pointed out. "You two have got no say in things, anymore than I do. Hopefully, Marcel and Rainette will be better within the next two days, and we won't be shorthanded for very long."

"And hopefully," Corhagen added, grinning, "there won't be any major disasters during that time."

Both men stared. "You just had to jinx it, didn't you?" Joss said flatly, causing Corhagen to lower his head slightly.

"Sorry, sir."

Joss sighed. "Just go," he ordered.

Corhagen nodded and marched down the hall past Cole, letting his arm brush up against the sidhe ever so slightly. Cole felt a twinge and grimaced.

"Call me if anything goes wrong," he said, not leaving Joss's side just yet. "Let me know how Staffelbach is doing."

"I think it'll be okay," Joss said hopefully. "He's been getting better. We haven't had nearly as many short-outs this week."

"Save, of course, for the time he accidentally leaned against the fire alarm," Cole pointed out to him, smiling. "At least he can touch a computer now without it catching fire. That saves a lot of time and money for everyone."

"Go," Joss ordered, though in a much softer tone than when he spoke with Corhagen. "I'll call, even if nothing serious happens. I'd like to know more about why Detective Carroll wanted both of you."

"I might understand her wanting me," Cole said as he walked off. "The real mystery is what she could possibly need with Corhagen."

Cole moved to catch up with Corhagen, more out of necessity than a desire to be close to the man. In the four months since they'd joined the Section together, his relationship with James had been strained, to say the least.

At one time, Cole had considered Detective James Corhagen among his closest and most trusted mortal friends. They'd met under less than stellar circumstances, when a rank amateur witch was dabbling in love potions to seduce her students. Cole had gotten mixed up in the whole ordeal, was wrongfully accused, and ended up helping to capture the real culprit in order to get the police off his ass. The result was that he and Corhagen had developed an uneasy truce with one another that evolved into a strange sort of friendship.

For several years afterward, Corhagen had worked as a police consultant specializing in occult matters. Corhagen ended up becoming a magnet for strangeness, meaning Cole was frequently on call. As a result of the sidhe's help, the young officer had ended up with a promotion and an unwanted attraction to the sidhe. Cole hadn't set out for this to happen, but he wasn't ashamed of it, which had been more than anyone could say for James.

After dancing back and forth in an awkward tango of ego and bruised masculine pride, Corhagen had run toward the heterosexual safety of his now-wife's arms. Cole spent a year not hearing from him and struggling to make ends meet without his primary source of income.

Then, on a cold day shortly after the first of the New Year, Corhagen had summoned Cole right out of the shower to a crime scene. That act had snowballed into Cole joining the force as one of the founding members of Section Thirteen. It had also led to Inspector Joss Vallimun, their leader, becoming his lover and roommate.

These days, Cole tried to have as little interaction with Corhagen as possible. The man's inability to get past his naïveté and shortcomings had left things tense. However, Cole told himself, it would only be for a couple of days. Working closely with Corhagen wouldn't be too difficult. Plus, there would be a third party to keep things interesting, and if James stayed consistent with his previous track record, this whole debacle had great potential for amusement.

So, it was with a slightly less annoyed expression that Cole slid into his vehicle with Corhagen coming in on the passenger side. The engine gave off a somewhat louder rumble than usual, and Cole couldn't help but think it was due to the mortal sitting next to him.

The space inside the car was rife with discomfort from Corhagen's end as Cole pulled out into the street.

"Feels funny, doesn't it?" Corhagen asked. "Working together again, I mean. Just the two of us."

"It won't be the two of us," Cole said. "We were assigned to work with Detective Carroll. It's her case we're being brought over to help solve."

Corhagen went quiet for a moment. "Yeah," he said at last, sounding less than thrilled at the idea. "Do you know the woman, incidentally? I'd never heard of her until this morning."

"We met last night," Cole answered, in an attempt at keeping things civil. "Rainette called Joss and I, asking us to check in on a friend of hers. It turns out, her friend had been murdered."

"Shit," James swore, looking grim as he stared out the window.

"Detective Carroll was the officer given the case," Cole continued, as though Corhagen hadn't interrupted. "The victim fit the MO of a serial killer pair that targets witches. Carroll was told to solve the case before the FBI could be alerted. She's desperate to catch the perps who did this so she can land a promotion."

Corhagen was staring at Cole now. "You learned all of that from her last night?" he wondered, looking surprised.

"No," Cole said. "Joss learned some of it from a janitor and filled me in before we showed up for work. The rest I picked up while sniffing around the crime scene."

"Sniffing around…." Corhagen's eyes doubled in size. "She saw you…."

Cole shrugged calmly. "There was nothing else for me to do," he said. "She wouldn't let me change in the bathroom."

"Great," Corhagen muttered. "It'll be all over the NYPD by tomorrow."

"I'm not worried," Cole replied at once. "They'd much rather gossip about me and Joss fucking than the fact that I occasionally have four legs and a tail."

Corhagen's face soured for a moment as Cole steered the car through traffic toward Precinct 1120. Surprisingly, Detective Carroll was waiting for them on the front steps, seeking shelter from the rain that was still pouring down as Cole pulled up along the curb.

Cole tooted the horn and flashed his lights, hoping to get her attention. Carroll hesitated in midsip of the Styrofoam cup of coffee she held, then hesitantly ran out into the downpour.

Corhagen reached around and popped the back door open for her to save time. "What the fuck kept the two of you?" she blurted out, jumping in out of the rain.

"We just found out we were being assigned this morning," Corhagen said when Cole didn't answer. "I'm James Corhagen, by the way, in case you didn't know it."

"She knows," Cole pointed out dryly, before turning out into the street. "Otherwise, she wouldn't have asked for both of us specifically."

"Oh, right."

Cole didn't allow the silence to linger for very long this time. "So, where to?" he asked Carroll, who was quietly sipping coffee in the backseat.

"The victim's body was taken to the morgue at St. Mary's Hospital," she replied between sips. "Let's head there first. I want to hear what the coroner found."

Corhagen shifted uncomfortably in his seat. "How long has the victim been dead?" he asked, casting a noticeable glance toward Cole.

"Not long enough," Cole cut back curtly. "We'll have to do things the mortal way on that front, at least for another day or two."

"What?" Carroll asked sharply.

Cole could feel her eyes drilling into the back of his head. "I can speak with the dead," Cole answered, eliciting a look from Corhagen, which he ignored.

Carroll frowned. "Like a psychic?"

"No," he replied, cutting a turn sharply at the corner of Fifteenth and Twelfth Streets. "I mean, I can raise the bodies of people who have been dead for a sufficient period of time and ask them questions."

For a moment, the car was filled with the sound of rain hitting the roof. Corhagen sat stiffly, expecting a bomb to go off. Cole remained unfazed.

"Is he serious?" she asked Corhagen.

Corhagen hesitated before answering. "Yes," he said finally. "He has the power to raise the dead."

Slowly, Carroll turned from Corhagen to Cole, her eyes narrowing sharply. "How?" she asked in a decidedly calm tone, once her gaze had again settled on the back of his head.

"It is the nature of my kind," he said as St. Mary's Hospital appeared off in the distance. "We all have unique gifts. That is mine."

"Along with changing into a dog?" Carroll cut in sarcastically.

"Wolf," Cole corrected. "And no, that ability was given to me by someone else many years ago. I wasn't born with it."

A smirk spread over the female detective's face. "Did you buy it online?" she asked jokingly. "Because, if so, I seriously need to reconsider my stance on some of those Internet auction sites."

"It was a gift," Cole said, his patience with the woman stretching ever so slightly as the car pulled up into the hospital parking lot, "from the Queen of All Faerie."

Cole caught a glimpse of the blanched look on Detective Carroll's face as he was climbing out of the car. A moment went by, and then she seemed to come out of it. Shaking her head, Carroll exited Cole's vehicle and tossed her cup into a nearby trash can.

"Is it always going to be like this?" she asked Corhagen once they were safely out of the rain.

"I'm afraid so," Corhagen replied, giving Cole a look as he marched up underneath the canopy, blithely ignoring the two of them now.

"Actually, scratch that," Corhagen said, shaking his head. "It'll get a lot worse before the day is over with. Right now, just be thankful things haven't gotten any weirder."

"And no scarecrows have shown up," Cole threw in.

This gained him a laugh from Corhagen and yet another glare from Detective Carroll. Surprisingly, her look softened after a moment, and she playfully smacked him on the back. "All right then," she said, almost a little too cheerfully. "Let's go talk to the coroner and maybe even the corpse, too. One of them is bound to have some answers for us."

Corhagen rolled his eyes as they entered the building one after the other. "We can only hope," he said, before the door shut behind him.

4

THE coroner was not happy to see Cole.

All of Detective Carroll's questions were answered quickly and efficiently, but the coroner's eyes darted toward Cole every other minute or so. The look there was less than friendly, bordering on hostile, in fact. It could not have been more obvious that she wanted him to leave.

Against his better judgment, Cole waited until she walked away before speaking.

"It would appear that word about me has spread around the community of corpse-handlers in the city," he mused, watching her leave.

"Your reputation precedes you," Corhagen jabbed.

"Do I want to know why?" Carroll asked worriedly.

Cole shrugged. "I like to be alone with the deceased when I work," he said. "Occasionally, the bodies will scream upon revival. I suspect that led to the employees present at the time coming to their own conclusions about what was going on behind closed doors."

Carroll blinked. "Screaming?"

"Being murdered is traumatic," Cole said pointedly. "How do you think your body would react to being killed and then resuscitated several days later?"

"I've asked," Corhagen threw in, only half joking now as the coroner's aide shot them a strange look. "He isn't making them yell like that for grins. The bodies really do react that way."

Detective Carroll looked as though she wasn't sure how to respond or whether she even wanted to. "Let's talk about something other than screaming corpses," she suggested, heading for the door.

"If you insist," Cole said, getting the door for her.

Carroll brushed past him as though he weren't there. "The body of the victim was stabbed first, before being burned," she said aloud, repeating what they'd just heard. "Going by the number of abrasions and bruises on the arms, shoulders, and legs, the coroner thinks she put up a struggle."

"With that many injuries, there's also a possibility that she was tortured," Corhagen said thoughtfully. "Did Rainette say anything about this coven sister, or whatever they call themselves, knowing something important?"

"She kept to herself, mostly," Cole said. "Katalina was from the same coven, and I never met the young woman once."

"Who is Katalina?" Carroll wondered.

Cole paused. "A friend," he answered curtly. "She was murdered several months ago. It was my fault."

Cole could feel the eyes of both staring at him as he stared off into the distance. "The way her apartment looked suggested there was a struggle," he said quickly, wanting badly to change the subject. "Nevertheless, she was attacked in her home, stabbed, and then set fire to while one of the two perpetrators spread bread crumbs around the body."

"Something about that's been bothering me," said Carroll, taking the cue as the trio made their way through the hospital corridor. "Why bread crumbs? I get the burning part, kind of, but why spread bread crumbs around the body?"

"How does burning the body make sense?" Corhagen asked.

"The victim was a witch," Cole explained, without thinking about the fact that it was Corhagen who asked. "I believe Detective Carroll is referring to the infamous witch burnings that went on in Europe some time ago."

"And the ones in Salem," Carroll added.

"Actually, they didn't burn witches in Salem," Corhagen corrected, looking pleased with himself.

Carroll frowned as they reached the front doors again. "Sure they did," she insisted, before turning to face Cole. "Didn't they?"

"No," he replied. "The government stripped the accused of their rights and locked them in prisons, hanged them, drowned them in lakes, and crushed them under heavy piles of rock, but no one was actually burned, with or without the stake, to my knowledge."

"Funny how so many people get that wrong," Corhagen said, laughing now.

Cole gave him a look. "And how did you come to know that?" he asked.

"I read," Corhagen said defensively. "You aren't the only one around here who knows how to use Wikipedia."

"Whatever," Carroll cut in, clearly bored with the subject now. "So we can confirm that the victim was assaulted, stabbed, then burned in her own home. Didn't you say something last night about a smell, MacColewyn?"

"The scents were familiar," he admitted. "But I still haven't placed them. However, as for the bread crumbs you mentioned earlier, it's probably a reference to Hansel and Gretel."

Detective Carroll glared at Cole for a moment, trying to gauge whether or not he was serious. When Cole met her stare, unflinching, she let out a long, pained sigh.

"Okay," she grumbled. "So, Hansel and Gretel are roaming the streets looking for witches to burn."

"Sounds plausible," said Corhagen as they reached Cole's car.

Carroll rounded on Corhagen as she beat him to the door to the front seat.

"You get used to it after a while," he explained calmly, moving away so as to climb into the backseat. "This sort of thing is normal for us."

"At least there haven't been any cake golems recently," Cole said, already inside with the keys in the ignition. "I, for one, am glad that's over."

"Cake golems?"

Carroll looked in the rearview mirror at James, who was struggling with his seat belt. "No kidding," he said over the sound of the buckle snapping into place. "Those things were weird."

Carroll was rubbing her forehead in frustration as Cole drove the car out of the parking lot. "I'm going to wish I'd never asked the two of you for help, aren't I?" she growled. "Are you seriously telling me that there are… cake golems, was it?"

"Not anymore," Cole said calmly, stopping as the light up ahead turned red. "We arrested the man responsible."

Corhagen piped up while they sat waiting. "And making women from cakes was by no means the worst thing he'd done," he said. "I'd rather not think about it, though."

Carroll gave her head a quick shake. "Let's get back to the case," she insisted. "Before this conversation gets even more off track."

"And here I was on the verge of telling you about Little Red Riding Hood," Cole said, amused, as the light finally changed.

"Save it for later," she barked as the car picked up speed again. "Now, the FBI file had a lot of info on these two. They frequently pose as husband and wife, so maybe they're staying at a hotel."

"If they're passing themselves off as a newlywed couple, we could check the honeymoon suites," Corhagen suggested. "That's something."

"I have another thought," Cole said. "We should check out Alice Tweedle's apartment again."

Cole spun the wheel and cut into a turning lane, which would take them back toward the deceased witch's home. Carroll gripped the door handle as they zipped along.

"What for?" she asked, once they were traveling at a more or less reasonable speed again.

"It's been long enough," he said. "We might be able to ask Alice Tweedle's ghost for details."

"Shit," Corhagen exclaimed. "I completely forgot you could do that."

Going by the look on her face, Carroll was doing her best to keep up but had run into a snag. "Slow down," she said, as Cole took another turn sharply.

Cole obliged by letting up off the gas.

"I didn't mean the car," she snapped in irritation. "I mean… what's all this about ghosts now? I thought you needed time to raise a body, like the stars had to align, or something."

"My power does not work in conjunction with the stars," Cole said. "It is a matter of time, the passage of the soul from this life to the next and the age of the corpse in question."

"Thank you," she said sarcastically. "That helps so much."

"I wasn't intending to raise Alice Tweedle's corpse," he explained. "What I meant was, we might be able to speak with her spirit. In the case of that, the body isn't necessary."

"Cole has power over all sorts of the dead," Corhagen tried, giving the back of Detective Carroll's head a sympathetic look. "The older the dead are, the easier it is for him to control them. Fresh bodies are out of his range, generally, but ghosts are a different story."

"You might be able to actually contact her spirit?"

Cole ignored the skepticism in Carroll's voice and continued onward. "Inside of her apartment, I should be able to make it manifest so that all three of us can see," he said. "Inside the victim's home, where she was murdered, no less, there is a strong spiritual connection."

Carroll went quiet as Cole hit a stretch of road with slightly less traffic and floored the accelerator. The chariot of the Wild Hunt roared in response to the noise of the other vehicles surrounding it, rising to the challenge. In moments, it had peeled out far ahead of them.

Carroll spoke up again as they entered a turnpike. "When I said that I wanted to bring Section Thirteen in to help me with this case, my superior advised me to rethink it. Something about you guys not doing things according to police procedure."

"Our work doesn't give us the luxury," said Corhagen.

"I'm beginning to see that," she replied. "So this is a typical day for all of you, huh? You fight monsters, raise dead bodies, and talk to ghosts?"

A great big grin split Corhagen's face as he nodded enthusiastically. "That's not even the really strange stuff."

Carroll shook her head at the smile still on Corhagen's face. "I thought you were supposed to be the normal one," she told Corhagen, which caused Cole to frown.

"That subject is up for serious debate," said Cole.

ALICE TWEEDLE'S home had been left more or less the way he and Joss had seen it the night before. It didn't look as though anyone from the Shadewater coven had come by yet. Cole was grateful, at least for the moment. What they were about to do wasn't an exact process, especially with a spirit so young, but ghosts tended to work under a whole different sense of time and rules than decomposing flesh. As a result, calling the soul of the Tweedle witch would most likely be easier if very little of her apartment were touched.

There was no one watching the door this time. Corhagen and Detective Carroll had gone to find the landlady so they could retrieve the key while Cole headed on up. To his surprise, the apartment door had been left unlocked.

Upon closer inspection, Cole saw that the door was cracked ever so slightly. Nudging it open, he peeked in, reaching for Aed Deigh at the same time, and sniffed the air. The room beyond smelled empty, yet the air hummed, as though whispering with some forgotten power. Cole had to remind himself that this was the dwelling of a witch. Spells had been cast here with frequency through the years, and Alice Tweedle's death would not have diminished that so quickly.

Convinced the coast was clear, Cole strode in but did not put his weapon away. His footsteps fell softly on the hardwood floor as he crossed the living area, sniffing the air as he went along. Cole reached into his pocket with his free hand, pulled out his phone, and hit the button for Joss's number. Two rings later, he heard his lover's voice come through, and let out a deep sigh.

"It's me," he said. "I'm back at Alice Tweedle's apartment."

"Hey," Joss replied, his voice practically dripping with affection now. "How's it going so far? Are you and Corhagen behaving yourselves with the nice detective?"

"How comical," Cole bit back sarcastically. "They're downstairs getting the key from the landlord. I went ahead and came up. The apartment door was left unlocked."

"Uh-oh," Joss said, suddenly very worried.

"The place is empty," Cole assured him. "It doesn't smell as though the place has been occupied since the forensics team left last night. I'm going to try and raise Alice Tweedle's ghost and see if she can answer a few questions, since my powers can't raise her body for another few days, at least."

"Will that work?" Joss wondered. "I don't remember you ever trying to raise the ghost of any murder victims before."

"Alice Tweedle was a witch," Cole reminded. "She was far more aware of the world and what goes on than the average New Yorker. It's possible that this will help make summoning her ghost much, much easier." Cole paused. "Or more difficult. If she has accepted her death, then there would be no reason for her to hold on to life."

"Right," Joss said, mentally scrolling back through what Cole had told him about ghosts. "They're pale reflections, fragments of a soul left behind.

"Well, good luck with digging up her ghost," Joss said, and it sounded as though he was saying good-bye. "I have to get back to work. I'll see you tonight, if not sooner."

"I miss you," Cole said, but Joss was already hanging up.

It sounded as though someone had been entering the room when the line went dead, so Cole wasn't offended by the abrupt cutoff. A few minutes later, Corhagen and Detective Carroll entered the room.

"Did you find the key?" he asked, enjoying the expressions on their faces.

"What happened?" Carroll wondered. "Did you break down the door?"

"It was open," he said, which earned him a sour look from Corhagen. "Someone left it unlocked and slightly ajar. It doesn't smell as though anyone has been here since the forensics team left, so I'm guessing it was just an oversight on someone's part."

"Wonderful," said Carroll, looking less than pleased now. "We just wasted valuable time. Well, get on with your hoodoo and see if you can't call the witch's ghost."

"My son loves that movie," Corhagen mused.

Cole ignored James and raised his left hand. Distracted by this, Carroll lowered the hand she had been about to smack Corhagen with and watched with eyes wide open as Cole summoned the bit of power he needed.

"Alice Tweedle," he said in a soft tone. "Witch of the Shadewater coven and fallen sister in service to the Goddess and Consort. By your name, I call upon your spirit. Answer my Hand of Power."

"That's it?" Carroll wondered as Cole opened his eyes. "I thought we were going to have to cut up a live chicken or something."

"I know," Corhagen said, keeping his eyes on Cole as well. "I was disappointed too when it was my first time. They make it look so much cooler in the films."

"I am officially ignoring you both," Cole declared. "And I think I have something."

The signal was faint, but being of the realm of the spirit, which Cole's power was tied to inexorably, his Hand of Power latched onto it with razor-sharp precision. A moment later, mist was flowing out from his clenched hand. Cole blew into it, sending the vapor through the air, where it congealed. A face formed from it, followed by the vague outline of a human body. Little by little, it grew more distinct, until the transparent form that had once been Alice Tweedle was standing in front of them.

Or hovering, as it were.

"Alice Tweedle," Cole said in a firm voice, getting the ghost's attention. "I have called you to the place that was once your dwelling. Can you understand me?"

Detective Carroll had gone pale. "What about that isn't impressive?" she wondered, leaning toward Corhagen slightly.

"Oh," Corhagen replied in a hushed tone, tearing his eyes off Alice. "I meant the first part. This half is always good for something."

The ghost of Alice Tweedle, meanwhile, had zeroed in on Cole the moment she registered his voice. A wind rustled through the room, stirring the curtains. Alice's face then distorted, and her hands became twisted, grotesque claws as her jaw stretched down, leaving her mouth hanging wide open. A horrible sound erupted from inside of it.

Cole stood there, unimpressed. "Knock it off," he ordered, clenching his fist again.

Alice snapped back to her previous form at once. "Spoilsport," she grumbled. "I'm dead. The least you could do is let me have a little fun."

"I thought you said she would be traumatized," Carroll said, interrupting them from several feet further back.

"Some ghosts handle death better than others," Corhagen told her, still standing in the same spot as before.

"And some develop warped senses of humor as a result," Cole finished, lowering his arm again. "Or become incredibly sarcastic. It all depends on the person involved, really."

"I prefer to embrace my new status with dignity, thank you," Alice replied haughtily. "After all, death is a natural state of being, not something to be feared."

"And it isn't as though you have a say in the matter," Cole pointed out.

Alice gave him the international symbol of friendship, which made Corhagen chuckle.

"I was told you might come here," she said to Cole, keeping her back to the others now. "They said that you would be asking about how I died."

"They?"

Alice stared down at Cole as though she weren't impressed. "My death was foretold," she explained, as if discussing a rather interesting pair of shoes she'd found. "I sought to prevent it. I even kept Rainette on the line because I thought she would call for help."

"She did," Cole said. "We got here after your killers fled."

"New York traffic," she grumbled. "I had to die because traffic got in the way of my plan."

"Who predicted you would die?" Cole asked, hoping Alice Tweedle's ghost was not the sort to be easily distracted. "And why didn't you just leave town?"

"I couldn't," she said. "I had a sacred duty to perform. That, I'm assuming, is the whole reason why they came for me. They wanted to know about the sword."

"What sword?"

This was from Carroll, who'd taken a brave step forward at hearing that. "Nobody found a sword anywhere in the apartment. If they had, I would know about it."

Alice said nothing.

"Go ahead," Cole said, gesturing. "Answer her. I'm curious to know about this, as well."

"The sword wasn't here," Alice's ghost explained, sounding a little bored now. "Only a piece of it. I was chosen by the Order to guard it."

Cole blanched, and Corhagen's face fell in shock. "You were a part of the Order?" Cole demanded. "Does Rainette know?"

Alice snorted. "No," she said flippantly. "No one in the Shadewater coven knew. I kept that a secret from them, obviously. Since the Shadewater wouldn't cooperate with the Order, they approached me to work as their spy. I traded information to them in exchange for money, better spells, and a piece of one of their holy objects."

Alice gestured around her still-damaged living room. "Even with the mess," she said. "Do you think I could have afforded a place like this on my own?"

"What is the sword?" Cole asked. "I command you to tell me."

Alice smiled. "There's no need to," she replied. "They knew I would have to tell you anything you asked if you managed to summon me. I wasn't expecting to come back like this, but it doesn't matter either way. The sword is one of the Four Hallows of the Tuatha de Danann."

The others went quiet, waiting for an explanation, but none came. Alice's ghost did not elaborate, and Cole's body went completely still.

"I would accuse you of lying," he whispered at last. "But that shouldn't be possible. Even a witch's ghost shouldn't be able to resist my Hand of Power, and I would sense it if you were trying."

"On the true name of the Mother of Darkness," Alice swore, with a glint of self-satisfaction in her eye. "I kept a piece of Claiomh Solais. The Hermetic Order of the Golden Dawn seized it years ago and divided it up."

"Why?" Cole wondered. "It seems as though the sword would have better suited the Order in its original form."

"You'd think so," she said, acknowledging his statement with a nod. "Apparently, there was some kind of prophecy surrounding it."

"Concerning what?"

"A prophecy?" Carroll asked, breaking in to intercept Cole's question. "Is all of this for real?"

"I don't know," Alice answered, paying the detective no mind now. "They wouldn't give me the full version, and I was…."

Alice hesitated for a moment. "*Deterred*," she finished at last, "from snooping around for more information. Something about the sword aiding a great king. And that's all I know."

"Okay, you know what?" Detective Carroll strode forward, her nervousness echoing in the loud footfalls she made against the floor. "Forget this shit. I've bought into wolf men, the dead rising from the grave, and the fact that I'm talking to a ghost. Now there are prophecies and kings?"

"I'm pretty sure she said there was just one king," Corhagen amended, stepping up behind her. "And like I said, you get used to it after a while."

"And a prophecy doesn't concern us," Cole said, turning away to face Alice's ghost again. "Nor does the sword, at least for the moment. Who murdered you, Alice Tweedle? Give us their names, if you can."

"I can't," she countered. "Because I don't know them. We didn't get a chance to sit down and have a cup of tea. They were a little distracted with the idea of killing me."

"So we just wasted twenty minutes talking to a ghost," Carroll concluded, throwing her hands up. "And being sold a bunch of garbage about a sword and a prophecy and some king. I thought you people were efficient."

"What's her hurry?" Alice's ghost wondered, watching Carroll with an odd sort of expression.

"Apparently, you were murdered by two serial killers that the FBI have been chasing for some time," Cole told her. "Detective Carroll was told to solve the case before they show up and take over the investigation. That is why we were brought in."

"Oh," the ghost replied with a shrug, as though it no longer concerned her. "In that case, I did get a pretty good look at them. Do I need to give a description?"

"No need," Cole said, as Carroll turned back around with a notepad in hand. "I can reconstruct them both from your fragmented memory."

Carroll's eyes widened as she looked up from her notepad. "How?" she wondered.

"It's another one of those things he does," Corhagen told her. "He doesn't use it much, but it helps every once in a while for things like this."

"I can draw the image out of you," Cole told Alice, who looked less than thrilled at the idea. "Just stay calm and try to relax."

"I'm dead," she reminded him, as he extended his hand toward her. "I can't get much more relaxed than this."

Wisps of vapor leaped off the surface of the evanescent body of Alice's ghost. The fragments gathered in Cole's hand, forming a ball of mist. Alice cringed, as though she found the process uncomfortable. Cole noticed this and raised an eyebrow.

"As a ghost," he said, with emphasis on the word 'ghost', "you should be immune to things like pain."

"It can still feel weird," she pointed out.

Grasping the misty ball in his fist, Cole added a drop of his own personal glamour to the mix before tossing the vapor to the floor. A cloud rose up from the spot where it landed. The evanescence swirled for a moment before congealing into two separate forms that stood side by side. Color bled into the white figures like a child's painting, at first. As it grew clearer, the shapes and tones became much more detailed.

Before the glamour of the two figures had fully formed, Cole had recognized them. "Mother of Darkness," he whispered. "It's them."

"IT'S who?" Detective Carroll called as Cole raced out the front door.

"Oh, don't mind me!" Cole heard Alice Tweedle's ghost shouting after him from inside the apartment. "I'll just haunt around here for the next few centuries. It isn't as though I'll miss anything important in the Summerlands!"

With a flick of his wrist, Cole banished Alice's spirit back from whence it came, silencing her. Behind him, he could hear Carroll and Corhagen's footsteps as they struggled to catch up.

"Slow down!" Carroll shouted from around the corner.

Reluctantly, Cole stopped and waited for the others. When both of them caught up, Carroll almost ran full tilt into Cole.

"You were saying?" he asked icily.

Carroll scowled as she regained her balance. "You recognized those two?" she demanded, staring up into his stony face. "From where?"

"A couple of months back," he answered evasively. "I encountered them briefly after I was suspended."

"Doing what?" Corhagen chimed in. His voice was far more suspicious, and the look he gave Cole was less than pleased.

"I don't know," Cole said. "We didn't get the chance to talk about it. Whatever it was they were sent to do, I doubt they had the opportunity."

"I meant," Corhagen elaborated, "what were you doing when you met up with them?"

"My job."

Cole said nothing else, earning him a disapproving frown from Corhagen, while Carroll glanced back and forth between them.

"So you've met them before," she summarized. "Is that why you said there was something familiar in that apartment?"

"Their scents," he answered, avoiding Corhagen's expression now. "I was close enough that time to smell them, but it was only that one time, so their scents didn't click with me when I smelled them in the apartment last night."

"And you're sure you don't know what those two were doing the first time you ran into them?" Corhagen pressed.

"No," Cole said flatly. "If their goal is to kill witches, they may have targeted someone in the area I wasn't familiar with. That is likely, but I also suspect they might have been paid."

"They're doing this for money?" Carroll asked skeptically. "I thought you said you didn't know these two well. What makes you jump to that conclusion?"

"Their work is professional," he said. "Their actions suggest a personal vendetta, but the quickness and ease with which they dispatched Alice Tweedle makes me think these two may work on the side as soldiers for hire."

"This is about the sword," Corhagen guessed, letting his anger at Cole fall to the wayside for a moment. "They might not have murdered Alice Tweedle because she was a witch. They just wanted the piece of that sword her ghost was talking about, right?"

"Possibly. And killing a witch was merely a bonus."

Carroll shook her head as Cole finished speaking. "Serial killers who work as professional killers for hire and have a vendetta against witches?" she wondered out loud, wincing as the thought struck her. "Ghosts that give out details about their deaths and pieces of a sword that fit into a prophecy? This is all starting to resemble a bad TV show."

"I keep telling you," Corhagen said, giving her a playful smirk. "This is a typical day for the Section. You ought to consider signing up."

"Not on your life," Carroll retorted sharply. "Not even for a raise and a promotion. You couldn't pay me to handle this kind of crazy shit on a regular basis."

Cole's phone rang before Carroll could go any further. "Yes?" he asked, answering it without checking the screen.

A loud crash, followed by a screech that sounded like rusty nails scraping on tin plating, echoed from the other end.

"Hello?" Cole tried again.

"Cole!" Joss's voice shouted from the other side over another loud crash. "Dammit, did the call go through?"

"Joss," Cole said as the line went dead. "Joss, can you hear me?"

"Can he hear you now?" Corhagen offered jokingly.

Cole shot him a very cold stare as he began scrolling through his history for the latest number. Before he could send the call, though, the phone rang again. "Joss?" he asked, answering for the second time. "Is everything all right?"

"Can you hurry this up?" Carroll asked, but Cole was already moving out of her grasp toward the elevator. "We're in the middle of an investigation."

"I'm answering to my superior," he pointed out.

"Right now, I'm your superior," Carroll said flatly.

"Since when?" Corhagen asked, giving her a stunned look. "I thought we were brought in to work together with you on this case."

"My case, though," she countered pointedly. "Therefore, I'm in charge."

"Quiet, please," Cole said to them both, feeling his patience stretch. "Forgive me, Vallimun. Could you repeat that?"

"I just wanted to know how the case is going," Joss replied over the phone as yet more shrieking reverberated.

"What is that noise?" Cole wondered. "It sounds kind of like nails raking over a chalkboard."

"I got a call a little while ago." Joss's voice became slightly ragged, as though he were running. Several seconds went by that were punctuated by gunfire. "Anyway, it's nothing major. They made it sound like it was a really big deal, but I've all but gotten things taken care of."

"What was it?"

"Just at…." A few more shots rang through Cole's phone. "Just some kind of shadow demon or something. I don't know, but the thing went down easy enough."

"Really? I've never heard of an actual shadow demon."

"Well, it's big," Joss said. "And scary looking enough, so I settled on demon. The shadowy part fits, though. It kept jumping around from one light source to another, but a few punches and several rounds were all it took to put it down."

"That's good to hear," Cole said. "You'll have to tell me about it later."

Later meaning, of course, when they were alone.

"Sure thing," Joss agreed, knowing full well what Cole had in mind.

"Where are you now?"

"Some rich stooge's apartment," said Joss, his voice much clearer now that the shrieking had stopped. "He took off as soon as I showed up. Listen, let me let you go so I can wrap this up and start filing the report that nobody's going to read."

"See you later," Cole said softly, before hanging up the phone.

Carroll was wide-eyed when Cole turned back to her. "Was that gunfire?" she asked, sounding legitimately concerned now.

"Yes," he said. "But Inspector Vallimun is fine. Apparently, there was a problem in someone's apartment with a shadow demon."

Both Carroll and Corhagen flinched.

"I'm as surprised as you are," he admitted honestly. "I was not aware that there were any real shadow demons. Shade constructs, maybe, but that is a new one for me. I wish I could have been there to see it."

"Is Vallimun all right?" Corhagen asked.

"He sounded fine," Cole assured him. "Just out of breath from the fight. If something serious had happened, we would have been called in earlier."

"Good point," said Corhagen. "Then I guess it's back to the murder investigation, huh?"

Cole looked at Carroll. "It is your call, Detective Carroll," he told her, giving the woman a somewhat smug look. "And your case, if I overheard correctly."

Carroll scowled. "Let's just go," she said. "I've had about all I can stand with spirits and sword prophecies, and… shadow demons."

The last one made her shudder. "From now on, we do this by the book. No more magic or weird bullshit fucking things up. Standard police procedures will solve this case, not talking to ghosts."

"If that's the case, what do you need us here for?" Corhagen wondered, following after Carroll as she marched toward the elevators.

"I was wondering that very same thing," Cole said. "Which disturbs me a great deal."

Carroll groaned as the elevator doors opened. "I should have listened to my superior," she mumbled, climbing in. "The world is insane enough without you people in it."

❺

"HI, HONEY. I'm home."

Cole shook his head as Joss climbed in. "I won't dignify that with a response," he said. "Let's just get out of here and go home where I can relax and have you fuck me into a blissful stupor."

The moment Joss was seated, Cole shifted the car into reverse and peeled out of the precinct parking garage. Joss managed to get his seat belt on before they were out into the street, where a number of cars began honking their horns.

Cole ignored all of them and kept right on going.

"What happened?" Joss asked as they sped toward what he assumed was the vanishing garage.

"After you called," Cole began, "I spent the rest of the day doing things 'by the book'."

"Oh," said Joss in a flat tone. "How did that work out?"

Cole's hands held the steering wheel in a vise grip. "You will note," he said coolly, "the utter lack of respect I currently have for pedestrians, fellow motorists, speed laws, traffic lights, and gravity right now."

Joss started laughing, then went quiet all of a sudden. "Gravity?"

"I'm pretty sure the wheels aren't actually touching the road at this point," Cole told him. "With the way I feel, it might be possible for this thing to achieve escape velocity and ride up the side of one of these buildings."

"In that case," Joss warned, as his fingers laced around the handle of the door, "would you mind slowing down so I don't piss myself? I'd rather not face any more horrors for the rest of the day."

It was Cole's turn now. "What happened?" he asked, making the tires scream as he turned sharply.

"Mostly paperwork," Joss answered, still gripping the handle. "Oh, and that shadow demon thing I told you about over the phone, or whatever it was. It was weird looking, and disappeared after I put several bullet holes into it."

"Sometimes, I wish all our problems could be handled that way."

"That's how you usually want to solve problems," Joss said pointedly. "I'm the one who has to remind you that shooting things and setting fire to them are bad ideas."

"And yet," Cole grumbled, "the one time I tried working as a competent leader and levelheaded individual, it completely blew up in my face."

"What?"

Cole took another sharp turn to avoid answering Joss's question. "I'm still not certain there are such things as shadow demons," he said instead. "I've heard of constructs made from shadows, and things whose auras were wrapped up in darkness so that they resembled shadows, but not shadow demons themselves."

"Weird," said Joss. "For some reason, I thought you'd know everything there was about it."

"Sorry. I'd love to hear all about it, but so far, it doesn't sound like anything I've dealt with before."

Joss settled back into his seat as Cole slowed down to a slightly more reasonable speed. "Where are we going?" he wondered after a moment.

"Home, I hope," Cole answered. "I've been driving around in big circles ever since we pulled out. Normally, the garage is just there, and the car finds it for me. Maybe it's because I'm under stress."

"Maybe," Joss said, reaching out to take one of Cole's hands. "Strictly speaking, now that you've slowed down some, I kind of like just riding around with you. I don't think we've done this before."

Cole gave Joss's hand a squeeze. "I'm sure we'll find it in a minute."

Sure enough, several minutes later, the two spotted the garage door nestled between an ice cream shop and a novelty item store. The car slowed down automatically as the door rose up to allow them passage. The garage was connected to the sithen somehow, which was supposed to dwell beneath Bowling Green Park. Joss had asked Cole before how the garage could be anywhere and yet still be a part of something miles from their home.

The short answer was that Cole himself wasn't completely sure. The sithen ran on physics not akin to the mortal plane, which meant a bit of rule bending was usually in play. As it was, he hadn't given enough thought to the idea to worry needlessly. Growing up in Faerie, one grew accustomed to seeing what humans would call bizarre things.

This was by no means the strangest event Cole had come across, in or outside of Faerie.

Before the car had come to a full stop, Mal had materialized in a puff of smoke. "You made it home!" he cried as Cole got out. "They're tearing the place apart!"

Cole stared calmly into Mal's panic-stricken face, then looked over to where Joss was standing. "Goblins," he said. "That's my guess, at least."

"Agreed," Cole said. "Mal, what happened?"

"They got into the kitchen," Mal explained as they trotted off toward the door leading directly into the sithen proper. "I made them a forest in one of the deeper levels, just like you said. For a while there, everything was the way it ought to have been."

Mal started hyperventilating. "Then they came up a flight of stairs," he gasped. "They said they were hungry. I told them the pixies were off-limits."

The floor began to dip and warp as Mal went on. "Not that I like them, per se," Mal was saying between gasps, "but I assumed you would want them alive for some later purpose."

Joss staggered as the floor beneath his left foot dipped sharply without warning. "Mal," Cole said, keeping his voice calm as he reached out to help Joss, only to be thrown backward by a ridge popping up between them.

"Mal," Cole tried again, more sharply. "You're warping the floor."

Mal looked around in confusion, then glanced down at the tile floor, which was moving back and forth like waves of gelatin dessert.

At once, the floor stretched back out to normal. "My apologies," he said. "Those little beasts you brought home have had my stomach in knots."

"They aren't that bad," Joss said, once he'd regained his footing. "A little smelly…."

"No, they actually tied my stomach in knots," Mal retorted, pointing downward. "It's on the thirty-fourth floor near the library."

Cole frowned. "We have a library?"

Joss looked just as confused as Cole. "Don't look at me," he said, wide-eyed. "I haven't lived here that long."

"Mal," Cole began, feeling his temper flare. "I was suspended for weeks and forced to watch an insurmountable number of hours of bad TV. During that whole time, you never once mentioned a library."

"Oh, I didn't?" To his credit, Mal had the decency to look embarrassed. "I was sure I left a note for you on the refrigerator. The pixies must have taken it down."

"Sure," Joss retorted.

"Have you cleaned up the mess the goblins made?" Cole asked, getting Mal's attention again. "I'll speak to them later, after I've had a shower. For now, try and keep them away from mine and Joss's rooms."

"Sir," Mal said, perhaps a bit too snidely, as the two walked off together, side by side.

Cole and Joss passed by the kitchen on their way to their respective rooms. Two of the goblins, one of which Cole recognized as Boogaloo, were sitting at the counter on high stools. A plate full of what looked like donuts nestled between slabs of pizza sat between him and the other goblin. On closer inspection, Cole realized it was Bugaboo.

"No time like the present," Joss said, slapping Cole on the back. "I'm going to take a shower. Good luck."

Cole shot Joss a dirty look as the man disappeared around the corner. A shifting in the sithen indicated that Joss was now too far away to hear anything Cole could shout at him in retaliation. Beyond that, he didn't feel up to it at the moment.

"Boys," Cole said, entering the vast room.

Boogaloo and Bugaboo looked up from their feast. "We need to have a serious talk," he said, while undoing his holster.

"I realize that annoying Mal might be fun." Bandersnatch and Jabberwock, Cole's specially-crafted twin guns, made a heavy thud against the counter as Cole set them down. "He has his amusing moments, but this is going to stop. I don't know all the details of what went on today, and, frankly, I couldn't care less. Whatever the problem is, we're going to settle things now."

"Um," Boogaloo began, raising up a single claw.

"Feel free to pass it on to everyone else," Cole interrupted. "As far as I'm concerned, this is how it's going to be from now on. If you don't like it, I'll just have to give Mal free reign to punish you."

Bugaboo snorted.

"Mal was once the ghost of a sorcerer that had been imprisoned inside of a book," Cole informed them both, wiping the grins off each of their faces. "Whatever he did to end up there, it most likely wasn't pretty. Inside the sithen, he can do anything. The only thing holding him back is my word."

Both goblins' eyes widened.

"I'm glad we're clear on this," Cole said, crossing his arms. "Now, was there a specific reason why you raided the kitchen earlier?"

Boogaloo shared a side glance with Bugaboo. "We were hungry," he said, as though it should have been obvious. "What else were we supposed to do?"

"I thought Mal gave you a whole forest," Cole said, feeling as though he were missing something. "There should have been plenty for you to hunt down there."

"Hunt?"

Cole noted the confusion on Boogaloo's face. "Yes," he said, growing frustrated. "Wood goblins are revered as hunters, correct?"

Boogaloo's frown made his whole face sag. "Why would we hunt for food?" he wondered, looking over at an equally confused Bugaboo. "Ordering pizza is way easier."

"Nagh!" Bugaboo agreed, nodding vigorously.

Cole shook his head, gathered up his guns, and walked away. "Never mind," he called out over his shoulder. "Enjoy your dinner, boys. I'll see if Mal can't set up your own kitchen for you."

"Like I don't have enough to do around here?" Mal asked, appearing in another puff of smoke.

"I could always check around and see if another ghost would like your job," Cole said, not stopping.

For some reason, the sithen had turned itself around so that Cole reached Joss's bedroom before his. Hearing the shower running behind the closed door, Cole kept on going, coming to his own private chamber a moment later. The door was already open, but one quick sniff told Cole he was alone. Whatever his feelings for the goblins, he still didn't like the idea of them nosing around in his room.

The hot water from the shower helped to soothe Cole's mood. Against his better judgment, he went over everything about the case one more time in his head while the jets sprayed the muscles in his back. As far as he was concerned, everything came down to tracking the two killers. Somehow, he imagined Detective Carroll would disagree, but Cole preferred the simple approach when it came to hunting.

It would be next to impossible to find them with so many other humans in the city. Their best bet seemed to be putting the goblins on the case and seeing what they dug up. The more Cole thought this over, the more ideal it sounded. For one thing, it would get the goblins out of the sithen tomorrow. Mal would have the place to himself to do whatever it was he did when alone.

Cole did his best not to think too hard about such things.

There were also the pixies in the fountain inside the great foyer. They'd moved in almost immediately after Cole had. During that time, they'd kept to themselves for the most part, leaving the fountain to harass Mal from time to time. If they could stay focused on the task at hand, sending them out might prove fruitful as well.

By the time Cole's shower was finished, he felt much better, but sick to death of mulling over police work. An idea struck him as he was toweling off, and, without covering up, Cole rushed out his bedroom door down the hall to Joss's.

"Get dressed," he ordered, not bothering to knock.

Joss was lying on his bed in a pair of tight boxers. "I could say the same to you," he quipped, giving Cole a lingering once-over that the sidhe appreciated. "What's wrong?"

"Nothing," Cole replied. "Let's get dressed and go out tonight."

The frown on Joss's face was disappointing, to say the least. "I just got out of the shower," he moaned. "I thought we could just stay in and rest."

"How much rest do you think we'll get with the goblins still trying to drive Mal bonkers?" Cole pointed out, even though the goblins had given up for the night, as evidenced by the lack of chaos in the rest of the sithen. It was a stretch as far as Cole was concerned, but Joss seemed to consider it.

"I want to go on a date with my boyfriend," Cole said. "A normal date, this time, I promise. No having sex on the floor of a fey bar."

Joss's mouth drew taut. "Well," he responded hesitantly.

"Hurry up," Cole said. "I'm going to go finish drying off and change."

"I didn't say 'yes', you know," Joss called out as Cole raced back down the hall. The laughter in his voice gave him away, however.

Roughly twenty minutes later, they were dried, dressed, and backing out of the garage. "I told Mal to keep the goblins occupied in the forest for now," he said as Joss settled in. "We shouldn't have any surprises when we get home a second time."

"We shouldn't be doing this, you know," Joss warned, though he didn't sound convinced. "We've gotta be up at the crack of dawn for training. And you've still got to solve that murder with Corhagen and the Carroll woman."

"Fuck it," Cole stated candidly. "I'm sick of all work and no play. We're going out to eat, catching a movie, and maybe closing out a bar."

"And having one hell of a hangover to go along with our exhaustion," Joss grumbled as Cole took off down the street.

"Joss," Cole said, mustering his patience. "You do remember that you're immortal now, right?"

Joss stayed quiet for the rest of the drive.

Money wasn't too tight, thanks to the sithen providing them with most of their daily needs. Mal could have easily whipped them up something, but the sithen butler had been happy for the night off. Plus, despite enjoying it, there was something about not having to cook every once in a while that Cole appreciated. That and the thrill of just being with Joss in public.

"What are we doing here?" Joss asked, closing the door.

"It's called the Dutch," Cole said, waiting for his lover to come up alongside. "The food here is supposed to be good. I thought we could try something a little different this time. Something other than bar food."

By some miracle, they'd found a parking spot not far down the street. Joss was giving the place a once-over and frowning.

"What's wrong with bar food?" he asked, mockingly offended.

"Nothing," replied Cole, reaching for the door. "A change of pace is good every once in a while. Now quit stalling."

The place was busy, but the hostess at the door was very accommodating. Cole slipped her a tip in appreciation as she led them through the sea of tables to a booth set up against a wall. Hanging above the table from the wall was a beautiful lighted lamp.

"I feel like I'm sitting in some sort of theme club for bohemians," Joss noted, looking around at the restaurant's clientele.

Cole watched Joss's face carefully. "If it bothers you that much, we can leave," he said seriously. "I wanted us to have fun, not for you to be uncomfortable."

"Nah," Joss said very quickly, smiling now. "I just enjoy giving you a hard time."

Cole rolled his eyes, which made Joss snicker. "I like being out in the open with you," he said, hoping to avoid some of his lover's teasing for just a moment.

The nod Joss gave in reply was a bit too quick, as though he were nervous. "It's no big thing," he said. "I don't mind being seen with you, if that's what you're wondering."

"I'd be more concerned about them," Cole said, gesturing to a random couple sitting at a table not far away.

"What about them?" Joss wondered.

"You're forgetting," he said, watching the crowd of hungry patrons closely. "I have spent nearly a hundred of your years in this city. There was a time when we might not have been welcome here. At the very least, we couldn't have done this."

Cole reached out and grasped Joss's hand firmly.

"Oh," Joss said, realization dawning. "Right."

Cole smiled. "You say that as if life has always been that way."

Joss tilted his head to the side thoughtfully, his forehead wrinkling slightly as he mulled over Cole's words.

"I always knew it existed," he said, giving Cole's hand a squeeze for emphasis. "There was a lesbian couple on the top floor of the apartment where I lived as a kid, and when I was married, we had two guys that lived together down the hall from us. For a long time, I just assumed other people had the same sort of experiences. No one ever really talked about it to me, so I didn't think otherwise."

Joss paused for a moment. "Not that I ever thought I'd wind up in a relationship with a man," he added, before throwing in quickly, "Not that I regret it or anything. I mean…."

"I understand," Cole said reassuringly. "We're still in that 'getting-used-to-one-another phase'. Is that what it's called?"

"It works," Joss said. "I guess we moved into things pretty fast."

Cole opened his mouth to speak but found himself cut off as an attractive older woman with dark skin appeared next to their table.

"Here ya go," she said sweetly, placing menus and glasses of water in front of each of them. "My name's Amber, and I'll be your server. What can I get you tonight?"

"Sloppy duck sandwich, hold the mint," Cole told her, refusing to let go of Joss's hand. "And a bucket of oysters on the half shell."

"The same," Joss said when she looked toward him with her pen at the ready. "And a glass of bourbon for both of us."

Joss threw Cole a quick look for confirmation, which Cole nodded once at.

"Great," she said, gathering their untouched menus up with one hand. "We'll have that out for you in just a sec, okay?"

Joss waited until Amber was out of earshot before speaking again. "How many times have you been to this place?" he asked.

"None," Cole said. "I read an article about it in the New York Magazine a while back. That was one of the things they recommended."

"Oh," Joss said. "Well, I just learned something else about you I hadn't known before. Apparently, you read the New York Magazine."

"It was back when Rainette and I were on that stakeout with Marcel," he explained. "She had a copy of it in the backseat of her car."

"Was that the one with the giant squid?"

"Yeah," Cole said, looking off to the side uncomfortably. "I think I've filled my quota of tentacles for the next fifty years, at least."

Joss laughed, and it was infectious enough to spread to Cole, who stroked his thumb along the side of his boyfriend's hand as they held one another.

"Tell me about before," he said, looking into Joss's eyes. "About when you were young."

Joss looked down at the table. "Not much to tell, honestly," he said in a withdrawn voice. "My parents got divorced when I was six. I spent a lot of time on my own while my mom worked to keep us fed."

"What made you want to become a cop?"

Joss looked over at his water glass as though willing it to change to bourbon. "My mom was raped," he said thickly, "by her boss when I was twelve. I swore I'd get the guy, even if I had to kill him myself, but she never let me go near the place afterward. The guy was connected, had people protecting him. There were rumors he was a middleman for one of the local drug lords."

The mention of mob connections caused Cole to stiffen. At one time, long ago, he'd been the chief enforcer for the Irish Mob.

"So I became a cop as soon as I was old enough to drop out of high school," Joss went on. "I got my GED, signed up, then started casing the place in my spare time. By that point, though, I had some messed-up priorities. I thought if I could nail the guy, it would be the one big break that would launch my career."

Joss looked up at Cole sadly. "I was going to avenge my mom and make a career out of protecting people all at the same time."

"I'm guessing things didn't go the way you planned," Cole surmised. "What happened?"

"He shot himself," Joss said, the bitterness in his voice thick enough to choke on. "There was a sting operation planned, and I'd been warned to keep my distance. I wasn't going to listen, but it never came to anything. The bastard got spooked, I guess, and ate his gun."

"I see."

Joss smiled humorlessly. "After that, I didn't have a reason to be a cop anymore, but I kept on doing it. Someone told me I should stop trying to think so much about what happened in the past, no matter how bad it was, and live in the present."

"Good advice," Cole said. "Who was it?"

"My superior. The one that told me to lay off the guy in the first place."

Neither said anything until their food arrived. Joss ate his sandwich and drank several refills of bourbon while Cole munched quietly.

"What about you?" Joss asked as they moved on to the basket of oysters.

Cole hesitated as he began peeling the meat off one shell. "There's a lot to tell," he warned, letting his fingers linger idly at the shell's edge. "I've lived a lot longer."

"We don't have to see a movie," Joss reminded. "I'd rather hear this than anything playing on screen, truth be told."

Swallowing the oyster in one bite, Cole tossed the shell aside and reached for another one.

"I was born in a place called S'fryld'ar," he said. "It is a somewhat mountainous region of Faerie located on the…."

Cole paused. "It's somewhat isolated," he said instead. "Not impossible to get to, but not a place that many people visited when I was young, unless they needed something. Or wanted something."

"A little off the beaten path?" Joss offered.

"Very much so," Cole said. "My mother, as you know, was from one of the Summer Courts. My father had brokered for an engagement so he could gain an alliance with her court. He'd been at war with the Frost Giants for years. Part of the arrangement meant the two of them participating in a rite."

"What sort of rite?"

"I don't know," Cole admitted, frustrated by the thought. "No one ever spoke of it in my presence for more than a second, and I wasn't able to find much information. It involved invoking the Goddess and Consort's power, but beyond that, I have no idea.

"To make a long story short," he said, between bites, "my mother left shortly after my birth. Legally, since her marriage to my father had proven a fertile match, she was bound to him. However, her parents brokered for her release in return for my father receiving further support from them. They were still married in the eyes of Faerie, but she was given what you might call today a 'free pass'."

Joss was listening now, fixated on Cole's words.

"I spent my early years at Wynterbreath," Cole said. "That was the name of my father's kingdom. The war continued, despite the help my mother's parents sent, and it was eventually concluded that my presence in his land was somehow detrimental to him. I was half Summer Court and weakening him."

"What'd they do?"

"I was sent to live with my mother." Cole's face turned sour at the thought. "It was supposed to be a temporary measure, but then my father was killed, and his brother seized the kingdom in my absence."

Joss processed this while Cole drained his glass and ordered another. "I made a friend at my mother's court," he continued, "but life there was far from ideal. My mother never had much use for me, and no one in the court wanted me around. Eventually, my friend was assassinated, so I decided I'd had enough and petitioned to join Queen Titania's wolves."

"And that's why you can shape-shift, right?"

It hadn't been so much a question as a statement of fact, but Cole answered Joss anyway. "Yes," he said. "I was allowed to join under the stipulation that I spend a year of Faerie time in Lord Oberon's Citadel of Pain. When that was over, and I survived the madness, Titania gave me the gift of wolf form and I began training."

Joss had chuckled at the mention of the word "madness," and Cole gave him a stern look. "It is not a joke," he said seriously. "Most fey that enter the Citadel lose their minds after a time. And remember, a year of Faerie time is very different from one year of mortal time."

"Right," Joss said, feeling embarrassed. "I'm sorry."

"For a while," Cole said, looking away now, "I was happy. Being one of Titania's wolves was the most difficult thing I'd done at that point, but she catered to all of us."

"Why did Oberon banish you?"

Cole sighed. "He claimed that Titania was doting too much on me. I don't believe that was the real reason, but being the Lord of All Faerie, he doesn't actually need any excuse to do something."

The memories were coming quickly now, and Cole took a moment to gather himself before going any further.

"I wound up in the harbor," Cole said. "It's funny, thinking about it now, but as I broke the surface of the water, I saw the Statue of Liberty. At that moment, it had looked like a marvel. I wondered what kind of world I'd come to."

Joss waited while Cole sat, lost in thought. "How did you get ashore?" he asked finally, breaking Cole's concentration.

"I swam," he replied. "Found work, was eventually banished from New York for failing to protect my boss, but you already know all of that."

"I remember," Joss said.

"I headed south," he went on. "Made my way to Florida and tried to forget about everything that had happened. Not long afterward, I ended up right back here in Manhattan."

Cole saw the look on Joss's face. "It's an even longer story," he said. "Ask me again some other time, though."

"I look forward to hearing it," Joss said. "It must have been serious, if you were willing to come back to Manhattan while the whole Irish Mafia was still gunning for you."

"I wish," Cole muttered. "At any rate, I drifted back and forth between Manhattan and Florida, as well as a few other places, over the decades. It was important for me to not stay in one place for too long. There was always the chance that someone could recognize me.

"That," Cole added, "and most humans find me unnerving."

"Because you're pale?"

Cole shook his head, and some of his hair spilled around him like a curtain. "They sense what I am," he said, staring off into the crowd again. "I understand that the human condition of albinism carries a nefarious superstition with it, but that isn't why humans mistrust me. Though they refuse to call me what I am, their instincts naturally warn them to keep their distance."

Joss followed his gaze and noticed quite a few people were watching them, as if unnerved despite the gap between their tables. For a moment, he wondered if it wasn't because he and Cole had been holding hands, but a closer inspection threw that idea out the window.

There was genuine fear in their eyes. Many were doing their best to hide it, but Joss saw the emotion for what it was. The people he counted off that were bothering to look up were scared shitless. What amazed him most, though, was that their looks encompassed him as well.

They were just as frightened of him as they were of Cole.

"I'm sorry," Cole said, snapping Joss back to reality.

"For what?" he asked, stunned.

"They feel it in you now, too."

Joss struggled to think of what to say and found himself coming up empty. Instead, he reached over and took Cole's hand in both of his.

The two decided to skip the film and head straight home. The sithen was quiet when they entered through the garage. Neither of them said a word as they made their way to Cole's bedroom. The lights switched on, automatically adjusting to a soft, low moonlit shade as Joss closed the door behind him. Cole began stripping out of his clothes, listening without turning around as Joss did the same. Each time he heard a piece of cloth hit the rug, something stirred inside him.

When Cole did turn around at last, he was nude, and so was his lover. The two reached out at the same time, pulling into each other's arms. Joss's skin carried the thick, sweet, musky smell that belonged solely to him. Cole placed a trail of kisses from Joss's collarbone down across his shoulder as Joss walked them both backward toward the bed.

For a long while, the two simply held one another close, feeling the strength in each other's arms and savoring the sweat and scent of their bodies. When Joss fumbled in the dimness for the vial of lubricant, Cole reached out and opened the drawer for him. Joss greased himself up, then added more to Cole's hole. In one smooth stroke, the head was past the tight ring of muscle that protected Cole's insides.

Joss worked himself in slowly, then faster. Cole was sidhe and had far different thresholds of pain tolerance. It had taken a little while, but each of them had gotten used to how their bodies responded. When Joss was all the way inside, he began to withdraw, slamming all the way back in after coming out only about halfway. Cole gasped into his lover's mouth, tasting him as Joss filled him up over and over again.

Joss reached down and bent Cole's legs up until they were hanging over his shoulders. From this position, he rammed deep, touching places inside Cole that made him howl. The sounds of their fucking reverberated off the walls. Cole came first, to his great shock, but Joss kept right on going. Farther and farther down, his cock stroked Cole's insides, until it felt like Cole might burst from the painful pleasure hitting his body.

His own cock was still hard, even after cumming. Cole reached through the thin space between their bodies and rubbed his thick knob, bringing himself over again just as Joss increased his pace to that of a jackhammer. Their mouths connected, Joss gave one last hard thrust, and both of them orgasmed.

Stars swam in front of Cole's face as Joss let go of his legs. The now-immortal inspector collapsed on top of him, settling his weight on the sidhe. As Cole's pleasure subsided, he raked a hand up through Joss's long, sunshine-spun hair.

"Everything will be fine, right?" he asked, suddenly very cold. "Nothing bad can happen anymore, now that it's just us."

Joss playfully nuzzled his face into Cole's neck. "Of course," he said teasingly. "What could possibly go wrong?"

MORNING came far too early, just like Joss had warned. Neither of them was in a mood for conversation as they climbed inside Cole's car and drove to work.

"We never did find out what happened to my car," Joss grumbled as he stared at the stiff traffic.

"It'll turn up," Cole said halfheartedly.

Cole gave a silent prayer that the sithen would eventually consent to give back Joss's vehicle. It had vanished from the garage right after he'd moved in, and neither of them had found a trace of it. Even Mal had been confused by the sithen's stubborn refusal. Cole could only assume it had been moved to some place just outside of Mal's range, although that should have been impossible. Mal was connected to every last square inch of their home, save for the temple located at the very bottom.

Cole suspected Mal might just be avoiding that area altogether. He couldn't really blame the ex-ghost for that, though, considering what they knew was down there.

No one said a word to them once they reached the precinct. Cole and Joss ignored any looks their fellow officers shot them. Most regarded the Section as a squad of crazies. At least, that was what Cole had overheard someone say once. For the moment, the both of them were too concerned with the task at hand to worry much about it.

The others were already waiting down in the training area. Since most of the Section was composed of people with unique abilities or who weren't human to begin with, they'd been working on getting everyone together on the same page as far as combat. More than one case had nearly ended badly because the team just wasn't functioning as a cohesive unit during a fight.

Thus, here they were now, weary-eyed and, in some cases, still struggling with the sniffles.

Rainette blew her nose loudly before tossing the tissue into a wastebasket and joining the others.

"I will be so glad to get rid of this cold," she muttered.

"You could have stayed home one more day," Joss said. "Are you sure you're feeling up to this?"

"I'll manage," she said. "Plus, if we ever find the bastards that did it to Alice, I want to be in fit condition to get in a couple of kicks myself."

"I will bring you their heads on a platter, if you would but ask," Marcel told her, his voice totally devoid of mirth.

"Thanks," she replied, smiling at him. "But I'm more of a 'flowers and a movie' kind of girl. It's sweet of you to offer, though."

Cole thought about this for a moment, then gave Joss a teasing look. "Should I have brought you the severed head of an enemy?"

Staffelbach, who looked positively diminutive standing next to Marcel, snickered.

"I'll pass on that too," Joss said, shaking his head as Staffelbach kept chuckling.

Corhagen's face grew taut, but neither of them paid him any mind. "We've got the place to ourselves for the time being," Joss went on, gesturing to the empty gym. "We might as well make the most of it."

"I guess being thought of as weirdos by the rest of the precinct has a few advantages," Staffelbach said, frowning as he took in the significantly deserted workout area. "Since they found out that this is when we meet, nobody else wants to come near the place."

"Thank heaven for small favors," Marcel replied.

"Agreed," Cole said. "Less of an audience works in our favor this time. We don't have to hide what we can do."

Corhagen cleared his throat. "I've been meaning to ask," he said, looking down at the ground. "Why exactly am I here? I don't... fly, or bench press cars, so...."

"You're still a member of the Section," Joss insisted, cutting him off curtly. "We work together best as a team, so you're here with us. Any other questions?"

No one had anything to say. "Good," Joss said. "Then let's get started. We don't have a lot of time."

For the first hour, the team took to the mats and sparred with each other. Corhagen challenged Cole and Marcel each time, alternating between the two. Apparently, he'd taken the fact that Staffelbach had gone toe to toe with the ogre while brainwashed as a personal challenge. As always, Corhagen did well at first but inevitably wound up beneath Marcel's heel in the end. In the case of fighting Cole, Corhagen managed to get in a lucky couple of punches when Cole mistakenly went easy on him. Following that, his anger and the past several months of Corhagen's snide remarks took over. Corhagen ended up on his back after a kick from Cole laid him out.

"You were going too easy on him before," Joss said as Staffelbach helped Corhagen up. "The whole point of this is to train ourselves against things that won't hold back."

"That's how he ended up on his ass there," Cole retorted.

Rainette sparred with Joss next for a bit, and did surprisingly well. As far as Cole knew, she hadn't had much experience with combat before the year started. Rainette seemed to take to fighting very quickly. She managed to evade a number of attacks by Joss and get in a few good strikes of her own. Their match ended in a draw, though, officially, none of them were bothering with keeping score.

Staffelbach showed the most promise. He tackled Joss, Cole, and went against Marcel again, one after the other. The young officer seemed to have boundless energy and never balked in the face of any of them.

Once the first hour passed, the group split off into teams of two. Cole went with Staffelbach to help him control his powers better. Rainette was giving Corhagen pointers on resisting magical influence while Joss taught Marcel boxing.

The month prior, Staffelbach and Cole had come across an entity that had gained a physical form with the help of nanomachines encrypted with an alchemist cypher. The machines had been stolen from a high-tech storage facility, and some had gotten infused in Staffelbach's body right before the creature attacked them. That was what they suspected had happened, at least. No one was entirely sure, and there was no one they could go to for confirmation.

Since then, Staffelbach had run into a few problems keeping his abilities under wraps. Anything he put his hands on ran the risk of warping into a completely different shape. In the case of electronics, they'd had a few close calls with things shorting out. Part of the reason for their new training regimen was so Cole could try and help the man get his new abilities under control.

It hadn't been easy at first. Staffelbach's powers seemed to come with a hair trigger, though practice and a lot of patience on Cole's part had yielded results.

"Let's go over some of the basics," Cole suggested, once they were over in a corner by themselves.

"Cool," he replied, squatting down on the floor. "How about a cube?"

Staffelbach placed the tips of his fingers against the hard floor. Sparks flew, and the air stank of ozone for a moment. A small cube made of the same material as the floor rose up out of it.

"Try something a little more complex," Cole suggested. "Like a dodecahedron."

The cube began to warp and twist, growing spikes out of it at uneven angles. "Let the image come," Cole coached. "Don't force it into your mind. Let it flow naturally."

Like rubber, the material snapped into a twelve-sided polygon. "Good," Cole said. "You're getting much better at this. Try a few more shapes."

Staffelbach went through his usual list of shapes: a sphere, a cylinder, a diamond, and an octagonal box. Cole watched as he rotated back and forth between the different shapes, before moving on to even more complex ones. The cube suddenly became a pony, a bowl, before settling on a superhero statue.

Cole studied the familiar face as Staffelbach grinned up at him cheekily. "I've been practicing," he said as Cole compared Staffelbach's face on the tiny statue to the real one.

"So I see," he said. "Can you make anything else that complicated?"

Staffelbach managed to construct a car that looked similar to the Batmobile from the old TV show, a skyscraper model, and a Ferris wheel. The last one, however, broke apart before their very eyes.

"Dammit," Staffelbach swore. "I keep getting the framework for that one wrong. How can I make a water cannon on my first try and fail so hard at this?"

"It's undoubtedly a mental issue," Cole said, crouching on the floor in front of him. "The first time your powers manifested, you were under stress. Your life was threatened, and magic responds to those situations very easily. The sidhe would often put their children through ritual duels for that very reason. Often, in the heat of battle, their Hands of Power manifested."

"Maybe I should just run headfirst into a fight from now on?" Staffelbach mused. "I could attack people with carnival equipment."

"Not a good idea," Cole warned seriously. "In that state, magic is often wild and unbound. You'd end up hurting someone, or killing yourself with your own power by accident."

Staffelbach looked at Cole. "You've seen that kind of thing before?"

"More than once," Cole told him gravely. "Untrained magic is a dangerous thing. That is why we're still going through the basics. Once you master them, the more complex things will become easier. It's the same as any other discipline."

"Right," Staffelbach said, looking down at the ruined pieces jumbled in a pile on the floor between them. "Back to the drawing board, then."

"You'll get it," Cole assured him. "Let's start again."

For the rest of their hour together, the two practiced as the sounds of the other Section members sparring or working out together reverberated through the room. When the second hour came to a close,

Staffelbach was on the verge of completing a pair of gauntlets to shield his arms.

"Keep working," Cole encouraged, giving him a pat on the back. "You're doing much better."

"I wonder if I could make some kind of jet pack," he said, more to himself than Cole. "For when I can make machines like that water cannon."

Cole left Staffelbach to muse, joining Joss by the water fountain. The two came close enough that Cole could feel the heat from their bodies. Joss looked up, eyes widening as he saw Cole standing there, and a smile crossed his face.

"I have to go," Cole said, darting his eyes over to where Corhagen stood making small talk with Staffelbach. "We have to go, actually."

Joss saw where Cole was looking. "Right," he said, nodding. "Give my regards to Detective Carroll. How much longer before you think this gets wrapped up?"

"I'm not sure," Cole said. "The sooner the better, though."

Corhagen was headed their way now. "I think I'll shower first," Cole muttered, heading for the locker room area. "I won't get a chance to do so again until we go home for the day."

The showers were not a facility Cole made use of very often. Finding the area deserted upon entering, he wasted no time stripping down. An empty locker had been left open near one of the open stalls in the very back, and Cole stashed his clothes there before climbing in. The water was cold, making him flinch. It was more from shock than discomfort, yet the reaction irritated him a little all the same.

He hadn't been under the spray very long when footsteps echoed down the path to the same open shower area. Cole listened, recognizing the shuffling sounds of someone stripping out of their clothes, and stuck his head back under the water. Whoever it was would just have to suffer his presence until he finished.

A moment later, the stranger stomped into the shower area behind him. Cole sniffed the area, recognizing the scent, and turned to find James moving toward another showerhead on the wall perpendicular to him. Corhagen kept his back to Cole the whole time, giving the sidhe more than an adequate glimpse of his backside.

Cole scowled and turned away. There must have been a dozen or so empty stalls the mortal could have used. He wasn't sure what Corhagen was trying to pull, but being so close together in the nude was aggravating. Like all sidhe in general, Cole was not bothered by nudity. However, Corhagen had never shared that sort of camaraderie with him. Most things about the male anatomy made the detective overreact, which made his presence suspicious.

Cole considered leaving then and there, but changed his mind before he could turn the water off. He had arrived first, and it was Corhagen's problem, not his. Whatever the man wanted, Cole saw no reason to let it interfere with him washing the sweat off his body.

Off to the side, James was doing his best to keep his back facing Cole as he coated his body in soapsuds. "What do you think of Detective Carroll?" he asked suddenly, turning toward Cole.

Cole didn't answer at first. "Why?" he asked at last. "We're only working the one case with her. Once the two witch hunters have been found, it's unlikely we'll see her again."

Corhagen fell quiet for a second, letting the sound of the shower water cover up the silence. "I think she likes you," he said abruptly.

Cole scowled.

"What do you want?" he demanded, turning around to give Corhagen the full view of his front. So long as Corhagen was playing games, he saw no reason not to press his advantage.

To his great shock, Corhagen did the same. "Nothing," the mortal replied, not bothering to cover himself as he ran his fingers through the soapsuds coating his chest.

Cole swallowed, struck by the sight of the hair there. He'd had a weakness for mortals with chest hair since arriving in Manhattan, almost a century ago. The sidhe had little in the way of body hair, and the unfamiliarity of it growing up translated into a fetish now. Corhagen had always been hairy—for as long as Cole had known him, at least. It was a trait both he and Joss shared, one of very few things they had in common.

Cole blinked, forcing himself to think of something else.

"I just thought we could talk," Corhagen was saying now. "Like we used to. We hardly ever do that anymore."

"And whose fault is that?"

The words left Cole's mouth before he could stop himself, though he wondered why he should care. Looking up, he saw Corhagen staring down at his feet guiltily.

"I've been an asshole," Corhagen admitted, taking several deep breaths. "I know that now. I don't know why I was, exactly. I just... I wanted things to be normal for so long. I needed things to stay normal."

Despite knowing better, Cole listened.

"I thought I had this whole thing figured out," James said, above the splashing of the water. "I was supposed to get up, go do my job, come home, and see my kids. That should have been enough."

Cole said nothing in reply.

"Lately, though, I've been wondering about that." James swallowed hard as he forced the next words out of his mouth. "I keep thinking about the things we did together."

A blush crept up Corhagen's neck. "And all that's happened."

"You wanted Joss out of the way so you could lead the Section," Cole accused softly. "You might not have planned any of what happened, but you didn't do a good job of hiding it."

"I thought the Section was my big thing," James tried, though he didn't sound very defensive. "I could do good, something nobody else was willing to do, and make my mark at the same time. Then it turns out that this has been around for longer than I have. Somebody else was already doing it, and then Vallimun brings it back."

"You thought it was your chance to be remembered?"

"And my chance to prove I wasn't crazy," James said. "I wanted to show everyone that this stuff, what we deal with, was real."

Cole felt sympathy for Corhagen then, much as he hated to. "They know it's real," he told James gently. "They just wish it wasn't."

Cole cut off the spray and exited the shower, hearing James do the same behind him. He hadn't thought to fetch a towel, but as he looked around, Cole noticed a second one laid out on the bench underneath the locker where his stuff was stored. Corhagen's was set atop his pile of clothes on the bench right next to Cole's.

Cole dried himself off as he heard James's footsteps behind him. Quietly, the two dressed. They could hear voices from the other end of the locker room. Nothing but the idle chatter of officers ready to start their day or coming off the night beat. Even now, members of the Section were avoided, but Cole only chuckled at this and resumed dressing.

Rather than going out, he waited until James finished. Every few minutes, Cole caught himself glancing toward the mortal, snatching peeks as James changed in front of him. He expected his former friend to make some sort of crack at his expense, an accusation about his uninvited staring or something in regards to Cole's old attraction for him. James remained quiet the whole time, however.

Once he had suited up, the mortal looked at Cole and smiled. "Ready to get this shit started?" he asked cheerfully.

Cole hesitated, then nodded. "Yes," he said. "I suppose I am."

It was a quiet walk to the garage. Neither of them said much, but Cole was even less bothered than before. It felt odd being back in this routine, being somewhat comfortable around each other. Some part of Cole wondered how long it would last before Corhagen snapped back and decided he was too abnormal to be around.

Before he could go very far down that road of thought, though, they were coming up on his car. To the surprise of both of them, Detective Carroll was waiting there, resting on the back bumper while drinking coffee.

"I thought you two were never going to show up," she said. "Let's get moving before the trail gets cold. We've got two psychos to hunt down."

Cole and James shared a glance before the sidhe unlocked his car. All three climbed in, one after the other, James taking the passenger seat while Carroll consented to sit in the back yet again.

"Any news?" Corhagen asked as they hit the street.

"Forensics didn't find anything we didn't already know," she said ruefully, gripping the empty cup in her hand as her eyes drifted to the back of Cole's head. "You were right in that these guys are pros."

"I guess they wouldn't have stayed one step ahead of the FBI for so long without getting very good at this kind of thing," James threw in.

"Section Thirteen," she reminded, scowling, "is supposed to be able to do the impossible. It is part of your job description."

"I wasn't aware we had such a sterling reputation with the rest of the NYPD," Cole said, smirking as he took a sharp turn. "My understanding was that we were the ruination of good cops everywhere."

"Yeah," James agreed. "Or something like that."

"You get results," Carroll stated. "For the most part, anyway. People may be skeptical of your methods, but no one can deny you get the job done."

"Plenty of people deny that," Cole pointed out, keeping his hands firmly on the wheel. "But thank you for the compliment, anyway."

James looked out the window thoughtfully for a moment as Cole continued driving. "What about the witches?" he asked, looking at Cole. "They'd help."

"I already thought of that," Cole said, though not unkindly for once. "They're in mourning right now. The only reason Rainette came in is because she knows us helping Detective Carroll puts the Section behind. She's going to be joining her coven later."

"So they're like a sorority or something?"

Cole looked back at Carroll's statement. "They are a coven," he explained. "For them, it is like being family, or part of a clan."

"Yeah," James said. "No matter what secrets Alice Tweedle kept from them, she was still a member of the Shadewater."

Cole gave him a look. "What?" James wondered, staring right back at him. "I know about these kinds of things. Rainette and I work in the same division, after all."

"True," Cole acknowledged, still a bit thrown.

"Could they find Alice Tweedle's killers?" Carroll asked seriously, leaning forward in her seat as she spoke. "I'm going to go on the idea that these are actual witches, since we've established that pretty boy here can raise ghosts and dead bodies."

"Yes," Cole answered, not bothering to look back at her. "They are 'real' witches, as you put it."

"Could they help, then?"

"Give them time to mourn," James advised her. "Then, sure. I'm guessing they'd love to help bring those two sons of bitches down."

"In the meantime, though, we should keep looking," Cole said. "If possible, I'd like to finish this without bringing the Shadewater coven into this. Curtailing the rage of a swarm of angry spell casters isn't something I planned on doing when I got up this morning."

"Good point," James mused, looking horrified by the thought. "What about that shard of the sword Alice Tweedle's ghost was telling us about?"

Cole thought for a moment. "The piece of the Claiomh Solais," he said. "Alice Tweedle's spirit was sure she'd been killed because of it."

"Something like that is bound to be worth money," James pointed out, looking pleased with himself all of a sudden.

"And you may know where to look?" Cole guessed as a cheeky grin spread over Corhagen's face.

"I did some checking last night," he said. "You know that hooker that used to stoolie for us back before you joined the force?"

Cole's face went still momentarily. "The girl with the missing leg?"

"She's almost thirty now," James corrected. "But yeah, her. It wasn't easy getting her to talk to me after so long, but it sounds like someone has been in the market for a sword that fits the description Alice's ghost gave us. They didn't call it by name, but it was supposed to have been broken up in thirteen pieces."

"Who?" Carroll demanded.

"I couldn't get a name," James said. "The lady deals with clients that have a taste for the 'exotic', as she calls it."

"Her term for being half-fey," Cole explained quickly to Detective Carroll. "It seems your contact friend hasn't given up on being in denial about her heritage."

"It's probably some bigwig with more money than God," James continued. "If they could afford something like that, they probably have a way of being contacted."

"I find it a little sad that one of the greatest treasures of the Tuatha de Danann would end up broken into pieces so that rich mortal eccentrics could squabble over it."

James laughed at Cole's dry tone.

"Then I guess this means we'll be visiting one of the places where mystical artifacts are sold and traded," Cole finished, shooting James a glare.

James's face fell. "Not that place," he groaned. "Please, no."

"Where?" Carroll wondered.

"THE Silver Chalice."

Detective Carroll winced in disgust at the dilapidated shack. "What's this supposed to be?" she asked, looking from it out to the docks behind them. "This building should have been condemned way before now. How is it even still standing?"

"Looks are frequently deceiving," Cole warned, enjoying her reaction.

"No kidding," James muttered. "That's what I thought the first time he ever brought me here."

"So you've been here before?" Carroll asked, giving James a look. "What is it?"

"A bar," Cole said. "A fey bar."

Carroll's face went flat before she cocked an eyebrow at him.

"It'll make sense in a minute," James assured her.

"Answer me already. What is it?" she demanded, hanging back slightly as they headed toward the half-collapsed building. "Some sort of abandoned place for weirdos who like spooky stuff so they can show up and conduct séances?"

"No," Cole said plainly. "It's a fey bar."

"As in, a bar for fey," James emphasized when it looked like Carroll was about to get very mad. "There are places like this spread out here and there all over the world, or so I'm told. The Silver Chalice is just one of them."

"Then it is a place for weirdos," Carroll insisted, as though she'd finally figured something impossible out.

"It isn't a place for weirdos," Cole said to her through a very tense frown. "The Silver Chalice is a fey bar."

"You'll see in just a minute," James explained as Cole marched right through a solid wall.

Detective Carroll's eyes nearly popped out of her skull.

"Just keep going," James encouraged, pointing to the spot where Cole had disappeared. "The wall's not going to hurt you. It's not even really there."

Carroll had yet to pick her jaw up off the floor. "But," she stammered. "That's impossible. He just…."

James couldn't fight the snicker rising up in his throat.

"So," she tried, desperate to rationalize the situation into something that made sense to her. "Is it a hologram?"

"It's magic," said James, nudging her forward. "Come on. We'll do it together."

Carroll shook her head. "No way," she said as James stood beside her. "You're not getting me with this sort of thing. This is a trick you bastards pull on other people to get a good laugh. Well, I'm not falling for it."

Cole's head reappeared halfway through the wall. "Is she coming or not?" he asked, growing impatient. "We haven't got all day, and there are still two killers on the loose."

"She's coming," James insisted, taking Carroll's hand. Carroll stared at their interlaced fingers with her mouth hanging wide open.

"Come on," he said, pulling her along. "I was a little freaked out the first time I saw this, but it doesn't hurt at all."

"Wait," Carroll protested, trying to pull free and failing. "No, stop. This isn't funny anymore, you two. Stop!"

THE noise cut off her protests. Carroll gasped as James loosened his grip, allowing her to yank free at last.

"What…," she began, before catching sight of the inside of the fey bar. "What is… what the hell is this place?"

"A fey bar," James and Cole said together.

"Are we going to have to explain this to her over and over again?" Cole asked. "Because it has passed being tiresome."

The room in front of them was bustling with noise, activity, and drunken fey of all shapes, sizes, colors, and variations. Pixies served drinks to customers, collecting coins and zipping them back to a waiting bartender in a far corner, across the sea of tables and chairs. The cornucopia of different fey sat beside one another, playing games or showing off trinkets. Some of said trinkets were offered up in the form of payment, or being used in wagers.

Carroll's face went slack as the full extent of where she was settled in. "I can't believe it," Cole just barely heard her mumble.

James looked over her head at Cole. "Was I like this the first time you brought me to this place?" he asked, looking nervous about the answer.

"Yeah," Cole replied. "A bit."

"But," Carroll was saying now, in between gasps. "But there's… it just can't…."

Cole reached out to steady her, which proved more problematic than he'd anticipated as Detective Carroll flinched hard enough to stagger backward into James. Corhagen grabbed her, keeping the detective on her feet, but this also meant his arms were wound around her, something Carroll protested against by thrashing about.

"She needs a drink," Cole said as James released her.

"We're on duty," James reminded him, while Carroll busied herself with straightening her blouse.

"You needed a drink your first time," Cole said, already steering them toward the bar at the other end. "Now she does too."

Carroll's eyes were wider than Frisbees as the two men cleared a path through the chaos. James had taken point, with Cole coming up behind Carroll, who had to be reminded every few steps not to stop and stare openly at something. Cole thought it was a miracle they made it to the bar at all. More than one patron of the Silver Chalice looked ready to rip both of Carroll's legs off until they saw Cole coming up behind her.

"What was that thing?" she demanded once they'd reached the bar.

James had already ordered drinks for the three of them. "That," Cole explained, taking a seat on one of the stools, "was a sea hag. There's a colony of them living just off the Hudson River. She must be down on vacation to be so far from home."

The bartender placed their drinks in front of them without a word. "That," Cole mused as James paid, "or it's some kind of family trouble."

"What kind of trouble?" James asked, keeping his stool pointed toward the bar. "The kind where we have to get involved?"

"Unlikely," Cole said while Carroll openly gawked at the room, her drink still resting on the bar behind her.

"Sea hags typically have more females than males in a family group," Cole said, spinning Carroll around to where she faced the bar. "There are only one or two men to mate with per every ten sea hags, so there ends up being a lot of competition."

Carroll was giving Cole a murderous look now. "It's okay," James said. "He's just looking out for you. This isn't the kind of place you should stare."

"They know you're human," Cole said seriously, getting her attention. "They'll have smelled it on you the minute you came through the door."

"We walked through a wall," Carroll reminded him.

"It's a door," he insisted, growing impatient again. "Maybe it didn't have hinges or a knob, but it was a door for getting in or out. The point is, nobody in here likes a human who stares too much. This is the only place fey can go and be themselves."

"You forgot to tell her that it isn't the nicest place for people, either," said James. "This is a bar for trading magical items and information."

Carroll's mind raced. "So that's what we're doing here, then?" she asked, as Cole took a sip from his cup. "We're looking for someone who can tell…."

James cut her off by kicking the side of her stool with his foot. "Not so loud," Cole whispered, giving James an appreciative nod. "We're just here for a quick drink, and maybe a look around. Nobody else needs to know our business."

Cole settled in his stool, taking sips from his drink every so often. James followed suit, getting up once to shrug out of his outer coat, which Cole watched him do with more interest than even he cared to acknowledge.

"Why do you wear that heavy thing?" he wondered. "April is already here, and that's too much even for New York."

"It looks sharp," James replied, grinning.

Carroll glanced back and forth from one to the other. "I'm sitting in a bar having a drink while I'm on duty with stuff out of my worst childhood nightmares playing poker behind my back."

James turned ever so slightly to his left for a second. "The one at the table over in the corner wearing that Stetson hat is cheating," James told her, chancing another glance. "From the looks of it."

"This is how we do things," Cole explained to her, a little more patiently this time, as he brought the glass up to his lips yet again to finish off the drink. "Sometimes, that means taking our time and letting the answer come to us."

Carroll's breath was coming in quick gasps now. It sounded to Cole like she was hyperventilating. Even with all the noise behind them, he could hear her heart slam wildly into her chest like a trapped butterfly.

"I could believe the ghost," she whispered, leaning down. "I mean, most of the people in my family told me they'd seen at least one when I was growing up. So it's not that I was in the dark about that, exactly. I just…."

Carroll turned her head, as if she couldn't help it, and gave the room behind her a quick sweep before jerking back around.

"It's all just…."

Cole looked past her at James. "I think she's having a panic attack," he said. "This might not have been such a good idea after all."

Carroll downed her drink in one gulp. "I'm fine," she declared loudly, slamming the glass back down on the counter. "Fine, really. Who do I need to talk to?"

Cole frowned. "What?"

Carroll at least had the sense to lower her voice, though the way she leaned into Cole negated any semblance of remaining inconspicuous.

"We came here to find out information," she hissed. "Who do I talk to?"

Cole watched her closely. "What drink did you order for her?" he asked James. "Because I think she's hit her limit."

"Spring Water," James replied, frowning down at her. "What else? I know better than to give fey liquor to a mortal who's never had it before. That's a lesson I learned the first time around."

Cole snatched Carroll's glass off the counter and sniffed it. A distinct odor drifted up through his nostrils. Lowering it, his eyes landed on a sign hanging high overhead on the wall opposite them.

Spring Water—2 gold or $5!

Special offer available between 11 and 2.

James saw what Cole was looking at and swore. "Well, I guess that explains it," he said, looking ready to kick himself. "Wait, so how come this stuff hasn't hit me yet?"

"No clue," said Cole as Carroll's eyes began to cross. "That's a mystery for later. We'd better go before the locals figure out there's a drunk mortal on the premises."

James hopped down at once, surprised by the fact that he could do so. "Maybe I've built up a tolerance to it by now?" he offered, reaching over to help Cole get Carroll down off her stool.

"Not unless you've been drinking the stuff daily," Cole replied. "And were that the case, you'd probably have pickled organs inside of you right now."

Cole froze in midstep just as James took hold of Carroll's limp arm. James looked over the heads of the various fey, most of whom didn't appear to notice the three figures that had just entered. A short, pretty girl with long black hair stood front and center. Flanking her was a gangly puppet as tall as a man and a jack-in-irons clutching a long, heavy chain.

It didn't look as though they'd been spotted, but then the girl, called Spinner, looked their way. Standing on her tiptoes, her eyes zeroed in on James and Cole, who were still holding Carroll up on her feet. The puppet, Pine Nut, and the jack-in-irons, Tobolt, saw them right after Spinner did. All three glanced back and forth at each other, then turned and dashed back out the entrance.

James stood there and blinked, still holding Carroll up. "I thought they were going to kill us," he said, a little relieved. "Not that I'm complaining, but why didn't th…."

His question was cut off as Carroll's body sagged into him unexpectedly. Cole was racing off toward the door, having left him to hold the detective up all by himself.

"Of course," he groaned, struggling with his newfound load. "Why couldn't I have gotten splashed with robot juice and developed superpowers?"

Cole leaped through the door out into the street, sniffing the air the whole time for a trail to follow. Their scent was distinct, and none of them had been given enough time to get very fair. To their credit, they hadn't stayed on the ground, where it would have been easier for him to follow. Backing away from the Silver Chalice, Cole began stripping out of his clothes as James stumbled through the invisible door with Carroll still in his arms, holding her up.

"I'm shifting," he explained, though James didn't look flustered from the sight of a nude Cole at the moment. "I need you to look after my weapons. Take Carroll back to the car so she can sleep off whatever was in that drink, and remember not to touch Aed Deigh if you want to keep both hands."

Before James had time to protest, Cole had shifted to his white wolf form. Rooting through his clothes, Cole yanked something out with his teeth, then went racing up the side of the Silver Chalice to the roof. Cole sniffed around, found their trail immediately, and took off across the rooftops of the dockside buildings after them.

Up ahead, they were visible, moving like the wind across row after row of buildings. Cole was tracking them less through sight and more by scent now. Spinner had shifted to her spider-goblin form. It had given her a distinct advantage over the other two, resulting in them falling behind. There was still quite a bit of distance between himself and them, though.

Bearing down, Cole let out a low growl and poured on the steam.

The trail stopped before a gaping hole. Cole had lost sight of the three when they'd crisscrossed over several gaps between buildings. Their scents, however, never faded. Cole shifted out of his wolf form and stood naked on two legs in front of the tear in the roof. Down below, through the gloom, he could make out an auto shop.

Most likely, it was Tobolt who had smashed a way through for them. The whole setup stank of a trap, which likely meant their entering the Silver Chalice was no coincidence. At one time, Cole would have charged straight in without hesitation.

Being a cop had brought out a cautious streak in him.

"I'm starting to think like a cop," he mused, chuckling at himself. "Joss Vallimun, what have you done to me?"

Cole raised the cell phone to his ear. He'd thankfully remembered to bring it along with him before leaving James behind. Sadly, it looked as though the miserable device was coming in handy for emergencies after all.

"It's me," he said, once James had answered his phone. "Is Detective Carroll safe?"

"She's still breathing," James said on the other end, though it sounded like he was wrestling with someone at the moment. "I think she'll be all right, assuming I can get her strapped in."

"Right," Cole said as shrill laughter echoed in the background. "I've got them. They ducked down through a hole in the ceiling of an auto repair shop about two miles down from where you are."

Cole paused, then ran to a corner of the building and swept the area. "The name of the place is Folsom Garage," he said, craning his neck to read the sign down below to his right.

"I can find it," James promised, sounding even more frustrated now. "I'll be there with backup soon."

"Call the rest of the Section too," Cole told him, hearing Detective Carroll mutter something to James in the background.

"Of course," James grunted.

A loud slap immediately followed this, and Cole distinctly heard Detective Carroll shout, "Bastard!"

The silence that came after was poignant. "Is something happening that I should know about?" Cole asked. "You aren't doing anything that I'll have to testify for later, are you?"

"I'm not that big of an asshole," James retorted, sounding hurt now. "She keeps trying to take my pants off. I've been strapping her into the backseat this whole time so she doesn't hurt herself or molest me."

Detective Carroll was snoring now. Cole took the opportunity to run back to the opening in the roof and look around at the inside.

"Hurry," he said. "I don't think they're planning to make a run for it just yet, but there's always a possibility that they've got an exit leading into the tunnel system."

"I remember," James said, shutting the car door. "Some sidhe are sensitive to sunlight, and the subway system is a great place for them to hide out. A little glamour and they look like your standard subway bum."

Cole heard a second door open. "Anyway," said James. "I've got your keys and am sending the call out now. Please tell your car not to swallow me whole during the drive."

"It won't," Cole assured him. "It knows you're bringing it to me."

Cole almost hung up, but a thought occurred to him. Despite the seriousness of the situation, he couldn't resist teasing James a little.

"I'm surprised you didn't take Detective Carroll up on her offer," he ribbed.

James made a grunting sound. "Maybe when she's not drunk off her ass," he replied while punching in the code on the computer that had grown itself in Cole's car less than a week ago.

"Has our moral stance on infidelity changed now?" Cole asked.

The bitterness in his voice surprised even him.

"Not exactly," James answered anyway as the car started. "I just don't have to worry about that anymore."

Cole frowned.

"Sarah kicked me out," James told him stiffly. "I'll tell you about it later, though. We've got bad guys to catch, and you need to get back to keeping the garage under surveillance."

"Yes," Cole said, unsure of why he felt so shocked at the moment.

"Over and out," said James, before hanging up.

Cole stood on the roof for a moment, still holding the phone next to his ear. Shaking it off, he snapped the phone shut as a breeze drifted through. James was on his way, and so was backup, but none of them might arrive in time. This was the best lead the Section had gotten in hunting Naryssa down since the year began. He couldn't let it slip past him, but this was also obviously a trap.

What he needed was more help, and the answer was obvious.

Cole opened the phone back up and dialed his house number. Mal answered on the second ring, sounding winded.

"Sir?" he asked, in lieu of a greeting.

"Mal," Cole said. "I need you to listen very closely. Three of Naryssa's children are trapped inside an auto shop directly below me. Can you follow the signal of the phone and pinpoint where I am exactly?"

Cole took a deep breath as he waited.

"Yes, sir," Mal answered after a brief moment. "What is it you need?"

"I need you to send the pixies in," he replied. "And the goblins, too. It's only me here right now, and this is most likely a trap of theirs. I can't afford to go in alone, but if we wait for too long, they'll escape and try again. If the pixies can help, see if they'll come and set up a barrier around the place so that nothing can get in or out."

"I've already asked," Mal assured him calmly. "They are on their way now. It won't be easy, but I believe the sithen garage can let them out less than a block from where you are."

"Good."

"And what about the goblins?" Mal asked as Cole heard one of them grumbling on the other end. "Do you have any instructions for them?"

"Have them guard the tunnels underneath the building," Cole told him. "If Naryssa's children are planning to escape through there, the goblins can track them. None of them are to engage the enemy. Make certain they understand that. I just want them to keep an eye on things down there and follow the three if they try to escape."

"Certainly," Mal said dryly. "We wouldn't want anything to happen to them, would we?"

Cole smiled.

"Oh," Mal added. "The pixies should be arriving now. I'll leave you to deal with them personally."

"Thank you, Mal," Cole said.

As he hung up, Cole spotted the winged fey flying through the air, their wings catching the sunlight like prisms, sending sparkles flashing all over the concrete.

"Good timing," he said to one as it fluttered to a stop in front of his face.

"Commander Sparklefly reporting for duty, sir!" the pixie shouted, giving Cole the middle finger.

Cole recoiled slightly from the gesture. "Thank you, Commander," he said. "Although, that isn't the sort of salute an officer should give their superior."

Sparklefly frowned. "Really?" he said, looking down curiously at the middle finger that was still extended upward. "Are you sure?"

"Positive," Cole said. "Human soldiers do not salute their commanders that way. At least, not until their backs are turned."

"Apologies, sir!" Sparklefly shouted.

"Sir!" the other pixies said, falling in line behind Sparklefly in rows.

"At ease," Cole ordered. "Have your men been informed of their mission?"

"Sir, yes, sir!" Sparklefly replied. "The perimeter will be secured in seconds, pending your order to begin."

"Then do so," said Cole. "Make sure nothing can get in or out."

Sparklefly saluted again, followed by the other pixies, this time using the Nazi heil sign. Cole winced as they flew off in groups, making circular patterns around the building.

"We'll talk about that later," he muttered while the barrier formed around the auto shop.

Several minutes later, as the barrier shined in the sunlight and numerous passersby slowed down their vehicles to openly stare, Cole's phone rang again. The number was from an unknown.

"We're in position, boss," said Boogaloo when Cole answered. "Nuthin's happenin' on our side of things, so far."

"Perfect," Cole replied. "I wasn't aware that any of you owned a cell phone, but this makes things much easier."

"This one's Beauregard's."

One of the goblins, presumably Beauregard, began shouting about not wasting minutes. "I had ta swipe 'is ta make the call," Boogaloo explained.

"Good," Cole said. "Now I know how to find you. Assuming nothing has happened down there, stick to the shadows and keep your eyes peeled."

"We know tha' drill," Boogaloo assured him.

"I'll call again soon if nothing else happens topside," said Cole, hearing sirens in the distance.

It sounded like his backup was on the way. "I have to go," he told Boogaloo. "Keep the phone on vibrate."

Cole hung up and wandered over to the edge of the roof that pointed toward the street. The pixies had fitted the barrier to where it clung to the building like a second skin, allowing him to walk right over it. The magic flowed over the surface like a waterfall made out of light, giving the building a gossamer exterior. It was no surprise to him that people openly stared. Even the cops down below were looking up, openmouthed, at it as they climbed out of their vehicles.

Cole spotted James down below, getting out of his car. Luckily, the building wasn't very tall. Cole jumped, managing to land on his feet, and came to a stop several feet past the front door. The cops gathered on the scene were staring with open mouths at him now, as opposed to the mystically sealed building behind him. Cole strode forward, head held high, and marched up to James.

James was holding Cole's weapons in both of his hands. Aed Deigh and both guns had been wrapped up in Cole's clothes for safekeeping. James held himself rigidly as Cole wordlessly took the bundle out of his hands, but didn't look away. It seemed to Cole like the Section Thirteen detective was having a very hard time not looking directly down at Cole's crotch. At this point, Cole was used to it and put on his pants first to help placate the man.

Once he was fully dressed, an officer on the scene approached. "So, what's the story?" he asked. "We got word that there were at least three wanted perps holed up inside."

The officer was speaking to James, for the most part, yet his eyes wandered over to Cole at every other word or so.

"That's correct," Cole said. "We're waiting for the rest of Section Thirteen to arrive."

"They're on the way," James told him. "Inspector Vallimun is bringing the whole team in."

"We'll need it," Cole replied.

The officer's face sagged into a deep frown. "So this is one of those cases?" he asked, cocking one eyebrow at each of them. "What have we got here? Escaped cultists or something? Did one of those teen vampire fangirls finally go off the deep end?"

The rest of the officers on the scene had gone back to watching the building as they taped off the area. Cole noticed, however, that one or more of them would look toward James and him every few minutes. By their expressions, none of them were happy to be here.

"I wish it were so simple," Cole told the officer standing in front of him. "Officer…?"

"Griffin," the man replied. "I've heard about you guys."

"We're famous," said James, smiling at Cole.

"Yes, we are," replied Cole, "but not for a reason you'd like."

The rest of Section Thirteen pulled up then, sparing Cole from having to answer any more of Officer Griffin's questions. Joss was in the lead, with Staffelbach, Rainette, and Marcel coming up behind him. Cole couldn't help but smile as his boyfriend joined them.

"The perimeter is secure," Cole told Joss.

"Which ones are they?" Joss asked, looking bleakly across the small crowd of cops at the sparkling building.

"Spinner, Pine Nut, and Tobolt," James answered. "I recognized them when we were inside the Silver Chalice."

"They came directly here," Cole said, "meaning they planned this from the start."

"So it's a trap," Rainette concluded, sniffing. "They wanted us to come here."

"Or at least me to come here," Cole countered. "It could be that they aren't interested in the whole Section."

Rainette looked less than happy about that. "It's always got to be about you," she grumbled, staring him down.

Marcel put a hand down gently on her shoulder. "All the better, then," he told her. "They won't be expecting all of us. This puts the team at an advantage."

Cole turned to Joss. "It's your show," he reminded. "Whatever you think is best. We are at your disposal."

Joss smiled, then turned back to the auto shop building. "One quick question," he stated, without looking at Cole. "As long as that thing is up, can any of them get out?"

"No," Cole replied. "And I've stationed some… others down in the tunnels below. That area is being watched, and no movement was reported so far. As far as I can tell, the three are locked up inside."

Officer Griffin, who had backed away upon seeing Joss approach, was nevertheless still within earshot. It was clear to Cole that the man was lingering nearby in the hopes of overhearing something. Rainette shot the man a withering glare, then abruptly ignored him altogether. Joss glanced his way for a moment, nodding once in understanding at Cole's need for discretion.

"Good call," he said, indicating that he meant the statement on both counts. "I guess that means we go in."

"Knowing it's a trap?" Rainette asked.

"It's a trap for them as much as us now," Marcel explained, letting go of her shoulder at last. "The barrier was something they hadn't planned on. If we go in now, they have nowhere to run."

Staffelbach, who until now had been decidedly quiet, didn't look happy. "Remember what they say about cornering wild animals," he said pointedly.

"Agreed," Cole said. "If we go in now, we're likely going to have a fight on our hands."

"And if we wait, that leaves them time to prepare," Joss countered.

No one argued, though none of them looked thrilled with the idea either. "In we go, then," said Joss, taking the lead.

Cole stepped back, letting Rainette and Marcel come up after him. James lingered a moment, then followed them, leaving Cole to bring up the rear with Staffelbach.

"Are you nervous?" he asked as another officer lifted the tape up so they could all pass.

"Not really," Staffelbach replied, swallowing a large lump in his throat. "I mean, we're pretty sure at this point that I'm not human anymore, so what's there to be afraid of."

Staffelbach looked over at Cole. "Right?"

Cole didn't meet his eyes. "I am no more human than you," he reminded him. "Furthermore, I've never been human, but I can't say I'm not unsettled by what we're doing. There are all kinds of things that could go wrong for me and everyone else."

They had reached the building. The sound of laughter could be heard around them, along with what could easily have been mistaken for running water. The barrier sealing the auto shop parted like a curtain, granting them passage. Joss reached for the door and found it unlocked.

"Thank them," Cole advised, before anyone could enter. "They'll appreciate it."

James turned around. "I thought you told me once that thanking a fey was rude."

"Only the upper fey," he said. "The pixies won't be offended at all."

Cole stood back with Staffelbach behind him as the others passed through the threshold, each whispering a small word of thanks.

"I am very nervous," Cole admitted, stepping forward as each Section member in front of them entered the building.

"But you're immortal," Staffelbach said, keeping his eyes fixed on the room around them as they entered together.

"Yes," Cole replied, closing the door behind him.

The barrier went back up, sending a shiver through his body. "But so are the things we're hunting," Cole reminded. "And they know how to kill things that are just as immortal as them."

THE inside of the auto shop was darkened, like twilight. The barrier was casting shade over the whole building, leaving Cole's team members with low visibility. Marcel would be fine, Cole knew, and he smiled with relief when Joss switched his eye patch over. That left Corhagen and Rainette for certain. Staffelbach was still an unknown, but they would have to make do. Cole could feel it stirring in the air with each step he took.

The party was about to begin.

Joss was rolling his sleeve up. The flesh from his hand poured away, revealing the silver and obsidian arm hidden underneath. The arm began glowing, sending wisps of power into the air like fog rolling off ice. Cole drew out Aed Deigh as Joss tapped his metal arm against a barrel. The sound concealed the noise of both blades snapping out at the same time.

"Knock. Knock."

Joss's voice was cool and calm, a sharp contrast to everyone else's mood. "I'm not getting anything yet," he said, turning his head from right to left with each step he took. "My eye isn't picking up their auras. Anything from your end, Cole?"

"Nothing," Cole said, sniffing the air. "There's too much metal and grease in the air. I can smell that they came in here, but pinning their location down will take time. It will be easier if we just search."

Rainette had summoned one of her liquid spheres. It was a spell of hers that called upon water's corrosive power. She could cast it multiple times, and was now splitting the sphere into three smaller orbs to conserve power.

Marcel took point by her side, prepared to give her cover if she needed it. Corhagen had pulled out his gun and was searching behind some of the equipment for signs of movement. Staffelbach, finally, was keeping his hands out in front of him. He hadn't drawn his gun yet, but Cole wasn't about to reprimand him for it. The best experience a fledgling with power could get was during combat. Cole gave him one small nod of reassurance. Staffelbach returned it with a smile before his eyes went back to sweeping the large area.

A loud crash came from somewhere off to the left. Everyone turned to see Corhagen recoiling in shock from a welding area.

"Rats," James said, moving even further away. "Sorry, I mean, this place has rats. I saw one over there."

Joss rolled his eyes. "We're hunting creatures that cannot die inside of a grease pit," he retorted. "I think rats are the least of our concerns."

"I beg to differ," Rainette said, looking revolted.

"Agreed," Marcel said.

Rainette gave her ogre boyfriend a look. "I find them unpleasant," Marcel insisted, staring back at her with a vexed expression. "How is that strange?"

"You're an eight-foot-tall ogre that can punch through solid walls," she reminded, giving the corrosive orbs in her hand a practiced spin. "How can rats get to you?"

"Quiet, you two," Joss ordered. "Let's stay focused on the problem at hand for right now. We can tell the nice people who own this place about their rat problem once we're done here."

The two fell silent, but then Marcel leaned into Rainette. "You are a witch with great magical potential," he whispered. "How is it you are unnerved by them?"

"They're unsanitary and spread diseases," she hissed back.

Joss glowered. "You two," he ordered. "Check the corners of the room. Separately."

Corhagen and Staffelbach each bit their lower lip to keep from laughing. As Cole watched them turn away from each other, something dawned on him.

"It's the middle of the day," he said, speaking directly to Joss.

Joss looked back over his shoulder. "And?" he wondered, a little impatiently. "Do I need to get you a watch so you can confirm that?"

"It's the middle of the day," Cole repeated, gesturing around them now, "and the middle of the week, but this place is empty."

Joss thought for a moment as the rest of the team continued their search, coming up empty. "You said it was a trap," he pointed out.

"Yes," Cole replied. "But I assumed the building was abandoned. When I was on the roof, I heard nothing that suggested the place was occupied."

The others looked at Cole now. "What are you getting at?" Joss wondered. "If the place was empty when they escaped in here, why is it bothering you now?"

"Because the equipment in this building looks used," Cole said, pointing a finger toward one of the machines for emphasis. "Some of it even looks new. If it's the middle of the day on a work week and this place was recently occupied, where are the workers?"

A light flashed in Joss's eye, and he swept the room. "I'm still not seeing anything," he said, alarmed now. "I kept thinking their auras would show up, but this place is empty."

"Could they have gotten out?" Rainette asked, moving away from the wall.

"They shouldn't have come in here if they had a better place to run," Cole said, thinking fast. "And the pixies barricaded it within minutes. The other exits are covered."

"So where are they?" Staffelbach asked. "And how did they know this place would be empty when they came here?"

"They didn't," Joss said, looking at each member of his team. "This wasn't a trap for Cole. It's a trap for all of us."

No one moved. Cole did a quick head count and saw they were spread way too far apart for his comfort. Rainette sneezed, and the noise made almost everyone jump.

"Sorry," she said. "I think the dust in here is making me worse."

"Something isn't right," Cole said, turning in a slow circle. "If this is a trap, what happened to the bait? And where is the hook hiding?"

The answer came to him at once. "In the one place where we still haven't looked," he said, looking up.

The others saw him staring up at the ceiling and craned their necks to peer through the rafters. There, between the wooden planks that helped hold the ceiling up, was Spinner. Next to her hung Tobolt and Pine Nut, and surrounding them were the rest of their family. Cole did a quick count and came up with at least twenty.

"They brought the whole family," Rainette said gravely, keeping her eyes fixed on as many of them as she could.

"Not all of them," Cole replied. "Thank Goddess for that."

"Just enough to take care of a problem we've had for a while," Spinner jeered, looking down at the six of them through all of her eyes. "Someone has been very naughty, trying to hunt us down."

"Can I do it now?" Pine Nut interrupted anxiously, his voice carrying a slight screech to it.

"Not yet," Spinner snapped.

"I think I see some familiar faces in the crowd," Cole said, providing a distraction as the other Section members closed in on the same location near the center of the room. "For those of you who weren't there when we first met, these are some of Naryssa's adopted children."

"We guessed that," Rainette quipped.

Cole shot her a look. "Everyone," he said loudly, "say hi to the kids."

"I'm afraid you people are all under arrest." Joss took over, his left eye shining brightly in the darkness of the building.

Quite a few of the half-fey above them laughed. "Arrest us?" Spinner asked. Her voice sounded like poisoned honey. "How do you plan on doing that?"

"The old-fashioned way." James spoke up.

"Corhagen, don't be a hero," Cole warned quietly, silencing him. "We are in a lot of trouble right now."

"You have the right to remain silent," Joss began. "Anything you say can be used against you in the court of law. You have the right—"

"That sounds fascinating," Spinner cut in, unable to contain her laughter now. "But we didn't bring all of you here so you could arrest us. Nanny Goodwynch asked that we take care of you so that you won't get in the way of the Triskaidekahedron's plans."

"We really need to get them to spell that," Raincttc grumbled.

"I'll ask," Marcel offered. "Does anyone have a pen?"

"The Thirteen Faces," Cole said, taking over. "We've heard of them. In fact, we met a few of their agents not too long ago."

"The Nihilgeister," Joss added, keeping his eye on Spinner. "And those tulpas that had those runes carved into their foreheads. One for each member of the Trisk…."

Joss stopped himself. "The Thirteen Faces," he said instead.

"We keep coming across that number, you know," Cole picked up, watching the crowd as they hung down from the rafters, looking eagerly at Cole now. "Any particular reason?"

"It is a symbol of the coming king," Spinner answered, to his surprise. "But Nanny wouldn't want you knowing much more about that."

"Then what's taking so long?" Rainette demanded. "We're all just standing here waiting for you to get started. Why don't any of you come down here and take us on?"

James swallowed. "We're not in that big of a hurry," he muttered.

"Yeah," Staffelbach agreed. "Sometimes it helps to talk things out instead of resorting to violence."

"We're not here to fight you," Spinner said, getting their attention again. "Nanny Goodwynch would never unnecessarily risk us coming to harm. You invaded our home and forced us to retreat."

"No one had better have touched my stuff!" Pine Nut shouted angrily. "I was just getting everything the way I wanted it."

Spinner smacked him with one of her legs before continuing. "By Faerie law," she said, "a trial by combat may decide who keeps the sithen."

"Except we aren't in Faerie anymore," Joss said. "This is the mortal world, so you have to abide by mortal laws."

"Mortal laws do not apply to higher beings," Spinner countered, bitterness touching her words. "We are above and beyond them. Especially since mortals do not acknowledge our existence."

Joss was close enough that Cole gave him a tap to the leg with his foot. "Play along," Cole whispered, before raising his voice. "Give us a moment to confer," he shouted up to Spinner.

Once they were facing each other, Rainette shot Cole a death glare. "What is going on?" she demanded. "Do they want to kill all of us, or just you?"

"All of us," Marcel told her. "This is their trap."

"Marcel is right," Cole said to everyone. "They've invoked an old law that gives the former residents of a place the right to reclaim it via a challenge, usually through rite of combat."

"What happens if you decline?" Joss asked.

"Officially, nothing," answered Cole, keeping everyone's attention. "We're not in Faerie. There's no one to enforce the law."

"Then why did she just challenge you?" Staffelbach wondered.

Cole glanced up at the rafters before answering.

"Because there's no one to enforce the law if Naryssa cheats by sending her children to make sure we lose," Cole said. "Naryssa sent her children to issue the challenge and probably ordered them to make sure I don't make it through the fight alive. Then they murder all the eyewitnesses. If anyone approaches her at some point down the line, asking about this little incident, there's no one to contradict her version of events."

"Then why issue the challenge at all?"

Rainette was the one who asked, but it looked as though everyone in the circle was thinking the exact same thing.

"Naryssa is very old," Cole explained. "I was kicked out of Faerie when I was young, but she's been alive for centuries, at least. After a while, you get set in your ways."

Rainette's mouth turned up into a sneer. "I get it," she said. "Like that aunt you can never reason with."

"A good analogy," Cole said, earning him a smirk from everyone in the circle.

"What happens if you don't fight, though?" Joss asked, serious again.

"They kill us," Cole stated flatly. "Or try to, at least. We could try to fight our way out of here, but they outnumber us. Naryssa sent this many for that very reason."

Several pairs of eyes flickered up to the rafters. "So you fight one of them, or whoever they brought to do the dirty work, and win," James said. "What happens next?"

"They kill us anyway," Cole said. "But that's okay, because while I'm fighting, it will give the rest of you time to do something brilliant."

The others looked at one another for a moment before turning back to Cole. "Like what?" Staffelbach asked nervously.

"I don't know," Cole replied. "You haven't thought of it yet."

Joss looked ready to smack him. "When you think of it," Cole went on, "fill me in so I know what the plan is."

"Are you prepared?" Spinner shouted from the rafter where she hung. "Our champions are waiting for you, sidhe."

The others took a step back, but Cole held onto Joss for a second. "Remember," he whispered in his boyfriend's ear. "Make it brilliant."

"Don't worry," Joss replied out the corner of his mouth. "I'm already thinking of something."

"Good."

Joss seized Cole's arm before he could step away. "Don't die," he warned, left eye flashing briefly in the dim light. "Because once this is over, I plan on kicking your ass."

Cole slipped his arm out of Joss's loosening grasp, smiling as he felt his boyfriend squeeze his hand for a brief second. He stepped forward in front of the rest of the Section and held Aed Deigh up over his head, saluting Spinner directly.

"I am ready," Cole declared. "I stand ready to defend Section Thirteen, my allies and my friends. Bring forth your champion."

Two figures fell from the rafters amid the gathered half-fey. Cole spotted them before they were halfway down and felt a surreal sense of déjà vu. One landed in a crouching position in front of him, the other behind him. Their kneecaps should have popped off. Such a feat wasn't possible for an average human, but Cole had no time to deliberate the fact. Before either had straightened up, the scents from their bodies reached him.

Their faces were the same as those in the glamour illusion Cole had created inside Alice Tweedle's apartment. Even their clothing looked the same. Both were dressed hell-bent for leather and armed to the teeth. Cole could make out guns and bladed weapons underneath the long coats trailing down to the dusty floor. Each one's face was the same as he remembered. Cole had to remind himself it had only been a couple of months since they'd first met outside the Order-controlled center.

The woman was smiling as she strode around Cole at a wide angle, stopping when she reached her partner. Cole stared into the face of the man next to her first before turning toward her.

"Hello, sweetheart," she cooed playfully, brushing a lock of blond hair out of her face. "Long time no see."

COLE gripped Aed Deigh. "Whenever you are ready," he said, taking his eyes off her only long enough to look meaningfully toward Joss and the others.

The three of them stood in three concentric circles now. Cole had scrawled them into the floor using the heat from Aed Deigh. It was the traditional ring for ritual combat. So long as Naryssa's children insisted on doing things by the book, so to speak, Cole didn't mind following the primary aesthetics.

The woman was smiling now. "I'm a little disappointed," she said, as though they were conversing over tea. "I'd thought you would be full of questions."

"We're here to fight, as far as I'm concerned," he retorted, keeping his guard firmly up, "not engage in idle chitchat."

"Enough!" Pine Nut shouted impatiently from above. "Begin, already."

"Yeah," Tobolt added. "Let's see a little sidhe blood, already."

"Shut up, you two," Spinner hissed.

The blonde woman's smile turned into a smirk as she rolled her eyes upward. "Impatient, aren't they?" she asked him.

Cole had been trying to remember her name for a few minutes now but kept drawing a blank. "Who are you?" he asked, looking from her over to the silent man standing next to her.

Her face turned, assumed a pouty expression. "He doesn't remember either of us," she said, looking at the man next to her.

"I remember you both," Cole interjected. "I mean, what are your names again?"

The woman blinked. "Oh," she said. "We don't have names anymore. It's just as well that you don't remember the ones we used when you first met us."

"Truthfully, I don't remember either," the guy next to her said, stretching.

"Will you two shut up and fight already?"

Spinner's voice echoed through the auto shop.

"In a minute," Cole shot back at her without looking up.

Cole looked at the two of them again. "I don't know why I couldn't smell it before," he said carefully. "Now, though, it's obvious. You two are brother and sister, not husband and wife."

"My perfume," she answered immediately. "We've had encounters with fey before, and it helps to know how to mask your scent."

Cole nodded in appreciation. "Even I didn't notice," he said. "So is this a living for the both of you? You go around murdering witches and other fey for cash?"

"Murdering witches is more of a crusade," her brother said, tensing up suddenly. "Killing fey is for money."

"A family's got to eat," his sister added.

Cole had his attention on both of them, yet, out the corner of one eye, he could see Rainette go rigid at the mention of this. Though the rest of the Section was standing a fair bit away from the makeshift battle arena, Rainette had nonetheless heard.

"You kill witches as part of a crusade," Cole said, keeping things going so that the attention was primarily on him, "then leave breadcrumbs around their burnt corpses."

"That was my idea," the brother said, smirking. "I thought it would make for a nice touch when we started out, all those years ago."

"Hansel and Gretel," Cole summed up, looking from brother to sister. "The human children's tale where the young brother and sister get lost in the woods and have to escape from the wicked witch."

"We escaped from her a long time ago," Gretel said, giving her silky hair a casual toss. "But the world is full of witches. We're just picking things up from where the story left off."

"Right." Cole cast an eye upward, then moved into an offensive crouch. "I think that's enough conversation for right now. Our spectators are getting restless."

"If you say so," Gretel replied casually.

Hansel looked her way then. "Do you want to go first, sis?" he asked, his voice growing smoother with each syllable.

"Mm," she mused. "You can have him first, if you want. I'll go afterward."

Cole smirked at the two of them. "It's been a while since I took on a brother and sister one after the other," he said, keeping his guard up.

This earned him a laugh from Gretel. "You've been a bad boy, haven't you?"

Cole shrugged as her brother stepped forward. "What can I say?" he retorted. "It was the sixties."

Hansel gave his left wrist a practiced twist. Out from under the sleeve of the coat popped a set of iron blades. They were spaced an inch or so from one another and ended in curved hooks, forming lethal-looking claws. Cole smelled the iron and instinctively moved back.

"It's not the first time my sister and I were brought in to murder a fey," he explained, approaching Cole in a semicircular movement. "Though this was a new twist: the fey paying us to kill one of their own."

"They aren't the same as me," Cole said. "I am sidhe. Most of the ones above us are half-fey and much lower on the bloodline scale."

Quite a few of Naryssa's children hissed at this. "They don't seem to like that," Hansel noted, coming in closer at a slow pace.

He and Cole had begun circling one another now, keeping their feet inside the constraints of the arena while Gretel watched from off to the side.

Hansel swung at Cole with his claws, but Cole brought Aed Deigh up in time to block.

"Most of them were taken from their families as infants," he explained in a low voice.

Hansel pulled back and struck several times against Cole's weapon. Cole blocked each attack with one end of Aed Deigh. Sparks flew from the red-hot brand, while flakes of snow scraped off the ice-covered opposite side. Cole danced back and forth, studying his human opponent's movements with each blow Hansel made. It was clear the man had done this kind of thing before.

Despite having superior speed and strength, Cole was having to push himself harder than expected to keep Hansel at bay. Whenever he struck, Hansel blocked, and the mortal's counterattack came much faster than the sidhe expected. Together, they spun back and forth in a blur of movement.

Abruptly, Hansel leaped back out of Cole's range, taking a spot next to his sister. "Your turn," he said, giving her a nod. "I've had enough for now."

The children of Naryssa roared in protest as the battle stopped.

"Bored already?" Gretel chided, ignoring the noise as she stepped forward. "I thought fighting a sidhe would be more entertaining for you."

"I'm only being fair," he replied, folding both arms in front of him. "Don't wear him out completely, though. I'll want another turn before long."

Cole waited as Gretel reached into her coat. She pulled out a glove with a long sleeve, came to a stop several steps in front of him, and slid her fingers into the material while her eyes stared deep into Cole's tricolored irises. The glove's fingertips had sharp talons attached to them. He knew without guessing that they were made of iron as well.

"I guess I should make this quick," she said, flexing her fingers. "It looks like the crowd doesn't appreciate the intermission."

The noise from overhead was still going on.

"They can wait," Cole said casually, with a half shrug for emphasis. "Unless you're in a hurry to get this over with."

"Not at all," Gretel responded, grinning from ear to ear now. "I wanted to do something like this when we first met, or had you forgotten?"

Cole looked at Joss involuntarily. Gretel noticed the movement and smiled as she realized what it meant.

"So he's the one you turned me down for?" Gretel didn't look offended, despite the slight put-out tone of voice. "He's handsome," she noted, giving Joss an appreciative once-over. "It doesn't look like he's much fun, though."

"I think some might agree with you," Cole said, taking a step forward.

Gretel calmly held her hands up in apology. "I meant nothing by it," she told him. "I just think you need someone a little more exciting in your life."

The claws were much shorter than her brother's weapon, and far faster. Cole found himself dodging her attacks, more than anything. Gretel had been fighting this way for a long time, judging by how easily she moved.

She was also the more limber of the two and avoided several of Cole's swipes as though he were moving in slow motion.

"You have been killing fey for a long time," he breathed as she brought out a knife with her other hand to block his downward strike.

The sound of the weapons clashing against each other rang in their ears. Cole saw that the blade was made of iron as well and had been forged with a hollow streak down the center so that it vibrated when struck. It was an odd thing for a blade maker to do, but Cole knew why. The sound of ringing iron was detrimental to lesser fey. Though his sidhe blood ran strong in him, the noise made him wince.

"Most humans can't keep up for very long," he spat out painfully.

"We've been doing this a while," she whispered in his face, before leaping back.

Gretel tagged her brother in, who circled Cole once before attacking his side. Hansel was almost as fast as his sister and knew how to make each attack count for something.

The point was for Cole to keep the fight going while the rest of the Section planned their escape. However, the duo were proving to be a more than efficient fighting team, compensating for one another's weaknesses perfectly and the other moving in whenever one grew tired.

"They aren't going to let any of us live," he hissed at Gretel when she took her brother's place again.

"Not my problem, really," she jeered back, hoping to get under his skin.

Cole spun around and sent a wave of icicles at her. Caught off-guard, Gretel flipped backward, letting them pass harmlessly above her body, but came far too close to the arena's edge. Cole took the advantage presented to him and sent a wave of fire out.

He'd deliberately aimed just to her left, giving Gretel time to move out of the way. Though she avoided incurring any major damage, the flames scorched the edges of her clothing, leaving her seared. Gretel let out a hiss of pain as she staggered to the floor.

Cole was on her in seconds.

"That includes you," he snarled softly, aiming the red tip of Aed Deigh at her throat. "I've fought Naryssa before. She doesn't like leaving loose ends."

Gretel started to get up, but Cole let the tip brush up against her flesh ever so slightly, causing it to scorch black.

"Each of her children watching us fight right now had a mortal parent," he whispered, sensing movement behind him. "Some of them had happy homes, but she slaughtered both sides and stole them."

Hansel was coming up in back of him now. Cole heard and spun out of the way, leaving Gretel on the floor to absorb her brother's blow. Gretel's eyes doubled in size as she brought her blade up to counter his attack. The claws coming out from the sleeve of Hansel's coat clashed noisily against his sister's knife.

Gretel stood, Hansel giving her a hand up, and the two turned on Cole together.

"Finally," they all heard Tobolt call out. "This is starting to get real interesting."

Cole held his ground as the brother and sister came at him from both sides. Surrounded, Cole set the floor on fire with the tip of his firebrand, forcing both back and leaving a gap between their bodies to escape through. Cole rolled along the ground, brought himself back up into a crouch, and sent a wave of fire and icicles behind him.

The blast was enough to slow them down, but Hansel and Gretel both proved quick enough to avoid taking more than a few slashes. Bloodied now, the two came at Cole in full force. Laughing, the sidhe slammed the tip of his ice-brand into the ground, spreading a layer of frost over the surface.

Cole stood up as both his opponents skidded toward him helplessly. As he brought Aed Deigh up to attack them head-on, Hansel did something unexpected: he fell backward and landed on his ass just as Cole was about to embed the ice blade into his flesh. Cole hadn't intended to give Hansel the full brunt of it. The man still had things to answer for, after all, and Joss would have been pissed at him for outright killing either of them.

Caught off his guard, Cole turned his eyes away from Gretel for a second as Hansel slid harmlessly past him. There was a flash of pain on his left forearm, leaving him instantly dizzy. Cole jerked his head sharply to the left in time to see Gretel holding her claws up. Blood was dripping from each iron claw, and, as Cole watched, it darkened from red to black.

His arm was on fire. The pain came in full force now, fast enough that it didn't immediately register with him. Cole jumped back automatically as Hansel swiped at the backs of his legs, but the damage was already done. Several deep slashes were running diagonally along Cole's arm. A wave of sickness struck as realization of what was happening hit him. Gretel and Hansel were each laughing as they closed in on Cole.

"I guess those old stories were true after all," Hansel said, bringing his claws up high overhead. "We knew cold iron worked well against fey."

"I wasn't sure it would affect a sidhe so well, though," Gretel finished thoughtfully, bringing the blood-soaked claw tips up to her mouth.

Cole watched Gretel stick her tongue out and winced as fresh pain shot through him. "Don't," Hansel warned, stopping her. "We don't know what that stuff does, and some fey are said to have poisonous blood, anyway."

Gretel frowned but complied. Both of them turned back to Cole as he sank to the floor. Hansel got in a strike to his side, leaving behind several deep slashes along his ribs.

"Finish him!" Spinner cried out.

The other half-fey cheered in response. Hansel and Gretel gave one another a nod and brought their claws down as Cole felt his strength fading. Cole forced himself to hold his eyes open. It was harder than he'd expected, facing death this way at the mercy of two witch hunters. Any other time, he would have been embarrassed, but the cuts on his side made it hard to breathe.

It occurred to Cole then that the two should have attacked him by now. Blinking, he forced his vision to clear and spotted someone standing in front of him, blocking Hansel and Gretel's path. Apparently, he'd been in too much pain to notice a chunk of armor stomping toward him.

"Get the hell away from him," he heard Staffelbach shout, "you sons of bitches!"

THERE was fighting.

Cole had been around long enough to recognize the sounds of battle. The problem at the moment was his inability to stand up and join the fray. He was pretty sure one side of the brawl consisted of his Section Thirteen friends, and it didn't take an old sage to work out why.

It was getting more and more difficult to string his thoughts together coherently, but Cole vividly remembered seeing Staffelbach standing over him. Where the armor came from was still a mystery, and, for all he knew, it had been a hallucination. With one punch each, Staffelbach had sent both Hansel and Gretel flying before either one could finish Cole off. This was what had set off Naryssa's children, he guessed, and brought them down from the rafters onto everyone.

And, as they said, all hell broke loose.

"I hope there wasn't poison spread over their claws," Cole wheezed. "Because this hurts a lot more than I remember."

"What's wrong?" Staffelbach asked, kneeling down in front of him.

Cole gave Staffelbach's armor a quick looking over before answering. Strangely, the suit reminded Cole of something out of a cheap sci-fi film or an old eighties comic book. Most of it was just wiring and tension rods holding together plates of metal covering his arms, legs, and chest.

Cole's eyes narrowed despite the pain. "Where did you get that?" he wondered, struggling to his feet.

Staffelbach gestured around them with one arm. "From all over the place," he said. "I just concentrated and transmuted the equipment here into whatever I thought I could use."

The surprise must have shown on Cole's face, because Staffelbach laughed. "I work best when I'm under pressure," he said. "Where are you hurt?"

Cole gasped as fresh pain struck him. "Here," he said, showing Staffelbach his arm. "And there," Cole added, turning so Staffelbach could see. "It's cold iron. Cold iron is one of the only things that work really well against anything from Faerie."

A scream cut Cole off before he could continue. One of Naryssa's children, an overbearing hulk that might have been half troll, came rushing toward them wielding a club. Staffelbach jumped in front of Cole before he could say anything, and thrust his fist out. What looked like a drill bit fired from the surface of Staffelbach's forearm and embedded itself in the half-troll's chest, dropping the creature in one shot.

"I'm really getting into this idea of using armor," he said, turning back to a stunned Cole. "I could probably make a few modifications to it so—"

"Behind you!" Cole warned.

Staffelbach didn't bother looking. He swung out his left foot and slammed the metal-coated appendage into the head of a giant cockroach that had an infant's face. Fire belched from the sole, causing the thing's head to burst into flame. The creature skittered away, howling in agony as the flames continued scorching its exoskeleton.

"Sorry," Staffelbach apologized. "What about your injuries?"

"They were made with cold iron," Cole explained quickly, keeping an eye out for any further attacks. "Cold iron weakens the fey."

"Can I help?" Staffelbach offered, raising Cole's injured arm gently to look it over. "I can transmutate anything, theoretically. Maybe that works on injuries too."

Staffelbach started to put his hand down over the claw marks on Cole's arm, but another attack from behind stalled him.

"This way," Cole said, gesturing as best he could. "Over by the wall."

With Staffelbach's help, Cole worked his way over to lean up against the nearest wall. Once there, Staffelbach placed both hands above Cole's injuries and concentrated. Several seconds went by, but nothing happened.

"It's not working," Staffelbach said, almost disbelievingly.

"The wounds are mostly superficial," Cole told him. "They'll just take a while to heal. If you can help keep Naryssa's brats off my back, I can fight."

"You're too injured to fight right now," Staffelbach told him obstinately. "Let us help."

"Watch."

Cole raised his good arm, the one that held Aed Deigh, and forced as much of his will into it as he could. The pain doubled, but Cole used that as well. Everything traveled down his arm into the weapon, forcing it to glow brightly.

Cole's hand shook as he pointed the firebrand into the fray. A burst of flame exploded out of the blade, searing several of the nearby brawlers.

"That's how," Cole gasped out, letting his arm fall slightly for a moment. "Hold them back for me, and I'll clear a path for the others so we can regroup."

The Section was being overwhelmed. To their credit, each one was holding their own against the swarm of half-spawn. Marcel was laying down a curb stomp, despite taking major hits, to give Rainette and James room to work. James was backing Marcel up with gunfire while Rainette launched corrosive orbs at her targets. Joss had gotten separated from them but was doing well, for a solo act. Cole had to admire his man for a moment before blasting a path through all of them. The result cut a swath through to both sides but left Cole drained.

Luckily, his team was quick on the uptake. Using his enchanted arm, Joss knocked Naryssa's children back away from him as he ran like a bat out of hell toward Cole and Staffelbach. Marcel made better time, thanks to James and Rainette's help. Cole thought he heard explosions across the room but couldn't be bothered. Joss was on him the moment he reached Cole.

"Are you all right?" Joss demanded, looking Cole straight in the eye. "What happened?"

"Iron weapons," he said weakly. "Those two did their homework."

"Speaking of those two, where are they?" Rainette asked as the children of Naryssa gathered around on all sides, blocking any chance for escape.

"Dunno." Cole forced himself to stand straight. "I didn't see which way they went."

"I'm afraid those two are the least of our concerns," Marcel stated, looking around at the slew of faces. "We seem to be at a disadvantage."

"It seems like any time I lead this team, it ends up being like this," Cole said. "But I suppose now isn't the time for apologies, either."

"You didn't know it was a trap," Joss insisted.

"I knew it was a trap," Cole replied. "I just wasn't expecting the trap to be quite so thorough."

Spinner was moving to the front now. "Get out of my way," she snapped angrily at two half-brownies standing in front of her. "Move!"

The two half-brownies staggered as Spinner forced her way through, nearly tripping over one's feet. "You can't get out of here," Joss told her, acting before the shape-changing spider goblin could recover. "This entire building is sealed."

Spinner shot Joss a glare before regaining her composure. "Then we'll just have to kill you," she retorted. "None of you were going to leave this place, anyway."

"It's sealed by a pixie barrier," Cole informed, fighting to keep his voice somewhat normal. "They can hold that in place for months. How long do you think it'll be before this bunch gets hungry enough to start munching on one another?"

"Gross," Rainette muttered, scowling.

"Seconded," Staffelbach said.

"Nanny Goodwynch taught us to get along," Spinner replied, scoffing at the notion. "Your tricks won't fool us."

Cole noticed the spider goblin's eyes didn't quite match the confidence on her face. "Instinct is instinct," Cole said. "No matter how hard you try and bury it, it's never too far from the surface. And the fey are all about survival of the fittest."

Several amid the horde growled, low and unearthly, yet Cole saw a number of them didn't look convinced.

"You can kill us, but it won't get you out of here," he finished, speaking to the whole group now. "And if it came down to it, do you think Spinner is the type to sacrifice herself in order to spare the rest of you?"

Spinner's face was livid. "Wicked, wicked sidhe," she hissed, her voice taking on an almost metallic tone as she leaped forward.

Cole moved to defend himself in spite of his injury. The others were already preparing to push him out of the way while Joss powered up his arm. Staffelbach was transmutating one of his metal arm guards into a sword. From the brief glimpse that Cole got, the blade looked to be made out of iron. The boy was learning fast, it seemed.

None of them got the chance to fight back, however. Something fell from the rafters when Spinner was about halfway across the gap separating them from her family. She'd gone for a dramatic flying leap, and this put her at a critical disadvantage from above. The figure in red landed on Spinner's head and flipped forward in a flash, leaving Spinner to crash-land on the floor, just a few feet in front of the whole Section.

Robyn stood up, brushing a hair away from her eyes as her bright red cloak billowed down behind her.

"Sorry to interrupt," she said, "but my client insisted we hurry, and his meter is running, so this needs to be wrapped up right now."

Rainette stared a moment, then looked toward the others. "Who's she?" she wondered, looking baffled by the red-hooded girl's sudden appearance.

The other children of Naryssa looked on, stunned. Many of them kept glancing down at the near-unconscious Spinner splayed out on the floor behind her, and back up again. Robyn paid them no mind, instead placing two fingers into her mouth. Out came a whistle that could have hailed for every cab on the docks. Cole winced in serious pain as something small and fuzzy fell down from the rafters, where he assumed she'd been until now. The creature, what little of it he saw, resembled an odd mix between a feline and a raccoon.

"Thanks, Murphy," she said, yanking on a zipper attached to the small creature's back.

Robyn reached in and pulled something that resembled an industrial-strength leaf blower from inside the thing named Scuzzy's guts. It should have been much too large to fit in there, and this was all Cole needed to figure out what the creature was.

"Got a new bottomless bag, I see," he commented, before the pain kicked in again. "Did your gran make this one for you too?"

"Fight now," Robyn said as Spinner got to her feet. "Talk later. Also, some of you might want to cover your faces."

Everyone took her advice, not willing to risk whatever was about to be fired out of the leaf blower. Robyn took aim as the wave of half-fey rushed her.

A wicked grin spread over her face. "I love this thing," Cole heard her say with some glee, before she pulled the trigger and everything was drowned out by what might as well have been a small jet engine.

"Seriously, who is she?" Rainette demanded over the roar of Robyn's weapon.

Cole looked up and saw the leaf-blower-like device blasting a stream of sunflower seeds into the faces of the approaching half-fey. Each of them howled and staggered backward, as though disoriented. Cole knew for a fact that this was precisely what was happening. Robyn had brought heavy artillery with her to the brawl.

This really shouldn't have surprised him, considering what had happened the first time they'd met.

Robyn kept up her assault until the blower ran out of ammunition. "I've got twenty more bags of the stuff in case any of you want to go again," she announced to the room.

The children of Naryssa looked dazed—those, at least, that could still stand. Unwilling to give up, Spinner forced herself back up onto her spindly legs and hissed.

"I will not disappoint Naryssa again," she clicked furiously. "She is mother to us all."

Robyn turned around to look at Cole. "These are the same nutballs we fought the last time?" she asked, crinkling her nose. "I thought they looked familiar."

"If you didn't know, what were you doing here?" Cole asked, his voice growing fainter.

"My client was looking for you," she said absentmindedly as Spinner struggled to make her way toward Robyn. "He said you were supposed to find his kid or something."

The moment Spinner drew near enough, Robyn kicked her leg out sideways and knocked one of Spinner's right out from under her. The spider goblin staggered backward on top of several of her unconscious brethren, who were snoring lightly.

"He couldn't come into the station?" Joss asked, keeping a hand on Cole so he didn't collapse.

"Thank you," Cole whispered, gently pushing him away. "But I need to stand right now."

"You can ask him yourself," she said pointedly, looking up above them into the shadows of the rafters. "He insisted on coming with me."

A dark figure swooped down in front of them. James jerked his head away immediately upon recognizing it. Marcel covered Rainette's hand with his enormous hand. The witch protested, but Marcel refused to compromise.

"His presence alone can affect your mind," the ogre warned as Rainette tried to force his hand away. "It is a nightflyer. One of the sluagh."

Rainette went rigid. "Fuck," she swore plainly.

The nightflyer hovered several feet above the floor, whipping his stinger tail back and forth as his leathery bat wings flapped out from the manta-ray body. Mr. McKnight looked directly at Cole for a moment before charging toward him. Joss moved, thinking the nightflyer was attacking, but Cole kept his lover at bay. Staffelbach paused when he saw Cole staring the creature down unflinchingly.

Mr. McKnight stopped dead in front of Cole's face just before they would have collided. "Where is my son?" he demanded. "You told me you would bring him back."

Cole wasn't fazed. "It's your lucky day," he told the angry nightflyer. "We just had the biggest break yet in the case of your missing son."

Following Cole's pointing finger, Mr. McKnight turned in midair toward the unconscious half-fey still lying around in heaps on the floor.

"These are the adopted children of the one who took your son," Cole explained. "Odds are, one of them knows where we can find Naryssa."

Mr. McKnight turned back around to stare at Cole again.

"The only question now is how we get all of them back to the station without there being too many questions," Cole finished.

Joss looked at Cole. "I have an idea," the inspector said. "But you're not going to like it."

"ALL things considered," Cole said as the doors to the wagon clanged, "this wasn't that terrible of an idea."

"I was more worried about how Marcel would take it, truthfully," Joss revealed, giving the signal for the driver to go.

The last paddy wagon, as Cole referred to them, pulled out into the street, leaving for their precinct while the driver and the officer riding shotgun stared grimly out through the window. The story was that Section Thirteen tracked down a suspect and ended up being attacked by a troupe of angry circus freaks. It had been a story they'd used when Marcel first joined their ranks, a couple of months back. Marcel had hated it, which explained Joss's hesitation.

"My feelings are of little consequence right now," Marcel said when Joss revealed why he'd been leery of the idea. "We're alive, and they are our prisoners."

Staffelbach had taken off his armor. Cole saluted the man with his injured arm, which earned him a sheepish grin.

"Nice armor," James congratulated, giving the rookie a thumbs-up. "I wish I could have been doused with experimental chemicals."

"You wouldn't like it," Staffelbach replied seriously. "It's cool having superpowers, but they're murder on my cell phone."

The team stood around together, looking at each other's faces. Cole was still reeling from what they'd endured and accomplished in such a short time. Naryssa's children were in custody, and they finally had a solid lead to her whereabouts.

"This is all well and good," Rainette said, as though reading Cole's mind. "But can someone please explain to me who *she* is?"

Everyone looked at where Rainette was pointing. "Her name is Robyn," Cole explained, as Robyn gave Rainette a quick, friendly wave. "We met at the beginning of the year. She helped me out of a couple of scrapes."

"What was that stuff you sprayed on them?" Staffelbach asked.

"Yeah," James chimed in, looking from Robyn to Cole. "I was meaning to ask that."

"Sunflower seeds," Cole answered for her. "Many fey are allergic and become disoriented if sprinkled with them."

"Really?" James looked surprised. "You never mentioned that to me."

"I have to keep some secrets to protect myself," Cole retorted, rolling his eyes. "When the weakness to cold iron got out, it was a big enough disaster."

The others found this funny, for some reason.

"Mr. McKnight, as he calls himself," Robyn said, looking directly at Cole now, "asked me to find you. He said you hadn't contacted him about his missing son in months."

"Because we hadn't heard anything until just now," Joss told her pointedly. "Capturing Spinner and the other children of Naryssa is the first big break we've had in the case. Naryssa's been keeping herself deep underground until now."

"This was the first big move she's made against us since we fought her over the sithen," Cole said.

Rainette looked confused. "If he was worried, why didn't he just ask?"

Robyn gave the witch a look, like it ought to have been obvious to her. "He's a nightflyer," she reminded. "The guy can't just walk into a police station and file a report. Most humans can't stand the sight of one, anyway."

Which was precisely why Cole had sent Mr. McKnight on ahead, along with the pixies. Mr. McKnight had consented after Cole vowed that they would speak later on that day, promising not to snack on any of the pixies in return.

The last thing they'd needed was for him to drive their backup outside the garage insane with his mere presence. Most cops had delicate psyches, thanks to years of working a daily beat, at least from what Cole had witnessed. Any member of the sluagh could have pushed them over the edge with but an effort of will and enough time.

"Plus," Robyn added, "he thought Cole might have been keeping something secret from him. He is a sidhe, after all."

Joss and Staffelbach both looked a little bemused by that statement. Marcel, on the other hand, actually gave a sympathetic nod.

"We really didn't have any information for him until now," Cole said quietly. "And even now, we still have to go down to the station and question them for Naryssa's location."

"Which we should do right now," Joss said. "Sorry, guys, but the job's not over yet. We still have a small boatload of suspects to question, and paperwork to fill out."

"Great," Staffelbach said. "Any idea how we're going to spin this one?"

"We'll think of something," James assured him. "We always do."

Though they were all banged up and in need of a good patching up, there was still work to be done. The others moved toward their respective vehicles. Officers were still lingering on the scene, mostly to help keep back the crowd that had gathered. Several were taking statements from the owners of the garage, none of whom looked particularly happy. Cole remembered the equipment Staffelbach had used to transmutate into his armor and chuckled at the thought of them trying to make sense out of it now.

"What's so funny?" James asked as they neared Cole's car.

"Nothing," he replied.

A thought occurred to him then. "Robyn," he said, turning around to face the petite girl with fey ancestry. "You were already inside the garage when Naryssa's children attacked us. The pixies had sealed the place off, so how did you get in?"

"From underneath," she said at once. "There was a trapdoor in the corner leading down into the sewers. When I saw the pixies had the place locked down, I thought about using the sunflower bazooka on them, but pixies aren't quite as susceptible to them, and they can be dangerous if you stir them up like that. So Mr. McKnight and I decided to check underground. Speaking of which, I should have told you earlier. Naryssa had a bunch of wood goblins guarding that place."

Cole stepped back slightly. "Were any of them hurt terribly?" he asked. "Because the goblins were working for me. I told them to stand guard down there in case Naryssa's children tried to escape that way."

Robyn flinched and gave Cole a toothy grin. "Oops. Sorry about that, but they should be fine. I didn't hurt any of them too bad."

Cole sighed and unlocked the door for James so he could go ahead and climb in. "Make yourself comfortable," he said. "I'm going to be a minute longer."

"Oh, can I get a ride with you?" Robyn asked as Cole marched back toward the entrance to the garage. "I'd rather not have to jump across rooftops again. It's supposed to rain again later."

"Backseat," Cole replied, not looking around.

It took Cole a minute to find the trapdoor Robyn had mentioned. Opening it turned out to be the easy part, though. There was no way for Cole to fit down there, given that he was so tall. Wondering how Naryssa expected some of her heartier children to fit, he stuck his head down and called out for Bugbear.

"Here, boss," Bugbear answered, sounding strained. "Some crazy broad came through kickin' and screamin' like a banshee. None of us could stop her. She had a nightflyer wit' her, and—"

"I know all about it," Cole said, cutting the wood goblin off before he could continue. "Robyn is a friend of mine, and the nightflyer just wanted to know whether or not I'd had any breaks in the case I was working on for him. Neither of them realized you were working for me."

"Oh." Bugbear's voice was utterly flat. "She's cute. Mind if I get 'er number?"

Cole ignored him. "Are any of you too injured to make it home?" he asked, squinting in the dark to see if any of them were lurking nearby.

"Give us some credit," Bugbear said, clearly offended. "She just got the drop on us. We'll be fine."

"Then go home and wait for me to call you," Cole instructed. "I'll have more work for you soon. Until then, stay out of the kitchen so Mal can work."

"Whatever," Bugbear grumbled lowly, though the echo from the sewer and Cole's sense of hearing meant it rang through perfectly.

With that taken care of, Cole returned outside to his vehicle. James and Robyn were already inside and buckled up. Robyn was sitting across from Detective Carroll, who looked to be slowly on her way to regaining consciousness.

"I completely forgot about her," he said, getting inside.

James looked back over his shoulder at Carroll, who was being poked at by a curious Robyn. "Do you think she'll be mad that she missed all the fun?"

"Nah," Cole said, pulling backward out into the street. "We just did all the hard work for her."

James started to laugh, then noticed the cuts on Cole's arm and side. "Are you going to be okay?" he asked, genuinely concerned.

"I'll live," Cole said. "They didn't strike anything vital, so I should be okay. It'll take a long time to heal, though."

Detective Carroll abruptly bucked up off the backseat and let out a shrill cry. "What?" she howled, jerking her head back and forth in alarm. "Where the hell am I?"

"Congratulations, Detective Carroll," Cole said, giving her a look through the rearview mirror. "You cracked the case. Those two serial killers have been caught."

It took a moment for that information to sink in. "Wait, what?" she demanded, looking from Cole to James. "They've been caught?"

Carroll's eyes drifted toward Robyn sitting across from her. Robyn smiled and gave the detective a wave as Carroll's eyes widened.

"Hi," Robyn said cheerfully.

Carroll's face fell flat with bemusement. "Who's she?" she wondered, pointing.

This made Robyn scowl. "I need a publicist," the red-hooded mercenary said as the car sped along toward the precinct, where the Section would at last find some answers.

Cole hoped, anyway.

THERE was a bit of a situation when they arrived back at the precinct. The captain had already dragged Joss into his office for a nice long shouting match. Having several wagons' worth of half-fey show up on his doorstep was a lot to take in, Cole admitted. The rest of the Section and the few officers willing to help were essentially forced to smuggle the whole pack of them in through the back. Were they human, this would have been a serious violation of protocol, as Joss liked to call it. Humans had a whole process to put criminals through.

Cole would have loved to see the looks on the other cops' faces if Naryssa's children had been paraded through for fingerprinting and mug shots.

Cole half wondered if some of Naryssa's children wouldn't scream violation of civil rights and demand to see a lawyer. Thus far, they'd been quiet, but this wouldn't last long. From the moment he entered the building, Cole could sense it. The whole place was on high alert. Every officer he passed dove to the side so as not to get too close.

In short, everyone was on edge and waiting to see how big of a mess the Section was going to make. It didn't help that the Section had a history of problems, one of which included a glen of oak trees appearing in the middle of the station. No doubt many were remembering the time Marcel had broken into the holding cell area back in February and gone on a rampage. Marcel had been under the influence of a mind control collar at the time, but cops were notoriously slow to forgive. Cole hadn't pressed the ogre for details as to how the rest of the NYPD were receiving him, but he imagined the answer was grim.

For the time being, any personal matters were being put on hold. Whether the rest of the NYPD were behind them or not, the Section had a job to do. It was the first time they'd ever managed to hold any of Naryssa's children. Joss wouldn't let an opportunity like this slide, and Cole was determined to stand by him.

It wasn't hard to figure out where the rest of the Section was. Naryssa's children were making a racket down in the holding area. Rainette, it seemed, had contacted her coven the moment they'd left the garage, asking for help. As many as ten witches were moving around from cell to cell, attaching charms to the bars, sprinkling water along the floor directly in front of each cell, and filling the air with incense.

The ruckus wasn't helping matters with the humans that had already been brought in. Some were attempting to antagonize the half-fey, while others curled up in balls as far from them as they could get, as though shell-shocked. More still were demanding to be released, screaming about being kept in a zoo.

Cole ignored all of this and helped where he could. Passing one cell with two humans inside, a man and a woman, Cole froze upon recognizing them as their mysterious fey-hunters. Robyn had already explained how she'd knocked the two out cold after coming up through the trapdoor. Apparently, the brother and sister had tried to escape before coming across her.

He wondered if either of them had given her a hard time. Then again, Robyn might have clocked both out of habit and nothing more.

"I want these two separated," he said, catching hold of Staffelbach as he passed by. "They're too dangerous to be kept together."

"Care to come in here and try it?" Hansel challenged, and it sounded more like flirting than a threat.

"You always try and steal the fun, brother," Gretel bit back playfully. "I wonder if the little one has the stones to come in here and do it himself."

"I don't need to," Staffelbach replied, getting both's attention.

Cole watched as Staffelbach entered the cell next to theirs. The young officer marched up to the bars forming a wall from his cell into Hansel and Gretel's and touched them. A circle formed beneath his hands as the bars melted away like liquid glass. The circle was gone before the bars completely disappeared, but Cole's eyes were fast enough to recognize the symbols inside it as some of those used in alchemy.

Staffelbach, meanwhile, had stepped aside to allow one of the two to pass. "Start walking, lady," he ordered, nodding to her.

Gretel gave Staffelbach a look, as if working out in her head how he had done that, then shocked everyone by complying. Once she had moved past him, Staffelbach restored the bars, then closed the cell behind him on his way out.

"Simple," he said to Cole as the lock clicked into place.

"You're getting pretty good at that," Cole complimented.

"Thanks. What's next?"

Cole looked around at the Shadewater witches, still busying themselves alongside Rainette. "Once the witches are done sealing the place, we wait for Joss to get back from listening to the captain squawk. There's something I've been meaning to tell Rainette."

Corhagen was marching back and forth down the holding area, waving incense sticks as though trying to land a plane with them and grimacing at the smell.

"I don't see how you can stand this," he said, stopping Cole as he walked past. "You're supposed to be the one with the supersensitive sense of smell. How come you're not climbing the walls with this stuff stinking up the air?"

"It's not half as bad as those cigarettes you used to smoke," Cole retorted, before moving on.

Something occurred to Staffelbach as he watched Corhagen. "How come you're not affected by that stuff, Cole?" he wondered.

Cole looked from Staffelbach to James and back again. "I am sidhe," he said. "A high-blood fey. Plus, the incense itself isn't dangerous to me. It's a part of the Shadewater witches' spell."

Understanding clicked behind Staffelbach's eyes. "That's why Marcel isn't here right now," he deduced, looking around for the large ogre.

"Right," Cole said. "He's waiting for us upstairs."

Marianne was finished a few minutes later. "It's all done," she assured Cole while taking the incense from Corhagen. "I'm not sure how long it will hold them, but this is better than nothing. Those bars would have already kept some locked away. The spell weaving just reinforced it."

"Thank you," Cole said earnestly.

"I'll call once we can come up with something more permanent," Marianne said, smiling broadly at Cole.

It was no big secret that Marianne had been interested in him for years.

"Thanks," Cole said again. "We'll keep in touch."

Corhagen was able to flag down an officer and rope him into escorting Marianne and her coven sisters out.

"Upstairs," Cole said, once they were out of earshot. "We've still got work to do."

James was watching the cells closely as they walked past. "How long do you think we have?" he asked, jumping as one blue-skinned half-trow launched himself into the bars.

"It will have to be long enough," Cole replied over the half-trow's cries. The creature had been thrown backward, thanks to the spell. "Even if the spell holds, the upper brass won't like the fact that we've brought two dozen or so fey in for questioning."

"I'm surprised we haven't been detained for it yet," Rainette muttered, keeping in step with the others. "Or that the Order isn't already on the case."

"Don't even joke," Cole warned. "I've been wondering about that too, and the answer can't be good. They wouldn't let something like this slip out of their chokehold for long, so that can only mean they're up to something."

They had reached the floor where Joss's office was located. Marcel was indeed waiting on them quietly in a corner, a book held carefully between his thick sausage fingers. One after the other, each member of Section Thirteen filed in through the door. Cole came in last, behind Corhagen, and claimed a space against the wall behind Joss's desk, near his chair.

Rainette had gone for Marcel, naturally, scooting her chair closer to him while pretending to be adjusting the skirt she wore. James sat down next to Staffelbach in one of the two seats positioned across from where Joss normally sat. It still struck Cole as odd that Corhagen would be so willing to share a space with a gay officer. Just a few months ago, he'd been unwilling to acknowledge their mutual attraction. Now, just going by how relaxed James was, one could easily mistake him and Staffelbach for friends.

It annoyed Cole more than he cared to admit, and despite how happy being with Joss made him, seeing the two of them sit together made Cole wonder why Corhagen couldn't have been that comfortable around him.

"We really need to get you a Kindle," Rainette told Marcel, snapping Cole out of his thoughts.

Marcel smiled at her and shook his head. "The buttons are too small for my fingers," he pointed out, holding up a finger for examination. "I would never be able to operate one."

Cole reminded himself that, for the moment at least, he and Joss were monogamous. Monogamy was a strange custom in the world of Faerie and not something that was practiced on a consistent basis. Joss had said he was open to the idea of something else in the future, but for the time being, their relationship remained a closed circle.

Looking over at Corhagen and Staffelbach sitting together, Cole wondered how much longer that would last. What really worried him was how much Corhagen could still get under his skin. Cole was beginning to understand why some humans complained about wanting to turn their emotions off. Right now, with the current crisis, that would have done him a world of good.

Cole let in a slow, deep breath, remembered the warrior training he'd received from his father's men a long time ago, and forced himself to stay calm.

"There's something I haven't told you yet, Rainette," he began, getting her attention away from Marcel. "Alice Tweedle was a spy for the Order."

Cole could practically see the thoughts running through Rainette's mind. Each one played out across her face like chapters in a story. Her face went slack with shock at first, followed by the denial that made her eyes widen slightly. Finally, anger settled in.

"You're sure?" she asked Cole. "You know what an accusation like that means."

"I'm well aware," Cole said calmly. "You know that I am. I waited this long to fill you in because you were grieving. I thought giving you and your coven a day or two would help ease things."

"Sorry," Staffelbach said, raising his hand. "I know this really isn't the time, but what did you mean by that?"

He was asking Rainette, but Cole answered for her. "The Order is considered the enemy of all fey that dwell in Manhattan," he explained.

"They're not popular with witches, for the most part, either," Rainette said, taking over very quickly. "The Hermetic Order of the Golden Dawn is looked at as a kind of neo-Nazi party for the supernatural community. Accusing someone falsely of being a part of them, even posthumously, is not a good idea."

"This is something I've wondered about for a while," James said, pausing halfway through the motion of raising his own hand.

Quickly, he lowered it back down. "How does the Order operate like that?" James continued. "I mean, if they're that bad, shouldn't someone have noticed?"

"They have money," Cole answered automatically. "The Order was originally formed in Britain, and by Craft practitioners from very old, wealthy families. A branch was set up in New York afterward, and this eventually became their main base."

"Just like the first Nazi party from human history," Marcel added in a dark tone. "The rich join together and decide who isn't needed. Then they begin sweeping the undesirables under the rug."

"It helps when the majority of Manhattan's population doesn't believe in pixies, or trow, or other such things living right next door to them."

"Bringing us to where we are," Cole finished. "Pushing back a giant with sticks and stones while the world faces the other direction."

Staffelbach's face twisted into a painful wince. "It's starting to feel like I've fallen into a bad comic book plot," he muttered.

Marcel shot him a look, which made him jump from embarrassment. "Sorry," he apologized quickly. "I just mean, it all sounds so surreal. There's some huge conspiracy going on right under everybody's nose, and the public don't even notice."

"That is how a good conspiracy is run," Marcel replied.

"Hiding in plain sight," said Rainette, staring out blankly into the middle of the room. "And they put one of their own into my coven to spy on us. I wonder how long Alice was theirs."

"Probably from the beginning," Cole said, trying to be reassuring. "I doubt Alice went to work for them after you came to the Section."

Rainette didn't look thrilled by this. "Regardless," she said sadly, looking over at Cole. "Alice was my coven sister. The rest of the Shadewater needs to know."

Then her voice became much more sardonic. "Thanks for letting that joy fall to me, incidentally," Rainette fired at him, though her eyes were playful.

"Saying it out in the open would have been disrespectful," Cole said, unfazed. "And a bad idea, since so many fey who hate us were being sealed inside their cages at the time."

"And you wanted me to know first," she stated, though not unkindly.

Cole nodded. "I felt you had a right to know."

Joss's footsteps were heard coming around the corner outside the office door. Cole heard them first and turned expectantly. The door opened less than a minute later, hitting the wall with a loud thud as their fearless leader strode in, looking a little worse for wear.

"That man is a pain in my ass," he announced to the whole room.

No one bothered guessing who Joss was referring to. "How long do we have?" Cole asked, and when Joss looked blankly up at him, he elaborated. "Until the captain wants them out of here."

"Funny enough," Joss said, moving around the desk for his swivel chair, "that isn't the issue. He's all in favor of finding out where the missing children are and recognizes that this is the first and best lead we've ever had. The problem is…."

Joss paused, glancing toward Marcel.

"Me," Marcel guessed correctly. "The first time I was here, things were…."

Rainette placed a hand gently on his knee, silencing him. "You were under the control of one of those black rings," she insisted. "We've already covered that."

"But the captain is still suspicious?" Marcel asked, looking toward Joss.

"His superiors are," Joss said. "And how they got wind of all this so fast I'll never know, but the bottom line is, they're not happy with us keeping so many fey locked in the cells all at once."

Joss cut a look toward Cole before continuing. "Not that they openly acknowledge them as fey," he added irritably, "but they hinted as much. There's also the little matter of a giant tree springing up in the middle of the precinct shortly after Marcel's black-ring rampage. They haven't forgotten that one either."

"When Danu moves, there's little I can do to dissuade her," Cole replied in resignation, which earned him a much sharper glare from both Joss and Corhagen.

Staffelbach, on the other hand, found this to be very funny. Rainette frowned disapprovingly as the young officer bit his lower lip to keep from snickering.

"They're waiting for a bomb to go off," Joss went on once the room was silent again. "So in all likelihood, we don't have much time. We've got to make one of them crack, and fast."

Cole pushed away from the corner. "Then let's not waste time," he said, placing a hand on Joss's shoulder. "Let the interrogation begin."

SIX hours later, and not one of them had cracked.

"They make this look much more interesting in those cop shows," Rainette grumbled irritably as she and Cole stood side by side.

Opposite them, on the other side of a two-way mirror, Marcel was looming over one of Naryssa's children.

"I can't believe he hasn't cracked yet," Rainette went on, looking through the window into the next room. "Marcel has growled, flexed his muscles, rained down threats, and none of them so much as blinked."

"It's harder when they've grown up with something much more intimidating," Cole said, idly sipping the cup of water in his hand. "Naryssa is half sidhe and half night hag. She's pretty much an embodiment of human fear. A grumpy ogre who's jittery from too much caffeine won't have the same effect."

"Well, keep in mind that I've never actually met Naryssa," said Rainette, looking at Cole oddly. "Is she really that bad?"

Cole took in a deep breath before answering. "In the time I've been on the mortal plane, I never encountered anyone so terrifying. She is a force to be reckoned with, and I don't say that lightly."

Rainette frowned and went back to staring through the glass mirror. This time, however, she was watching the half-fey being interrogated by her boyfriend.

"Why do you think she does it?" she asked after a moment. "Naryssa, I mean. What does she gain from taking children from their parents?"

"Naryssa believes that children who are born of mixed heritage can never belong in the mortal world," Cole replied promptly, sounding almost bored. "The children will either be rejected by their peers or reviled by the parents that spawned them. To her, murdering their parents is a mercy, because the children won't suffer under their hands."

Marcel was backing away now. The door to the main interrogation room had opened, allowing Joss to enter. Cole observed the man he had found himself bound to in his immortal life. To his own embarrassment, Cole felt himself smile. Sentimentality struck him at such weird moments.

"That's a messed up logic," Rainette said, referring to Naryssa. "It almost sounds like you sympathize with the lady."

Cole barely heard her. "Rainette," he began reluctantly. "I need to ask you something that must stay between the two of us."

Rainette cocked her head at Cole's tone. "What is it?" she wondered. "If I'm being fired, now's not really the best time to be informing me."

"No," Cole said. "To my knowledge, you aren't."

Cole looked down at her as Joss began grilling the half-fey. "What made you ask that?" he said.

Rainette shrugged. "I haven't had much luck keeping jobs," she said casually. "It seems like something goes wrong sooner or later. Honestly, I never pictured myself as a cop, so I thought maybe I'd forgotten to file paperwork in the right folder."

"They don't fire people on those grounds," Cole replied. "Not usually, anyway, or else I seriously doubt I'd have lasted this long."

Rainette laughed, and hearing it made Cole pause. Once, the two of them hadn't been on the best of terms. Having Rainette smile at him as he took another sip of water felt peculiar. Cole wondered briefly what Katalina might have had to say about this situation.

Thinking of his deceased friend caused a pang in Cole's chest, like a hot needle stabbing him just below his heart.

"You're thinking about Katalina, aren't you?"

Cole's eyes widened in surprise.

"I can tell," Rainette stated, holding his eyes with her gaze. "You always get real quiet whenever she crosses your mind. It doesn't happen often, but you're pretty obvious about it when it does."

Cole turned away from her and looked through the glass at Joss, wondering. "Does anyone else notice?" he asked, hoping he sounded casual to her.

"Don't know," she said, following his gaze. "Why? Is that important?"

Cole polished off his water and set the cup down in a chair off to the side. "Joss isn't human," he stated, and the words sounded forced to his ears. "Not anymore, thanks to me."

"The Goddess elevated him," Rainette reminded him. "You were just the instrument through which her power worked."

"I know," Cole said, "but that happened because I asked her to do it. One day, and for all I know it will be very soon, she will call upon me to return the favor. The Great Lady does not offer favors to her children unless they are willing to do for themselves and her in kind. It is not her way."

"Preaching to the witch that burned the choir," she chimed, smiling.

Cole's mouth turned up into a half smile. "Joss was raised human, and now he is immortal," he went on. "Because I needed him. Now, I worry he won't be able to accept what he is."

"That he's going to live forever?"

"That he will outlive everyone and everything he knows," Cole told her as his eyes clouded over in defeat. "In a hundred years, this city will not look the same, but Joss will. He may not be so thankful then, once all that he grew attached to in this time changes."

"And you're worried he'll blame you," Rainette summed up, getting the picture. "You think Joss is going to leave you someday."

"I need him," Cole said insistently, keeping his eyes fixed on the man whose bed he shared. "Everyone else I know is mortal and will one day pass on."

"Thanks for reminding me," Rainette said, giving Cole a look that reminded him of the mutual dislike they'd shared years before.

"Forgive me," he apologized. "I realize this is an uncomfortable topic for discussion, but ignoring the fact will not make anything better. The fact is, all mortals die at some point."

"And you think you're the only one in the room with this kind of problem?" she countered, still glaring angrily. "Marcel and I haven't been dating long, but he and I have had this conversation so many times I've gotten sick of it."

Rainette's face softened as she looked to where Marcel was standing in the other room. "I didn't expect this to happen," she said quietly before brushing a finger underneath her eye. "Any witch worth her sea salt knows that dating one of the fey is a bad choice. It comes with too many problems to list."

"Preaching to the choir," Cole reminded. "Not so long ago, I was pining for Corhagen."

Rainette snorted. "Like he's over losing you yet," she bit back playfully, laughing all the while. "Everyone can see he's still sending you goo-goo eyes when your back is turned. He just hasn't got the balls to admit it."

"And he is married," Cole added, almost as an afterthought, "with children."

"To a nutcase that shouts after him any time he leaves the apartment," she concluded, still chuckling to herself.

"They're separated," Cole informed her as Joss stormed out of the room, leaving Marcel alone to deal with Naryssa's stubborn adopted offspring.

Rainette whirled around toward Cole a second or two later. "What?" she exclaimed softly, remembering that the mirror keeping the two rooms apart wasn't terribly thick.

"Corhagen told me earlier today," he explained, while Marcel went back to work trying to intimidate the half-fey. "I haven't had the chance to press for details, but it would seem Sarah threw him out."

Rainette sputtered for a moment, trying and failing to get herself under control. "Bet Corhagen's kicking himself now," she said between fits of giggling. "Serves him right for not coming out and admitting what he was feeling for you."

Cole smiled as he heard Joss approach. "Thank you for saying that," he told her, "but I'm spoken for now."

"Since when are the sidhe monogamous?" she asked, wide-eyed in amazement, as Joss entered the room.

Joss looked up at Rainette's statement. "What's going on?" he wondered, looking back and forth between them as his forehead wrinkled in weary confusion.

"Nothing," Cole said. "I take it the questioning wasn't going well."

"You could see for yourself that it wasn't," Joss pointed out, sounding pissed as he let the door slam shut behind him. "It's been seven hours, and I'm ready to call it a night."

"At least you've got an immortal's stamina," Rainette countered. "Us poor humble witches have to go home and sleep at some point."

"No dice," Joss countered fast, though his eyes were sympathetic. "I need every member of the Section on this. One of these bastards has to crack eventually."

"What if we used human magic?" Cole asked, looking toward Rainette thoughtfully. "There are all sorts of mortal spells for binding the lesser fey."

Rainette looked from Cole to the mirror, where Marcel was looming over the half-fey closely. "It would work," she began, despite looking doubtful, "in theory, I mean. I was under the impression that most, if not all, of Naryssa's children are half-fey, so it will depend on how strong the human side of their bloodline is."

Joss looked even less thrilled by the thought. "That's coercion," he said sadly. "I know it's magic and not science, but you're still talking about using an outside source to influence a suspect without their permission."

"Wouldn't that be a gray area, though?" Rainette was looking less opposed to the idea now as she stared past Cole at Joss. "New York Police procedures don't cover magic and enchantment."

"But they are clear about using anything that might force a criminal, even a suspected one, into giving up information without their consent."

Joss's face softened as he spoke. "I know what you're trying to do," he finished, smiling gently at her now. "And I appreciate it, but we're going to have to settle for doing this the hard way."

"As always," Cole muttered.

Joss smiled dryly at his boyfriend. "I've been doing this sort of thing for a long time," he reminded them both. "That bunch will crack eventually. No one likes being cooped up in those rooms for very long. Someone's bound to break from it. We just have to be patient."

A thought flashed over Joss's face. "Didn't you tell me that lesser fey have a harder time adjusting to human surroundings?" he asked Cole.

Cole's mouth turned downward slightly at this. "Some do," he said. "It all depends. A lot of fey in Manhattan adjust to the climate here after a while, but they all prefer Faerie, or the closest they can get to it."

"Central Park was a popular hangout for a long time," Rainette threw in. "So was Times Square, for some reason, before the city decided to shoo out the riffraff there."

"I was just thinking that being locked up in this building with so many humans might speed the process up some," Joss explained, thinking quickly.

"It might," Cole said. "On that note, however, I need to go up to the roof for a little while. There's someone up there waiting for me."

"Who?" Rainette asked as Cole moved for the door.

"Mr. McKnight," he replied, stopping as he reached for the doorknob. "I'd called him earlier, after our meeting in Vallimun's office, and asked him to meet me up there after dark with Robyn. He wanted an update on our search for his son, remember?"

Cole said the last part to Joss specifically, who nodded. "When you see Robyn, tell her I'd like to have a word with her before she leaves."

"What for?" Rainette asked.

"I want to hire her as a full-time consultant for the Section."

Cole froze at Joss's words and turned around. Rainette was looking up at her superior with wide eyes.

"Why her, of all people?" Cole demanded, giving voice to what Rainette was clearly thinking at the moment.

Joss narrowed his eyes, like it should have been obvious. "She hunts fey professionally," he pointed out. "And she knows the dirty dealings of the fey underworld. You've been our number one guy on that front since the Section reformed, but I can't expect you to carry the weight all the time."

Cole looked away slightly. "I didn't mind," he muttered.

"I know," Joss said, aware of the smirk on Rainette's face as she watched them exchange quick looks with one another. "I think we need more than one expert on hand with us, just in case. Even you can't run 24-7 with everyone, and it's unfair to expect that."

Cole looked away again. "Maybe," he said. "Are you sure you're not trying to shuffle me out the door slowly?"

"I would just get a broom for that," Joss teased, earning him a smile. "Go, and send Robyn down to my office once you're done. Assuming she'll come, text me so I'll know to meet her there."

"Okay," Cole said, opening the door. "But I think you're crazy for thinking she would sign on with us. Someone with her skills doesn't work for chicken feed."

"Maybe not," Joss called out as Cole began to shut the door behind him, "but at least the union finally got us that dental plan. That's something."

"Good idea," Cole retorted, keeping the door cracked just enough so Joss could hear. "She can knock someone's teeth out, then go get a cavity filled."

"Just go," Rainette told him. "They're up on the roof, and it's starting to rain. This water witch thinks it's going to pour soon too."

Cole wasn't sure if nightflyers were bothered by bad weather, but it seemed prudent not to find out by keeping McKnight waiting. As Cole passed by one of the spare interrogation rooms, Corhagen stepped out in time to block his path. Instead of going around, Cole waited as the mortal shut the door behind him.

"Anything on your end?" James asked hopefully.

"Nothing yet," Cole said as James followed slowly beside him. "But Joss thinks one of them will break soon."

"Hopefully, before they run out of coffee in the lounge," James said wearily. "We might be at this all night."

Cole didn't respond.

"So where are you headed?" James pressed. "I thought we were supposed to stay in groups of two in case something went wrong downstairs, like last time."

"I have to meet someone on the roof," Cole explained, lowering his voice ever so slightly as they passed a group of plainclothes officers. "Mr. McKnight wants a progress report. He hasn't heard from us in months."

James took the cue and waited until they reached the empty stairwell to speak again. "What about afterward?" he asked, his words echoing through the enclosed space.

"One thing at a time," Cole said. "Joss wants to have a word with Robyn once I'm done with her on the roof. He's hoping she'll come on board as a full-time consultant for the Section."

"Oh."

James slowed to a stop in the middle of the intermediate landing. "Whenever you've got a minute, there's something I need to talk with you about."

This made Cole pause. "About before?" he inquired, turning around to look back down the steps at James.

James wasn't looking at Cole. "Yeah," he said awkwardly. "Speaking of which, Detective Carroll is doing okay. I meant to tell you earlier. She found me before the interrogation started. It looked like that stuff she drank hit her pretty hard, but she's feeling better."

"She caught her two elusive serial killers," Cole said, keeping his eyes fixed on James.

"With the Section's help," James added, looking up to find Cole's tricolored eyes glowing slightly as they drilled holes down at him.

"She can have them," Cole said, not looking away as James cleared his throat loudly. "Section Thirteen has bigger problems to contend with at the moment."

"No shit." James's eyes were lit with fear. "So," he stammered nervously. "Later, then?"

"We'll see," Cole replied, before continuing his climb up the steps.

Even without looking behind him, Cole knew James lingered on the platform between steps for several minutes after he left. The stairwell was narrow, meaning the man's scent lingered in the air. Cole found himself thinking of the handful of times when he'd breathed that scent into him, craving it. The scent seemed to circle around Cole long after he heard James's footsteps clunk loudly back down the way he'd come.

Cole knew it was foolish to think he could have gotten over Corhagen so fast. It was even more foolish to think they had a future together. Cole was with Joss now, and Joss was immortal. That should have been enough.

Except it was lingering traces of James's scent that he breathed in as Cole reached the door leading to the roof. As he listened to the sound of the rain picking up behind the door, it was James that made Cole's cock harden. It was James Cole was thinking of as he opened the door to confront Mr. McKnight.

"Shakespeare almost had it right," Cole muttered as he stepped out into the rainfall. "What fools these immortals be."

THE building storm above them didn't bother Cole, nor did it seem to be having any obvious adverse effect on Mr. McKnight. Robyn was the only one present who seemed annoyed by the fact that they were slowly getting soaked.

Mr. McKnight was less than pleased, and Cole honestly didn't blame the man. Back at the beginning of January, shortly before Cole had joined the NYPD, McKnight's son was taken by Naryssa. Mr. McKnight had escaped Naryssa's fatal curse thanks to a technicality, though the grief of losing his only child had been more than painful enough for the exiled sluagh.

McKnight had been the only parent to survive Naryssa's attack. Since then, the Section had been less than successful in locating the nightflyer's son. McKnight had gotten impatient, it seemed, which accounted for Robyn's presence.

The bottomless bag she had somehow converted into a sentient, furry construct was currently shivering beside the red-hooded girl's leg.

"Let's make this quick," Cole said to McKnight, looking away from the shivering creature. "The head of Section Thirteen wants to have a word with Robyn once we're done, and the weather doesn't appear to agree with her."

Robyn gave Cole a disdainful look. "You try wearing one of these," she snapped back at him irritably. "The material is heavy when it gets wet."

"Noted," Cole said.

"Agreed," added the nightflyer. "You have some information for me, sidhe, regarding my missing son?"

"Not yet," Cole began, which earned him a hiss from the nightflyer. "But we captured several of Naryssa's children and have been interrogating them."

The nightflyer considered Cole for a moment. "And this is what took you so long to meet with me up here?" he demanded.

"Yes," Cole said. "I was hoping to have more for you by now, but the half-fey that Naryssa uses as her proxies are being stubborn."

Mr. McKnight considered this further. "How much longer?" he asked. "I do not enjoy the idea of having to wait on the roof for the rest of the night."

"You could have gone home and returned later," Cole pointed out. "I offered to call when I had something."

The nightflyer hissed again, and this one reminded Cole of the sound of metal scraping over broken glass.

"My son is missing," the sluagh predator said, flying right up into Cole's unflinching face. "The night hag stole him from me, and if all of the mortals' hell needs moving, that is what I will do to ensure he is returned to me."

A thought occurred to Cole as the nightflyer flapped his leathery, bat-shaped wings, causing droplets of water to scatter everywhere.

"Maybe you can help us," Cole said. "Mr. McKnight, would you be willing to ask one of Naryssa's children directly?"

McKnight was clearly thrown by the request. "I would rip the information from their lips personally," he vowed as his tail whipped back and forth through the wet air.

"That may not be necessary," Cole told him quickly. "The children of Naryssa are half-fey. Their human blood would most likely be weak against your presence. That just might be the advantage we need."

"Why him?" Robyn wondered, interrupting.

"Even the sidhe feared the sluagh in Faerie," Cole informed her knowingly. "If Mr. McKnight's presence can make humans temporarily lose their minds, a half-fey should at least have a harder time keeping secrets with him around."

"Will it get me my son back?" McKnight asked.

"Yes—" Cole said.

"Then when do we begin?"

McKnight had spoken before Cole could finish and was moving back and forth through the rain the way a fish swam, clearly eager.

"Most likely sometime after he works out a way to get you downstairs without causing a riot in the building," Robyn piped up gleefully, looking past McKnight at Cole. "How are you planning on doing that, by the way? He can't just fly straight down, or else I wouldn't have waited this long out in the rain."

Cole looked at Robyn, dripping wet from head to toe as she stood, shivering slightly, under the torrent.

"Money is money," she said with a shrug, anticipating his question. "And a girl has to eat."

"We can clear a path to the interrogation room," Cole said, after thinking for a bit. "At this time of the night, there won't be as much traffic in the corridors as there is during the day. I'll call ahead and inform Joss… Inspector Vallimun. Once that's done, Robyn, go and wait for him in his office, if you would."

"I'd love to," Robyn said, stretching lazily with her arms high over her head. "But this little hood is soaked and in need of a hot bath."

"Inspector Vallimun wants to hire you as a full-time consultant for Section Thirteen," Cole said, making her freeze up. "We need another person who is familiar with the fey to help prepare the other members of the team."

Robyn looked stunned by this. "A girl has to eat," Cole reminded her, smirking at the expression on her face.

Robyn seemed to consider this for a moment but then shook her head. "He can't afford me," she declared with confidence. "Besides, how would it look from a professional standpoint if I started cooperating with the police?"

The fuzzy beast huddling against her leg sneezed, then turned his head away in protest. "Would it hurt to hear him out?" Cole pressed.

"You could dry off while you're inside, at least, and have a cup of hot coffee. And we could call you a cab afterward so you wouldn't need to run home in this weather."

Mr. McKnight cast an irate stare at Robyn while she thought it over. "Do what you will," he said. "I am going inside just to get out of the rain."

Cole moved aside at once so the nightflyer could pass. "You might have said something earlier," he informed as McKnight whooshed past. "I didn't realize the rain was bothering you. We could have at least stood inside the stairwell."

McKnight turned around so that his eyes were facing Cole. "Why would anyone voluntarily conduct a meeting on a rooftop while it was raining?" he asked incredulously.

"Because they didn't want to be overheard," Robyn said, moving past him. "Let's go, already. I'm tired of listening to the water squish in my shoes. We can sort the rest of this out inside, where it's dry."

Once the three of them were standing in the stairwell, McKnight swooped up overhead near the ceiling and shook himself off, making it rain indoors down the vacant shaft formed by the flights of stairs hugging the walls.

"Much better," he mused, lowering himself back down.

Cole waited as McKnight landed a foot or two from where he and Robyn stood. The nightflyer rose up on his haunches and looked directly at Cole.

"While I'm thinking about it," Cole began. "Why didn't you just call and ask me to meet you somewhere discreet so we could talk? You could have asked about your son's case that way instead of hiring her."

"I'm glad he did," Robyn cut in as she wrung out her red cloak. "Business has been kinda slow for me since we raided Bowling Green together."

A thought occurred to Robyn as she let go of the red material. "That doesn't mean I'm thinking about coming to work for the Section, though," she added warningly.

"I cannot afford another husk to wear at the moment," McKnight said to Cole, ignoring Robyn completely now. "They are custom made to fit most of the fey that own them, and husks for nightflyers are especially tricky to make."

"It didn't have to be in broad daylight," Cole countered.

McKnight let out a hiss, as though frustrated by the direction the conversation was going. "You are a sidhe," he stated flatly. "The sluagh have been mistreated and used as shock troops by your kind for generations of Faerie-kind. How was I to know any information you gave me was true?"

Cole blinked and turned to look at a suddenly sheepish Robyn. "He hired you to kidnap me?" Cole demanded, though it sounded less like a question and more like a threat.

Robyn shrugged coolly. "I told him it probably wouldn't be necessary, but he's been waiting to hear something for months, and you never said anything."

"There were other problems," Cole said, as he looked back at McKnight. "None of us forgot. The Section is a small division of the NYPD, and our caseload has been packed since we formed. There were a lot of distractions."

"Distractions?" McKnight didn't bother concealing his anger. "Things that were more important than returning my son to me?"

"Unfortunately," Cole affirmed, though he hated saying it. "There was a hostile takeover of Staten Island during a snowstorm and a problem with some imaginary friends at a TV studio. Beyond that, though, Naryssa did an impressive job of hiding herself, so we just haven't had many leads until today."

Cole paused to take a breath. "Oh, and there was also a tentacle monster."

Robyn's eyes doubled in size at this. "Tentacles?" she asked warily. "Wait, you mean here in Manhattan?"

"It's gone now," Cole replied flippantly. "It exploded."

Robyn thought this over while McKnight cleared his throat to direct Cole's attention toward him again.

"Our people have been enemies," he stated matter-of-factly. "Is it really so strange that I wouldn't trust you completely?"

Cole met McKnight's eyes unflinchingly. "We aren't in Faerie anymore," Cole pointed out, anger bleeding carefully into his words. "For better or worse, I am a member of the NYPD now, and was tasked with locating your son for you. That is my mission. If I'd had any information on his whereabouts before now, you would have been the first to know outside of the Section."

McKnight didn't look reassured.

"Whatever happened in Faerie can stay in Faerie, for all I care," Cole continued, clenching his fists. "If I am too sidhe to bring your son home, that is a problem you need to sort out for yourself."

Cole left McKnight looming on the upper platform with Robyn, taking each step two at a time in his rush to get downstairs. Before he was halfway down, Cole remembered that Joss had wanted to speak with Robyn. He didn't hear her footsteps following him, nor did his ears detect anything that sounded like a nightflyer's wings flapping. Cole had already given Robyn the message from Joss. As far as he was concerned, that was the most he was capable of without dragging the girl to Joss's office by her feet.

Robyn wasn't the type to come quietly, so, all in all, Cole was happy not to have it come to that. Much as he hated acknowledging it, McKnight's comments about his heritage had struck a rough cord in him. It had been a while since anyone had reminded Cole that he was sidhe in such a way. The other fey living in exile in the mortal world were all too happy to see Cole whenever it was convenient. However, at the same time, none of them ever cared to associate with him except on a professional level.

At one time, he had taken their money, resolved whatever problem they'd hired him for, and gone on his merry way with a little more cash than he'd started out with. Cole had very few of what he could call friends in the fey world. The other outcast denizens of Faerie didn't like being reminded of their current status. In most cases, the fey in Manhattan had been exiled because of a sidhe. Cole reminded them of where they'd come from and why they were in the mortal world.

Generally speaking, he didn't blame them, but none of that made it easier to take. Somehow, the nightflyer had gotten under Cole's skin with his words. It left him agitated and yearning for his home in the sithen.

It also left him yearning for another's touch. When the sidhe were upset or stressed, they tended to crave physical contact. Cole was reminding himself of this as he exited the stairwell in a rush, mostly to avoid thinking about who he wanted to feel touching him. Joss's face came to mind at once, but so did Corhagen's. One was someone he could spend the rest of his immortal life with. The other was all too mortal and someone he thought he'd given up hope of being with.

It looked like the fire Cole had kept burning for Corhagen the past few years hadn't gone out as easily as he'd first thought. That made him angrier, and all the more frustrated as a result. Suddenly, Cole wanted to go home and sleep for a hundred years so that his problems would pass him by. It was juvenile, and a shameful thing for a former member of sidhe royalty to think, but at the same time awfully tempting.

When Cole reached the hall where the interrogation rooms were located, he found Detective Carroll standing outside with Corhagen and Joss. Carroll spotted him approaching and gave Cole a small smile along with a nod. She looked somewhat happy to see him, despite the drugged-out look on her face. Faerie drink hadn't agreed with her, it seemed, yet she was standing on her own two feet.

"I was wondering where you'd run off to," she said as Cole came to a stop in front of her. "Blondie here said something about you going up to the roof. Did no one tell you it was raining?"

Cole noted he was still dripping wet and shook himself off. In his haste to get away from McKnight, he'd neglected to dry off completely. No doubt there was a puddle trail of water leading to this very spot. Someone was going to have a time cleaning it all up, but Cole didn't care.

"I gave Robyn your message," he told Joss first. "Whether she will come or not, I can't say, but I thought you'd want to know."

Joss nodded.

"Guess who showed up while you were on the roof," Corhagen said, pointing toward the door to the interrogation room next to them.

"What?" Cole wondered, slightly wide-eyed at the thought of something else going wrong. "What is it this time?"

"The Feds showed up," said Joss in an incredibly dry tone. "They're in the room right now with our two mystery killers."

Joss nodded at the door Corhagen was indicating for emphasis.

"Hansel and Gretel?" Cole asked without thinking.

Carroll crinkled her nose. "That's actually their names?"

"It's what I called them," Cole said while Corhagen chuckled softly. "We weren't able to get much information out of them before."

"They're the Feds' problem now," Joss explained, though he looked unhappy at the thought. "Since they're wanted across the country, it's a federal matter."

Cole noted his boyfriend's tone and frowned. "You don't sound enthused," he said. "Isn't it better if they're taken off our hands?"

"Maybe," Joss admitted. "But something in my gut tells me they have information we need."

"In other news," Carroll interjected, looking from Joss over to Cole, "I just got word from the captain, here. Apparently, the chief was impressed by how fast I was able to capture these two with your help."

"We didn't mention the part where she was passed out in the backseat of your car," Corhagen informed him quickly, with a guilty look on his face.

"I wasn't the one who got her drunk," Cole pointed out.

Carroll, meanwhile, let out a long sigh that got all three's attention. "It seems I've gotten my promotion," she told them. "It hasn't been finalized yet, but since our serial killer duo was caught so fast, the Chief thinks my talents are being wasted."

Something about the way she said that made Cole feel uneasy. "Where are you being transferred to?" Corhagen asked before Cole could.

"Here," she said flatly. "You're looking at the soon-to-be Inspector liaison between Section Thirteen and the rest of the NYPD."

TO HER credit, Detective Carroll hadn't sounded thrilled by the notion. No doubt, Cole suspected, because the last liaison for the Section had mysteriously vanished. Agent Willhiem had been working for the Hermetic Order of the Golden Dawn through Internal Affairs before officially disappearing. Cole had put a bullet in him, then left the bastard to die as a pocket dimension the Section had infiltrated collapsed in on itself, thanks to some magical tampering.

According to the official word Carroll was given, she was being put into the new position because of how well she'd worked with Cole and Corhagen. Someone upstairs had been impressed with how quickly Carroll was able to track down the two elusive serial killers that had evaded capture by the FBI and thought she was perfect.

Cole thought the poor woman was signing her own death warrant and had said as much, which earned him a look from everyone.

"This makes you the new mole," Cole had explained. "Your job is essentially going to be reporting our every move to the upper brass so they can go over it with a fine-tooth comb."

"I figured," she had answered coolly. "The Section has a divisive reputation, to say the least. You get results, but not without costs. Some think you'd all be better off on a shorter leash."

No one said it, but the look between all three men spoke volumes. The thought had been especially clear in Joss's eyes when he looked over Carroll's head at Cole.

Detective Carroll was no fool. She didn't expect to have much luck reining Section Thirteen. The problem was, the brass, and the Order by extension, thought otherwise.

That, or she was being set up to take a very big fall on someone else's dime.

For the time being, though, there was little anyone could do. Carroll could have turned down the promotion, but that would have placed the ambitious detective in a very precarious spot. The Order wanted her as a spy, and passing up an opportunity like this could cripple her career. The Order would retaliate, and the most efficient way of doing that was to ensure Carroll never went any farther in the NYPD than she was currently.

At the very least, she was being cooperative for the moment. Following their conversation, Carroll disappeared through the door into the mirror room adjacent to where the two witch killers were being held with the Feds. Seconds after Carroll had closed the door behind her,

Robyn appeared with a very heavy and lumpy mailbag being dragged behind her. Cole saw the sack move and knew what must lie inside.

Pulling Joss aside, he explained the situation in his boyfriend's ear.

"It's worth a try," he finished. "That is, assuming one of you can get him inside the interrogation room without being seen."

Joss's only reply was to nod.

"We'll think of something," he assured Cole. "I might as well have a talk with him too, while he's here."

"About what?"

The bag Robyn was dragging let out a disquieting noise, like a very low howl, which caused several officers passing through the corridor to stop and stare.

"It's full of broken toys," Robyn explained quickly. "For the Christmas in July project. We're trying to get a head start this year."

One lieutenant didn't look totally convinced. "I never heard a toy make a sound quite like that before," she said, eying the bag the whole time.

"It's an old Teddy Ruxpin," Robyn went on, unflinching. "Someone put a tape recording of an old horror radio program in it. Now it sounds like a person is dying whenever you switch it on."

The sound came again, making the lieutenant shudder. "Some of the things kids come up with nowadays are wild," she mumbled, before walking off in a hurry.

Cole rolled his eyes once the coast was clear. "Take him to Vallimun's office," he said, pointing, "before someone else hears and wants to make a donation. The bag you're carrying looks heavy enough."

Joss was watching the furry creature clipped to Robyn's waist. The bottomless bag that had somehow been given semi-sentience blinked once and trembled under his watchful gaze.

"Why didn't you put it in there?" Joss asked, gesturing at the creature.

Robyn looked down at her furry, mismatched friend. "Oh," she said, understanding. "He didn't want to. Said it looked uncomfortable. I just happened to have the mailbag with me."

McKnight, still inside the mailbag, growled low.

"Come on," Joss said, motioning at Robyn to follow him. "Let me show you to my office so Mr. McKnight can get some air. It doesn't look like that bag has been washed in a while."

"It's a mailbag," she retorted, sounding very much like a child suddenly. "If you washed it, the ink on all the envelopes would smear."

Cole sighed.

"Have fun explaining that to her," he said to a departing Joss. "I'm going to have a look with Detective Carroll at our two witch hunters for a moment, then grab a quick shower in the locker room. It looks like we're going to be here all night."

"Looks that way," Joss answered before disappearing around a corner. "Have fun. Keep me posted in case something interesting happens."

Cole left Corhagen out in the hallway. Inside the room, Carroll stood in front of the two-way mirror, close enough that her nose was almost touching it. Carroll didn't acknowledge Cole as he approached, preferring to keep both eyes on what was happening in the other room.

"Humans generally only stare that closely when they're looking for something they can't find," he noted quietly.

In the next room, the Feds were talking softly with Hansel and Gretel. Cole guessed that the three suited men there knew they were being observed. Two were sitting at the table on the side opposite the two witch killers, while the third stood off to the side. Instead of watching the scene in front of him, however, the third federal agent was looking directly at the mirror.

"He knows we're here," Cole stated, looking the man over for a moment.

Carroll stared over at Cole, then turned to see what he meant. "I suppose you're right," she mused, sounding unconcerned. "I'm more worried about what's going on with those four at the table. They've been talking since before I came in here. I think the Feds are trying to bargain with them."

Cole considered this as Gretel spoke in a low, even tone. With the wall and the mirror separating them, it wasn't easy, but his ears picked up most of it.

"They're not making a deal," he told Carroll as Gretel finished speaking. "They were asking about the pieces of the sword."

Carroll leaned away from Cole in surprise. "You can hear them?"

"A little," he said nonchalantly. "They want Hansel and Gretel to crack before they're brought in to federal headquarters."

Cole saw the confused look on Carroll's face and elaborated. "I suspect the federal agents are looking to get promoted as well," he said.

Carroll looked less than pleased by the statement. "I didn't ask to sign on with Section Thirteen," she stated angrily. "You guys may get results, but this place is too strange for me. I never planned to be a part of police investigations where we consult with ghosts and raise the dead on a regular basis."

"You get used to it."

Detective Carroll gave Cole a withering stare. "God, I hope not," she muttered, before turning back to the mirror.

Cole watched the Feds continue with their fruitless attempt to break both witch hunters. After a moment, however, something occurred to him, and he turned back to look Carroll over.

"How is your head?" he asked delicately. "From the drink you had, I mean."

"Fine," she spat out, though it didn't sound that way.

"Detective Corhagen really did think he was ordering plain spring water for you," he tried, which earned him a look from her in return.

"I know," Carroll admitted begrudgingly. "I thought at first that this was just some sort of hazing ritual you guys put people through, but from the way he kept apologizing, it sounds like an honest mistake."

"When did he apologize?" Cole asked as one of the agents in the next room slammed a fist down hard on the table in front of Hansel, who merely laughed.

Carroll didn't answer at first, as she was giving her full attention to the scene unfolding. "Earlier, before you showed up in the hall," she answered very quickly at last. "What's up with those two?"

Carroll nodded toward the two witch hunters for emphasis. "Don't they look a little too calm to you?" she asked insistently. "It looks like they're waiting for a bus to show up."

Cole shrugged. "Maybe," he admitted, not concerned. "Their weapons were taken away before we locked them up. They haven't got a means of escaping at this point, so it's probably just a front they're putting on."

Carroll didn't look convinced. "Did you ever find out anything about the sword?" she pressed, giving Cole the barest glance before zooming back in on the two sitting calmly before the Feds.

"Claiomh Solais," he clarified for her. "The Sword of Light."

"Alice Tweedle. Her ghost, I mean."

Carroll was talking rapidly now as she kept glancing back and forth from Hansel and Gretel to Cole.

"They killed her because she had a piece of it. Did they find any of the pieces on them?"

Cole frowned. "I don't think so," he said, startled by the thread of eagerness in her voice. "Most likely, they kept the pieces hidden somewhere else. Anything that valuable would have a hiding place."

Carroll's eyes showed a flicker of disappointment. "I guess you're right," she said, sighing. "They wouldn't have risked losing them after all that trouble."

"It isn't trouble for them," Cole countered, keeping his voice even. "These two kill for pleasure. They hunt and kill witches because they enjoy it, and I'm curious as to why."

Carroll snorted. "Good luck working that mess out," she said derisively. "I leave that business up to the criminal psychologists."

The two of them watched in silence as the federal agents stood at the same time. It looked as though the interrogation was over. Cole thought briefly that the agents would be taking the witch killers away now, but both remained in their seats while the agents stormed out the door.

"Looks like it isn't over," Carroll said quietly.

"Not yet," Cole replied, stepping away. "It looks like someone needs a promotion badly. Since it's the intermission, I'm going to shower quickly before the second act starts."

Before he reached the door, Carroll called out to him. "Finale," she corrected, smiling. "The second act occurs halfway through. If this were a play, we would be coming up on the finale."

Cole stood facing her with the door open and chewed on this for a moment. "It seems a little underwhelming, if you ask me," he replied, before exiting.

JOSS'S meeting with Mr. McKnight and Robyn had evidently ended already. The office was unoccupied when Cole slipped by, though he wasn't shocked. Robyn hadn't seemed like the type to come and work for the NYPD out of the goodness of her heart.

Then again, Cole mused as he made his way downstairs to the locker room showers, neither had he up until a few months ago. As he entered the showering area, Cole wondered if he'd have made the same choice without Joss's side offer. It had come out of the blue for him, but, after Corhagen's initial rejection, he'd been looking for some company.

The locker room was occupied by a surprising number of cops. Cole stepped through without breaking his stride, eager to get clean and leave. The atmosphere was less than hospitable, and quite a few men gave him looks of pure loathing as he passed.

Cole ignored it, having long since gotten used to this sort of reaction, and found an empty locker off to the side, far away from the others. He took his weapons off first, then stripped out of his clothes, using them as a bundle to wrap Aed Deigh, Bandersnatch, and Jabberwock in.

With all of his stuff put away, Cole strode naked toward the showers. He could still feel the looks from his so-called fellow officers. Most of them were mixed with envy or lust.

None of it meant anything, of course. Being a sidhe, most humans were attracted to him on some level. He'd noticed it becoming more frequent, recently, especially with men, though that mystery remained unsolved. Cole suspected it had to do with him living in the sithen. It was the closest approximation to Faerie he had encountered since his banishment.

Of course, none of the humans would have believed such a thing. To them, the world was made up of indivisible lines that offered very few exceptions. Therefore, the attraction he felt coming from the other NYPD officers was somehow his fault, at least in their eyes. Thus, he paid them no mind. For the moment, he didn't feel like egging anyone on. As Cole reached for the shower knobs, he heard the cops outside slam their lockers shut, slap their clothes on, and make a beeline for the exit en masse.

The water was nice, even lacking the purity that the sithen offered. Cole stood under the spray and let the jets wash over him, turning every minute or so to let the water cover him on all sides. Now wet, his long hair took on an odd grayish tint. In the dim light, it almost looked black in spots. Cole ran his fingers through it a few times, then turned around so the spray could massage his back.

James was standing in the entrance to the showers with nothing but a towel on, watching Cole closely, with a heated look.

Cole waited, but the mortal said nothing.

"Mind if I join you?" he spoke at last, just as Cole was about to face the wall.

Cole hesitated briefly, then gazed back toward James, feeling his stomach flutter as their eyes locked with each other.

"It isn't my shower," Cole replied after realizing he'd been staring. "I'm just borrowing it for a moment. Do whatever you like."

Cole turned again, this time not stopping, and glared at the tile covering the wall in front of him, where the showerhead hung. He could hear James's footsteps echoing clearly throughout the room, and the sound was making his cock stir. Swearing quietly, Cole let in a deep breath and started to will the beginnings of his erection away.

His actions startled him a second later, however. James had entered of his own volition, and if Cole being aroused at the time was something he couldn't handle, Cole wasn't obligated to metaphorically hold his hand by coddling the mortal's sensibilities. Letting the air out of his lungs in a whoosh, Cole reached over for the soap, only to feel his hand brush over James's outstretched fingers.

"Sorry," James said quickly, before Cole could, though the mortal didn't pull away very fast. "Here, I'm done with it."

The soap dispenser was nearly empty. Cole piled the lather into both hands, needing every last drop because of the mane he sported, and began working the suds into his flowing locks. James required maybe a third that much, and was already rinsing his head before Cole had finished.

James didn't leave, though. The mortal detective remained under the spray, letting it pound into his scalp the whole time Cole methodically washed the shampoo away. By the time he was done, Cole's whole body was covered in suds, and the water had begun cooling. Cole suspected James was standing under an ice-cold spray by now. If what was going on between the man's legs was an indication, though, he didn't mind.

"Can I ask you something?"

James's question made Cole groan inwardly. So many of their strained conversations had started by him asking that.

"Would you wash my back for me?" James went on, not giving Cole a chance to reply. "After all the running around town we did, I was sweating like a hog. It needs it, I'm sure, but I can't reach behind me well enough."

Cole waited, sure this was a joke on James's part. James expectantly turned halfway around, keeping his back presented, and Cole finally walked up behind him. It occurred to him that James had been nude in front of him for several minutes now without so much as flinching.

Being this close, Cole had a wonderful view of the mortal's ass, which looked positively scrumptious.

Cole felt a slight charge as his fingers touched the skin on James's back. "Sarah and you have separated," he stated, feeling his breath quicken as his fingers moved up and down over the surface. "Would it be a problem if I asked why?"

"No," James replied, his voice lower than normal. "We've just been fighting a lot. The pregnancy has been harder on her than usual, and I get that—"

James stopped short as Cole's fingertips dug slightly into the muscles in his lower back.

"I get that part," he continued, after clearing his throat. "But she's angry all the time, and acts as though this is somehow all my fault. Mostly, we've just been fighting a lot, and it was getting to be bad for the kids."

James started to turn toward the spray, and Cole pulled his hands back.

"When she told me to get out, I only intended to be away for the night," he went on. "The more I thought about it, though, the more it seemed like the best thing to do, at least for right now. Her sister is staying with her, and I'm still visiting, so it's not like I've turned into a deadbeat father or anything."

Cole didn't reply.

James smiled then, and it looked like every muscle in the mortal's face was screeching in pain from the effort.

"So, how are you and Vallimun coming along?"

Cole didn't answer. "Why are you here?" he asked plainly instead. "Here and now with me in this shower stall, why are you here?"

James looked cornered all of a sudden, like a deer caught in a vehicle's headlights. Cole had worded the question deliberately so as to leave the mortal with fewer exits.

"You could have waited," he continued, when James wouldn't answer. "A year ago, you probably would have waited for me to finish. You would have charged into a burning building to avoid being naked in the same space as me, so why is this suddenly different?"

An answer came to Cole at once. "Is this your way of getting back at Sarah?" he demanded, growing angry now, which made the water from both their faucets warm slightly.

James jerked at the rise in temperature, but Cole wasn't about to let the subject die so easily. "Am I supposed to be your revenge on her for tossing you out?" he pressed.

"No," James said, a little louder than necessary for such a small space. "I just finished telling you. We're living apart right now because that's what's best for the kids. You know how I feel about my kids."

"Yes," Cole said, folding both arms defensively in front of his chest. "They were the excuse you gave several times for why it wouldn't work out between us. When you bothered giving me a reason at all, that is. Now, though, they aren't as much of a factor in your life."

"What's this about?" James wondered, looking genuinely scared as he took a few tentative steps away from Cole. "This doesn't make any sense."

Cole followed James, unwilling to let the man slip away so easily this time. "You wanted me to wash your back," he said, once they were standing face to face under the same spray. "There was a time when I would have bled in exchange for touching you. Now you stroll in, naked as a summer rain, wanting to chat like we're old friends and this is a typical Saturday night."

James looked hurt by that statement. "We are old friends," he said, flinching as water splashed in his eye. "Cole, I've known you for almost as long as I've been on the force."

"Then what happened?" Cole demanded, inches from James's face. "Why now, of all times?"

"I… don't know what—"

"Stop lying to both of us."

Cole's words cut James off before he could finish denying it further. The phrase whipped across James like he'd been slapped, and his eyes almost appeared to fill with tears. Blinking several times, James took in a long, deep breath to steady himself and clenched his hands.

"I… don't know," he tried, finally. "I just don't know anymore. This wasn't supposed to be what I wanted, and for a while, I thought I had what I did want figured out."

Cole uncrossed his arms and lowered them. As he did, the water splashed over his skin, dotting him and James both with fresh beads. Cole noticed that James's clenched fists were directly below his hands now. An infinity went by in his mind as he debated with himself over what to do. When Cole finally brought his hands down, James opened his own so that their fingers linked together.

James squeezed as his voice shakily returned. "I keep having the same dream, over and over again," he began. "You're always in it, and so is Vallimun. He wasn't always in it, though. It used to be just you. I've had it for years, but it's been a lot worse recently."

"More frequent?" Cole tried.

James had spoken before of having dreams and suspecting them of being prophetic. At times, it did seem that way, though it was never a skill Cole relied on much.

"I'm being chased by this shadow," James was saying. "It starts out like that every time, and it's always the same shadow. There's something familiar about it too, like I saw it somewhere a long time ago and can't remember. Sometimes I think I'll recognize it if I turn around, but in my dream, I'm always running. I can never seem to stop running."

Cole leaned into James slightly and gave his hands a gentle squeeze. The water coming from the shower was even warmer now, bordering on hot.

"I keep running through places I've been before," said James, squeezing Cole back. "My apartment, my wedding to Sarah, the hospital when she was in labor, and the school I was assigned to where we first met."

Something flashed in James's face. "I see that one a lot," he said, locking eyes with Cole to help him understand. "That school is there in my dream all the time, usually near the end. And you're there too, but then...."

"What?" Cole pressed.

"You're trying to kill me," James said. "And then I wake up."

When Cole brushed his face up against James's, the detective didn't pull away. James pushed his stubble into Cole's cheek as their hands tightened against one another's. Cole could feel their hard cocks pushing back and forth into each other. When James lunged his hips forward unexpectedly, the movement drew a moan from Cole.

Their hands went everywhere. Cole pressed his mouth into James's as he felt the mortal touching him all over. Cole let his fingers trace paths through the water coating the soft flesh as James dug his fingertips into the hard muscle in Cole's back.

Soon, Cole had James pressed against the cold wall. The water from both of their showerheads had turned hot, filling the room with steam. Each man's tongue danced back and forth while Cole dipped down between James's legs. Giving the thick cock there a few tender strokes, the sidhe moved past to tug at the balls for a moment, before moving along further still to the real prize.

James gasped as he felt a finger press into him. "Do it," he whimpered pleadingly. "I've wanted you to. I can't stop thinking about you doing it to me."

There was no lubricant to make the entry easier. This was not the sithen, where such things could be delivered to Cole's hands via magically-appearing slots in the walls. Cole wet his fingers, using the shower water, then pressed back down into James's ass again. Rather than helping, the water seemed to make penetration rougher. James was a trooper the whole time, though, and once Cole was past the outer ring of resistance, it was as though the ass opened to receive him by magic.

James was still trying to keep his mouth pressed firmly into Cole's as he leaned forward into the sidhe's body for support. James had hiked one leg up to give Cole better access, and now bucked his hips up and down, riding the three fingers spreading his hole.

When Cole turned him around, James didn't fight. The mortal placed his arms high above his head against the wall, as though waiting to be frisked, and waited as Cole moved between his legs. The head of Cole's cock popped through with only a little hesitation. James flinched, but then let out a long, slow groan that rose in time with Cole's own grunts. Their noises became a chorus as Cole drew himself back out slowly, then punched forward. Keeping the same rhythm, Cole repeated the movement again and again, drawing curses and gasps of encouragement from James.

Their bodies moved together fast. Someone could come along at any moment, and both men were feeling the urgency. This was about primal lust, at least for now. It was about cooling a thirst that had been burning inside the both of them for months.

It was better than the dreamscape where they'd coupled together with Joss under the influence of Queen Titania's spell. Cole felt his whole body burn with need and the heat of the shower water. The air was thick, saturated with sweat, moisture, and the desire for more.

James came first, with Cole following soon after. The mortal gasped as he felt the cock stuffing him blast round after round of seed into him. James's own cock painted the tile white for a few brief seconds before water washed the evidence away. Cole's arms were looped under James's pits, gripping him as they rode out the rest of their orgasm together.

Cole's breath was hot against James's neck as he leaned forward. "Never again," he breathed, letting the words sink into James's ears.

As Cole pulled out, he repeated them.

"Never again," he said, keeping a hand pressed into James's back between the shoulder blades. "No more running for either of us. Not anymore."

James started to speak, but was cut off as a sharp noise tore through the air. The sound rained down from somewhere outside the showers, alternating between silence and a bitter shrill.

"What the hell?" Cole asked.

"It's the alarm," James said, his face turning grave. "Something's happened. No one said anything about there being a drill today."

"Is it a fire?"

James frowned. "Do you smell smoke?"

Cole sniffed the air and, getting only whiffs of steam and sex, moved to the entrance. "I don't smell smoke," he said, dread clouding his voice. "I smell fey. Half-fey, to be exact."

"Naryssa's children." James had gone pale before he could finish speaking. "They're loose!"

NOT feeling at his best fighting naked, James had lingered behind to throw on some pants. Cole, however, had gone straight for his locker—not to get clothes, but his weapons. Foregoing anything else, he charged for the door, steadying himself as he hit a wet spot on the floor and charging out into the hallway that led to the gym area without waiting for James to catch up.

There was no fighting in this sector of the precinct, but Cole could smell blood, sweat, and the stink of Naryssa's adopted brood up ahead. With both blades extended and Jabberwock in one hand, Cole rounded a corner into a fray where several cops were attempting without success to hold back what looked like Spinner in her spider-goblin form.

Spinner was never one to let herself be deterred by a mortal, and this instance proved to be no exception. Several cops had latched onto her, only to find themselves flung through the air into nearby walls. Others were keeping their distance, but Spinner's spidery legs made this tactic just as futile.

As Spinner swept one leg out sideways, causing the officers to fall like dominoes, she happened to look up in midcackle and spot Cole coming toward her.

"You!" she cried out over the recovering officers, who winced in pain upon finding Cole naked and unfazed. "We've been looking for you," Spinner continued ranting, paying the cops no mind for now. "I will—"

Cole didn't give her the chance to finish. He brought his blade up and sent a jet of fire straight into Spinner's face, setting it ablaze. Before she could recover, Cole was leaping through the line that the cops had formed, firing Jabberwock into each of Spinner's eyes, causing them to burst like swollen canker sores.

The spider goblin shrieked, but Cole didn't let up. Using the advantage he had, he plunged the frost-covered blade into her stomach, dragging it down with the weight of his body, until her bowels were spilling out onto the floor at his feet. Behind him, several cops retched at the stink that rose from the punctured intestines.

Spinner was still alive. There was enough fey in her to keep Death from taking her soul, so Cole resumed firing at her, aided by the other officers and James. Corhagen had joined them at last, dripping wet and concealed by a pair of pants. Spinner's howling continued through the flames licking hungrily at her face. Bullets punched through her thrashing body as she swatted at them like they were flies. The attacks seemed to be doing little more than irritating her, but none of the officers let up.

Cole jumped out of the way as Spinner's legs jerked wildly. Her arms were smacking her head, fighting to extinguish the blaze. This was making it hard to get in close. Cole took aim at the joint of one leg and, after several misses, lodged a bullet there. The spider goblin's body sagged, putting her off-balance and leaving her gaping belly wound wide open. Seeing it, Cole charged, thrusting the flaming end of Aed Deigh upward and burying the blade once more into her guts.

Cole felt his eyes burn, and a tingling prickle formed in his right hand. The wounds there, left by Hansel and Gretel's iron claws, seemed to flash briefly. Cole was brought back to the situation at hand as fire roared to life inside Spinner's body. Her scream mutated into a guttural roar while her innards became ash.

Still, she fought.

Cole was thrown backward by one of her legs before he could disengage. James was the one he landed on. Up ahead, Spinner stood, looming over them as the other officers backed away. One man turned around and grabbed James by the shoulders, yanking him up off the ground. James kept both arms locked under Cole's chest, refusing to let him go. After a moment's struggle, the officer gave up and left them there.

Spinner, however, was no longer a threat. The spider goblin had gone perfectly rigid. A poisonous stench filled the hallway as her corpse burned. She was still alive and in incredible pain. Her roars had diminished to weak whimpers now. Aed Deigh was still buried inside her, the frost tip sticking out of the deep vertical gash in her abdomen. Fire came rushing out of the wound in small spurts.

Cole and James both watched. James was unable to look away, whereas Cole blinked several times, assuming he was seeing things.

The fire coming from her gut wound burned black.

"Black flame," he whispered, glancing down at his injured hand, which prickled in time to the flames' movements.

Cole got to his feet and helped James up before giving Spinner his full attention once more. The spider goblin had staggered backward into the wall. Her legs jerked and kicked out uncontrollably. Silently, Cole raised his hand and closed it into a fist, pushing power through it at the same time. The black flames eating Spinner alive from the inside roared, consuming her carcass. James turned his head away, unable to watch, as Spinner gave one last feeble plea to be spared.

The cuts on Cole's hand flared a bright red as the last bit of life ebbed from Spinner's corpse. Cole watched as the cuts darkened, before lightening to a soft pink. In seconds, they were scars.

His right hand still burned. Cole flexed it automatically, then held up his left hand, which felt unnaturally cool. Side by side, he held both hands in front of his face as power poured through them.

"The Hand of Cold Death," he whispered, "and the Hand of Black Flame."

James was staring in confusion. "Okay," he said blandly. "What does it mean?"

"'It is time for you to enjoy your gifts'," Cole quoted, remembering back to the night down in the sithen's lowest chamber. "I have a second Hand of Power."

Cole looked up in surprise and found James looking at him.

"Only the most powerful high sidhe lords have two Hands of Power," Cole said.

"What does that mean?" James wondered. "Is that good or bad? And if it's bad, can it wait until after we're done with this mess?"

James's words had pierced his stupor, snapping Cole out of it. "Right," he said. "We need to find the others and clear the building. See if you can't track down Rainette and Marcel. I'm going to look for Staffelbach and Joss. We'll meet upstairs once we track everyone down."

"What about them?" James asked, jerking a thumb in the direction where the other officers had fled.

Cole took a quick look down the corridor. "If you find any officers still fighting," he said, "get them out of here. They're not going to be of much use against this many half-fey. Spinner was a bitch to put down, even with my help."

"No shit," said James, already on his way. "Stay safe."

"You too," Cole replied before he had time to think about it.

Cole took the hallway back the way he'd come, opposite of the way James had gone. It should have been the last thing on his mind. Somehow, Naryssa's children had gotten loose and were going on a rampage. Yet, the thought stubbornly persisted.

He'd had sex with James. They'd made love together in the shower. Cole was seeing Joss, and, by human standards, he'd been unfaithful to his lover.

There were far bigger problems for the moment, but his guilt wouldn't fall back.

"Later," he insisted, almost pleading with himself. "Right now, one disaster at a time, please. Single file, no pushing."

This battle wasn't going to last nearly long enough.

THERE were blood-soaked bodies everywhere.

Naryssa's children were giving no quarter. Many of the precinct's officers that had been on duty when the coup started were littering the hallways. Some had been torn in half. Others had bled out from wounds in the neck and legs that had been made by teeth. Cole made himself keep going despite the dead surrounding him. Had their bodies been long cold, he would have summoned them to help the living. Unfortunately, the smell of their still-warm corpses lingered in the air as he strode past.

Each time Cole came to one of Naryssa's children, he dealt with them in short order. Some, he was able to take down by surprise. Others spotted him first and fought back. There had been a head count during the initial lockup, and Cole was keeping a tally of his own to compare.

As far as he was concerned, the time for mercy had passed. None of them would escape this place with their lives.

Pine Nut the marionette was one he came across while searching the lounge area. The fetch had just finished decapitating an unarmed secretary when Cole arrived. He'd heard her screaming, but not in time to save the woman.

Pine Nut was cackling like a jackal when he spotted Cole. "It's about time you showed up," the human-sized living toy said sneeringly as his blood-covered strings whipped around him. "I was beginning to think you'd turned coward and run off."

Cole fired Jabberwock into Pine Nut's forehead, making his neck snap back.

"Ow," the wooden man whimpered, bringing his head forward. "That actually hurt."

"So will this," Cole said in an icy voice as he raised his right hand. "I hope you've made peace with whatever gods still listen to you."

Pine Nut cackled again as black fire rose from between Cole's long fingers. "What am I supposed to do?" he jeered, even as his eyes remained fixed on the flames. "Beg for mercy? A few harmless sparks aren't going to—"

Pine Nut never finished his sentence. Cole quickly dropped his gun into the belt holster, the only piece of clothing he wore, and pulled out Aed Deigh with practiced ease. Tossing it into his flame-covered hand, he concentrated as the black flames leaped out into the firebrand. Power roared in his ears, hungry and eager for fresh victims.

"The black flame was said to have been used as a method of execution by the high sidhe during ancient times," he said, taking aim as worry finally creased Pine Nut's face. "I think this is fitting."

There was a roar like a jet engine starting. Pine Nut's screams were just barely heard over the noise as the flames closed in. Not one to go down willingly, the fetch marionette leaped out of the way and made a break for the door before the fire could reach him. Cole didn't even push his will into the flames to make them give chase. The fire turned of its own accord, eager to pursue its target.

When they finally touched Pine Nut's wooden body, the flames consumed him in a matter of seconds. Pine Nut screamed even as his ashen limbs began falling apart. A horrible cracking sound filled the room each time a piece broke away. Cole watched the whole time, not blinking. Once the body fell silently to the floor, a smoldering pile of kindling, he turned and walked away.

In each part of the precinct Cole came to that held some of Naryssa's children, it was the same. The baby-faced cockroaches were left splattered against a wall. A half-troll was bisected and left screaming on the floor as his lower half froze over. If he remembered them clearly, Cole took great care to prolong their pain for what time he could spare.

More than once, one of Naryssa's adopted children was left shattered in icy pieces on the tiles as he walked away in search of his next target.

Others, he was more merciful with, and let the flames from his right hand cook them alive.

Near one of the evidence lockers, Cole located Rainette. A female half-nightflyer was leading several of her brothers and sisters against the water witch. Cole recognized the half-nightflyer from when he'd first encountered Naryssa, but her name escaped him. Rainette wasn't giving the attacking half-fey any leave. It looked like more than one had smoking holes in their flesh from where her acidic water orbs had struck home.

A few blasts of ice and fire scattered them, clearing a path for Rainette to run through. The bastards had cornered her, and one gave a swipe at her leg as she passed. Rainette turned around and gave the long-fingered beastie a face full of acidic orb before moving again. Cole laid down additional cover with his guns, firing a couple of warning shots up above them as well to keep the nightflyer woman at bay.

"I hope that wasn't too forward," he told Rainette once she was by his side. "It wasn't a comment on your skills, but you looked like you could use a hand."

"Shut up," she barked, taking cover behind him. "Where the hell's Marcel?"

"I don't know," Cole said between shots. "James is supposed to be looking for him. Have you seen Joss or Staffelbach?"

"I saw Staffelbach a little while ago," she said, backing away in step with Cole as the fey began moving toward them. "But we got separated. As far as I know, no one's seen Vallimun since before all this started. What the fuck happened, anyway?"

"Someone let them out of their cells," Cole explained. "This is only a guess, but I would be willing to wager the blond brother and sister duo had something to do with it."

"So this was a trap?" Rainette raised both hands and called water from the pipes in the floors. "And we fell for it?"

The water burst out of the floor into the air, cutting off the encroaching fey in midstep. Squinting her eyes in concentration, Rainette focused her power into the water, causing it to boil. Steam filled the air as the cries of Naryssa's children filled the hall while hot water rained down on them.

"That seems terribly cliché," she finished.

"I'm not proud of it myself," Cole stated, waiting with Aed Deigh's ice brand while the water died down.

Once the wall of hot water had fallen back, Cole lashed out with wave after wave of icicles that cut through the half-fey's flesh like a butcher's knife. Up above, the half-nightflyer was making a dive for them. Rainette caught her in the chest, though, with a corrosive orb. The flyer zigzagged helplessly through the air while struggling to knock away the acid, which hissed as it ate through her skin.

Cole put Aed Deigh away and fired both guns, riddling the flyer's body with holes. Blood poured down, and Cole quickly jerked Rainette back out of the way.

"A nightflyer's blood is almost always poisonous to humans and the sidhe," he explained, before resuming fire.

"Got it," Rainette said, looking Cole over. "By the way, this isn't the best time, but why are you naked?"

"I was showering downstairs when I heard the noise," he explained, getting in one last good shot before the half-flyer hit the floor and skidded to a stop against a wall.

Rainette's eyes drifted over Cole's ass for a moment. "Would it have killed you to save the day wearing pants?" she wondered, looking away.

"No," he replied, slamming the firebrand end of Aed Deigh down into the half-flyer's skull and killing her instantly. "But you might have died for it. I didn't bother because it would have wasted time."

Rainette stared in shock as Cole straightened up, turning his attention to the other half-fey. "She was down," Rainette blurted out in a sudden burst of fury. "You just killed her in cold blood!"

"Yes," Cole stated flatly without turning to meet her accusing eyes. "And she killed who knows how many. I'm putting an end to this."

Rainette's face went from shocked to horrified as Cole moved in on the rest of Naryssa's children, who were backing away from Cole now.

"We're cops," she shouted as he raised his right hand. "You're supposed to work on the side of the law. I know what they've done, but there are limits to this sort of thing, Cole."

"And they were the ones who crossed them," Cole said.

Black flames curled out through his fingers, licking the air hungrily. "I have come into my second Hand of Power," he said softly to Rainette as she paused in midstep, intending to approach him. "I have the Hand of Black Flame, the judgment flame that burns the wicked to ash."

Rainette didn't move. The other half-fey children were backing away more quickly now. Cole didn't take his eyes off them.

"There are many kinds of fire in Faerie," he said, keeping his voice low and smooth. "All kinds of colors, with many different purposes. Black flame was once used to execute those guilty of crimes. Only the righteous could pass through it unfazed."

One of the half-fey hissed at Cole.

"When a sidhe comes into a Hand of Power, it must be consecrated," he went on. The other fey had slowed, afraid to move.

"Cole…," Rainette tried, struggling to keep her voice clear and crisp.

"Go find Marcel," he told her. "I won't ask you to participate in this, or even witness it. Find your love and see to him. James may have already found him by now. If you see the others, tell them I'm all right. I'm going to find Joss once I'm done here."

Rainette didn't move.

"I realized something tonight," he whispered, as the fire in his hand stretched yearningly toward the half-fey now cowering in fear. "I am a sidhe, yet I've been trying to live by mortal guidelines. I cannot pretend to be something I'm not, so I won't from now on."

Swiftly, Cole raised both arms up over his head, cradling the fire in both hands as though it were a precious stone. The sound of Rainette's feet hitting the tile as she raced away from the scene filled his ears for a moment. Cole then lowered both arms, sending the fire out to bathe the whole flock of Naryssa's adopted spawn. Their cries filled the hallway, bringing a satisfied smile to his face.

Cole waited until the last one had fallen before leaving. After making sure the holster belt around his waist was secure, he dove forward, shifting into his wolf form. The air felt thick with the stench of blood and burned corpses. Now using his nose and ears to guide him, Cole took off past the smoldering remains and darted left. Gunshots and howls could be heard in the distance, telling him a fight was going on.

A cloak was spinning through the air as he came up on the scene. Attached to it was the small frame of Robyn, who had twin revolvers that belched fire and noise as she pumped bullets into the snarling half-breeds reaching for her heels. Cole shifted forms again and drew both Bandersnatch and Jabberwock to lay support fire.

Robyn landed on her feet, dropping into a crouch as she skidded to a stop down past her attackers. Without speaking, she and Cole charged toward one another, opening fire into the swarm. There were half-brownies, and what might have been one or two human-pixie combinations. Briefly, he wondered how that had come about, then dragged his attention back to pumping them full of magical lead.

Robyn's furry companion flipped up through the air into a spin. The zipper on its back had come open, and out through it fell an oversized grenade, which Robyn caught expertly in one hand.

"Fire in the hole," she cried out, before yanking the pin free with her teeth.

Cole looked around wildly for a place to take cover. Up ahead, past where Robyn was, someone had left a door open. Cole leaped forward, snatched her up in both hands, and charged for it as the half-fey spawn rose up again.

The door had just shut behind them when the blast knocked it clear off its hinges. Cole and Robyn both were thrown forward, the panel of wood smacking their backsides hard as it crashed to the ground. Shrapnel buried itself in the broken door, which had shielded them, while chaos reigned out in the hall.

Cole could hear the half-fey's cries easily as he pushed himself up off the floor. "I'm beginning to get a little irritated with the way you keep blowing things up around me," he grumbled.

"Beggars can't be choosers," Robyn retorted, sliding easily out from under the door ahead of him. "Where were you before now? I've been looking everywhere."

"I was down in the showers," he said, shrugging the door off as he got to his feet. "Someone let Naryssa's children out of their cells."

"I noticed," she retorted dryly. "I was in the office with that Vallimun guy, listening to him make his pitch."

"Where is he?" Cole demanded, watching Robyn peek out through the fractured doorframe. "I haven't seen anyone other than you and Rainette since I parted with Corhagen earlier."

"I can't remember half the names of your teammates," Robyn informed him absentmindedly as she motioned Cole forward. "The Vallimun guy left with me when the trouble started. Mr. McKnight stayed behind in the office where he'd be safe. He should still be there, if he was smart."

"What about Vallimun?" Cole pressed.

Robyn and he both reentered the hallway, which barely standing after the grenade. "He said something about going up to the roof," she answered, grabbing Cole by the arm. "I can take you up to him right now. He's probably worried."

Cole hesitated for a moment, reluctant to let anyone else fight his battles for him. "Okay," he decided, after a piece of the ceiling crashed down on top of the pile of injured half-fey. "Let's go. I could use some backup. Why did Vallimun say he was going to the roof?"

"He didn't," she replied as they broke into a run. "But I think that was where those two blond nutcases were going."

Robyn's furry companion skittered up behind their heels and underneath Robyn's red cloak. It leaped, grasped hold, and crawled the rest of the way up to her shoulder. Robyn continued as though oblivious to it, but gave the creature a quick but gentle pet once it was secure.

"You never told me its name," Cole said curiously.

"Murphy," she answered, knowing what he meant. "His name is Murphy."

The following corridors were much less congested. Cole and Robyn came across one or two groups of NYPD officers who had fashioned barricades for themselves from whatever they could get their hands on. Amazingly, none fired on him once he came into view. Cole wondered if they recognized him as one of their own, or were just too stunned from seeing a naked man wandering around after everything else that had happened.

"Get out of the building," he instructed, hefting the toppled desk up and out of the way so one group could pass. "The halls should be clear by now. We haven't run into any more of them for a little while."

"What are those things?" one young-looking officer demanded, clutching his Beretta tightly.

"Why are you naked?" another asked, pausing as he moved past.

"Sorry, people," Robyn broke in, waving her arms wildly. "No time for twenty questions. Stick to the back hallways and stay out of sight."

Once the group was out of their way, Robyn hesitated. "Why *are* you naked?" she demanded finally. "It's been bothering me since we ran into each other, but I assumed there was a reason."

"I was in the shower," Cole said impatiently. "Let's go."

The worst was ahead of them now. Nothing was blocking the door leading to the stairs, but the narrow shaft holding them was ideal for an ambush. Sure enough, he and Robyn had just entered and were ascending the last flight leading to the roof when Tobolt came crashing down.

"In the name of my mother," he roared, filling the shaft with his echo, "I will—"

"I so don't have time for this," Cole muttered, pulling out Aed Deigh.

"No kidding," retorted Robyn, who then watched wide-eyed as Cole blasted a wave of flames the color of tar into a descending runt jack-in-irons.

"Die," Cole declared, bringing the firebrand downward in a swooping motion.

The black flames from his right hand encased the Faerie blade, cleaving Tobolt in half with one stroke. Cole spun around, bringing the blade with him, and cut both halves of the jack-in-irons' head off before the body could waver.

In one last smooth motion, Cole reached out with his right hand and forced what was left of his power into the flames clinging to Tobolt's carcass. The fire rushed over the corpse eagerly, reducing it to cinders in a matter of moments. As both pieces fell to the wayside, Cole collapsed to one knee.

"Wow," Robyn said, breaking the silence. "I never knew you had the power to do anything like that."

"I didn't before tonight," he gasped out, taking slow, even breaths. "I came into a new Hand of Power: the Hand of Black Flame."

Robyn observed Cole as he struggled with his waning strength. "A new Hand of Power is hard to control," he said between breaths. "It eats up more power, and I haven't been using it sparingly. My magic is almost gone."

"Really? That's good news."

Cole cocked an eye at her. "Not really," he grunted. "If Joss is in fact up on the roof, and Hansel and Gretel are there too, then this is very bad. I'm about to waltz into a fight with them while I'm not at full strength."

"Is that all?" Robyn snapped her fingers, summoning Murphy to her open hand. "I have just the thing in here to make that problem much easier."

Cole watched as Murphy's zipper opened. "I keep forgetting how crazy prepared you are for situations like this," he mumbled.

Robyn smiled down at Cole. "My grandma taught me well," she told him. "A woman who is prepared never has to worry about any man getting the drop of her."

Cole watched as Robyn reached an arm down into Murphy. The creature didn't seem fazed by this at all, and waited patiently while Robyn fiddled around inside of it for a moment before pulling something out.

Cole's eyes widened slightly at the smell of iron. Robyn drew out a thick length of black iron chains, and without so much as flinching, swung one end around to where it snagged Cole across the chest.

The impact left him gasping for breath all over again. Robyn smacked him again, this time across the back of the head, causing spots to swim over Cole's vision. The next thing he knew, she had straddled his back, using the weight to pitch him forward onto the floor, and was winding both ends of the chain around his arms and legs.

"Nothing personal," she said, after checking to make sure the chain was secure. "But a girl does have to get paid, and with the economy the way it is, I can't let something like personal feelings get in the way of earning a paycheck. Grandma taught me better than that, too."

"SORRY," said Robyn, holding the door open with one foot. "You're way too heavy for me to do anything but drag you up the stairs."

Cole struggled in response, which only served to make the iron chains dig excruciatingly into his flesh.

"Those were stored in a freezer for three weeks," she added, before hauling his body out onto the roof under the pouring rain. "Just for good measure."

"It's about goddamn fucking time!"

Robyn looked up sharply at the voice, letting the door slam shut behind her in the process.

"We were beginning to wonder," Hansel said, softening his tone somewhat.

"I didn't find him as fast as I expected to," Robyn explained, dragging Cole along behind her. "And some of the brats below got in my way."

Gretel laughed as she offered to take the chain Robyn was dragging Cole along by from Robyn's hands.

"You'd better hope that Naryssa crow doesn't find out about it," she said warningly as Robyn obliged by accepting the offer. "She's awfully protective of her kids."

"She shouldn't send them to an NYPD precinct as a part of some messed-up Trojan horse plot," Robyn retorted, lowering her hood slightly to keep some of the rain away from her face. "Is everything else ready?"

Hansel gave her a curt nod as Cole felt himself being dragged over the rough gravel strewn across the roof toward what looked like a transmission tower.

"The pieces were right where you put them," he informed Robyn in a cool tone. "Our boss will be pleased."

Robyn abruptly looked past Hansel to the transmission tower, where Gretel was positioning Cole. "I think I'll stick around," she said, keeping both eyes on the sidhe. "He wanted me to make sure you didn't do anything permanent to that one."

Hansel looked over his shoulder at Cole. "He doesn't trust us?" Hansel asked, smiling slightly as Robyn glared. "I don't blame him. My sister and I aren't the types to instill confidence in people. You shouldn't worry, though. We're only here to finish the job."

Robyn reached down to scoop up a shivering Murphy, who had taken refuge from the rain beside her leg. Murphy let out a soft coo as Robyn lightly ran her fingers over the top of his back where the zipper was.

"I'm still amazed Naryssa was willing to trust you," she said, following Hansel as he walked calmly over to his sister.

"Assuming all went well downstairs," Gretel said, hearing Robyn over the rain, "Naryssa will have gotten what she wanted."

"Maybe." Robyn leveled her eyes at Cole's right hand. "By the way, I left his weapons in the stairwell. One of them hurts you if you touch it, so I thought we'd be better off with it away from this."

Hansel didn't answer her. "Are we ready?" he asked Gretel instead, once she'd stood up. "The storm isn't supposed to last for much longer."

Gretel looked Cole over and gave a nod of her own. Cole was strung up on the tower near the base. The chains wrapped around him were now securing him to the infrastructure. Rain splashed in his face, and he raised his head to stare straight up the metal monolith. There, higher above, illuminated by flashes of lightning, not far away, was Joss.

The sight of his lover stirred Cole, and he once more fought against the iron chains.

"Was there anything in our employer's instructions about how to get him to summon the wild magic?" Gretel wondered, looking Cole over. "I know the 'fire from heaven' is crucial, but that's remedied easily enough."

"I don't remember anything about either of them having an on switch," Hansel mused sarcastically as another flash of lightning lit up the rooftop.

All three stood with a noticeable gap between their bodies as rain continued to pelt them. Robyn's foot tapped impatiently while Murphy cringed against the rough petting she was now giving him.

"Well, someone had better think of something," Robyn said finally, over a crack of thunder off in the east. "This is getting embarrassing for all of us."

"Maybe we should call him," suggested Gretel, looking from her brother to Robyn. "Do you still have his number?"

"You call him," Robyn said defensively. "He's a busy guy, and I don't want to have to explain to the man why this project didn't get off the ground in time. That honor can go to either one of you."

Hansel snorted derisively. "This would be easier if we could at least hurt the white-haired sidhe," he grumbled. "Why in the world did the boss man want him spared, anyway?"

A light flickered in Gretel's eyes, and she smiled as another flash of lightning broke across the sky overhead.

"Let's hurt the other one," she said, looking excited. "We need blood anyway, and two sidhes have to be better than one."

"We don't know that the other one's blood will work," Hansel said, looking up the tower past Cole where Joss was suspended. "Wasn't he mortal until not too long ago?"

"It would still work," Gretel insisted, positively beaming now. "Hurting him has got to get some sort of reaction out of MacColewyn."

"Do whatever you think will work," Robyn said warningly as she backed away. "Just don't kill him. And I'd be careful about using his name out loud."

"Why?"

The question came from Hansel, who had been reaching for the tower. "What can saying his name do?"

"Some sidhe could draw power from mortals who spoke their names aloud," Robyn informed him. "I would think you of all people knew that much."

Gretel was already beginning the climb up the tower. "Ignore her," she advised. "And watch your step. The tower is slippery."

Hansel grunted as he followed suit. "We would have to do this in the rain," he mumbled. "After this, I won't want to do another job in this town for a while."

"We could always try Canada," Gretel offered, pausing so her brother could catch up. "You enjoy the walks in the woods there."

"True," Hansel mused. "But we always get lost."

COLE'S breathing quickened slightly as he listened for the sounds of Hansel and Gretel's feet scaling the tower. Once he was sure they were focused on not falling, he began working his right hand around to where it was clutching the chain. The iron burned just by touching him, and any slight movement on his part caused the chain to dig into him. It was excruciating.

Cole let out a sigh of relief when he felt his hand close around the chain's links. It was black fire housed in his right hand. Fire that was intended to burn the wicked to the ground. Danu had told him he was to have more gifts. Regardless of the color, fire was still fire, and it was all he had to break his bonds. His weapons were gone, and the chain was impeding his ability to summon the dead.

Then again, that might not have worked anyway. The dead below, inside the precinct, were all fresh kills. Even if the chains weren't stopping his magic, the corpses wouldn't have heeded his summons. The only power left was his Hand of Black Flame.

Cole had already used up most of it. A Hand of Power burned a lot of magic during its first few hours of manifestation. A fresh kill or a ritual could reignite it, but there was still the immediate problem of the chains holding him in place. Cold iron inhibited Faerie magic, and the sidhe were most certainly no exception.

Cole's magical reserves were dry, and he was wrapped up in cold iron chains while chilly April rainwater smacked him in the face. Overall, it seemed as though he was cosmically screwed.

Robyn's betrayal had taken him by surprise. After many years on the mortal plane, he'd let himself get soft.

Robyn, meanwhile, was walking toward him.

"Here's the thing," she stated without preamble. "There's this sword that was broken into pieces. Those two were collecting the pieces for somebody, and the sword needs reforging under the fire of heaven with a high-powered sidhe's blood. They know not to hurt you, but the same doesn't go for the one up top."

Cole inhaled as much air as the chains would allow. "So you kidnapped Joss earlier so I would comply," he guessed.

Robyn shrugged. "I thought he would work just fine," she confessed nonchalantly. "He's supposed to be sidhe now, and I'd love to hear how you managed to swing that, incidentally. They weren't convinced it would work, though, so he became our hostage. If you cooperate, nothing very bad will happen to him."

Cole looked past where Robyn was standing. A circle had been dug into the roof. Inside the circle were several runes symbolizing the Faerie hierarchy. The shards of the Sword of Light, all thirteen of them, had been laid out, fanning in four directions, with the hilt taking center stage.

"The tower," he surmised. "It will act as a lightning rod for the spell. And my blood is the key to putting the pieces back together?"

Cole smiled as Robyn nodded in the affirmative. "I'll do it," he told her. "See if they will come down from the tower. I'll give all three of you my word of cooperation."

Robyn looked skeptically at him.

"I will be the sidhe that reforges one of the four great treasures," he said pointedly. "What other fey in Manhattan could boast that?"

Robyn was still frowning, though it looked like she believed him a little more now.

"I will give whatever vow will placate you," he said. "If your orders were not to harm me, then the ritual itself doesn't require my life. I reforge the Claiomh Solais, Joss and I go free, and we call it a night. Cooperating with you is the best way to end this."

Robyn's mouth twisted into a frown. "Sorry," she declared after a moment's deliberation. "I don't buy it. You have to be up to something."

Cole hissed as a piece of his skin stuck between two of the chain links. "Ordinarily, I would be," he confessed. "I've been trying to distract you long enough to burn through this chain, but it isn't working. I'm almost out of magic, and whatever little is left has been snuffed out by the chain."

His honesty seemed to startle her.

"Okay," she said, setting Murphy down on the ground. "Hold on a sec."

Murphy clung to Robyn's leg as she brought both index fingers up to her lips and let out a loud whistle that should have signaled half the cab drivers on the island.

"Get down here," she called out loud enough to be heard above the still-rolling storm. "I've got something to tell you."

A moment later, Hansel and Gretel were on the ground. "What?" Hansel demanded irritably. "We were just getting started."

Robyn pointed toward Cole. "He says he's willing to help," she informed. "Assuming you haven't hurt the other one too much, get him down so we can finish this and dry off."

Gretel looked over at Cole for a moment. "Are you sure?" she asked. "He could be bluffing. I hear the sidhe were never very trustworthy."

"He's probably got something planned," Robyn readily admitted, earning her a surprised look from everyone, including Cole. "But if that's the case, keeping him tied up won't help for very long, and I'm sick to death of standing out here in wet shoes."

"We can make the other one break," Gretel said with confidence. "It shouldn't take too long."

"And in the meantime, we're still standing on top of a police precinct," Robyn reminded her. "Those bozos downstairs won't keep the NYPD occupied for too much longer, and someone is bound to notice that they're gone."

Hansel frowned.

"You have a point," he acknowledged before meeting his sister's eyes. "And honestly, I want to get out of the rain too. Let's bring him down."

Cole tried to be patient as all three began undoing the chain and twisting it back off his body. Each time the links brushed into his skin, it pinched, sending pain through him.

"Careful," he barked weakly when one particularly jagged piece scraped him.

"We're almost done," Robyn said, speaking to the others more than Cole. "The chain will have weakened him, but keep your eyes peeled for any tricks."

"Will do," Gretel assured her. "We're all ready for this job to be over with."

"People need to pay us," Hansel mused thoughtfully as the chain came off Cole's body. "And witches need to die. Let's finish this."

Cole staggered down off the tower to his knees, breathing hard. "Give me a minute," he gasped. "My blood won't be any good to you if it's been contaminated."

Cole could feel Hansel's gaze pierce him as the mortal man looked him over.

"You seem fine to me," said Hansel in a reproachful tone.

"He's fine," Robyn insisted, nudging Cole with her foot. "Get up, you. We haven't got all night to do this."

Cole stood, his knees not wanting to cooperate with him, but stubbornness and sheer willpower held him up.

"You need me to bleed over the circle?" he asked, looking over one shoulder. "That's all?"

"That's all," said Robyn, petting a content-looking Murphy again. "Get to it."

Cole stepped forward unsteadily until the tips of his toes were barely touching the circle's edge. "I need a knife of some kind," he told them. "Preferably one that isn't made of iron, though."

Two sets of footsteps approached. Cole turned halfway and saw Gretel holding out a plain steel knife while Robyn held him at gunpoint.

"Thanks," he said calmly, taking the knife from Gretel.

"I thought the sidhe didn't believe in thanking others," Gretel said questioningly while Cole turned back toward the circle again.

"They don't," he replied, "as a general rule, but I've been around humans for a while. Some things rub off."

"I think it's one of his little quirks," Robyn said quietly to her.

Cole ignored them both and sliced the knife down his wrist in a slightly diagonal motion, spilling his noble blood out over the pale white flesh meant to hold it in. Droplets fell over the crook of his forearm down onto the roof in the space reserved for magic. The circle thrummed the instant his sidhe blood touched it. The air just above the circle grew warm, and steam rose to meet the still-falling rain.

"That really ought to do it," Gretel mused.

"Good," her brother chimed in, coming forward at last. "Now could we perhaps cover the naked man so I don't gouge out my eyes?"

Cole snorted, then moved off to the left where he was out of the group's way, yet simultaneously more in Hansel's line of sight.

"Better?" he asked, knowing full well it wasn't.

The circle was hammering now, like the beat of a child's heart. The air smelled of flowers and the earth right after a fresh summer shower. Beneath that was the scent of fallen snow and ice in the wind. The combination of summer and winter together clung to the air as the pieces of the broken sword glowed.

"It appears to be working," Cole noted calmly.

"Yes," said Hansel, who glanced toward Cole, winced, and looked away quickly.

Gretel smiled, amused, as the pieces of the sword began to melt.

"Is it supposed to do that?" Robyn wondered. "I thought we were putting it back together, not melting it down."

"Shh," Gretel replied, though not in a particularly unkind way.

Cole watched as well, observing closely as the melting pieces slowly oozed over the surface of the roof toward one another. The rim of the circle began glowing as well, a bright gold and silver color that cast shadows across the rooftop.

"Step back," said Hansel suddenly, pulling on his sister's shoulder as he followed his own advice. "Next is the fire from heaven, and you know what that will mean."

The pieces had completely melted now. The others had moved back as far away from both the circle and the tower as possible without falling off the side of the building. Cole, however, remained where he was. The air had a faint hint of ozone to it now. Glancing up, Cole's eyes adjusted just in time to see lightning cut across the sky above the precinct building.

The clouds were illuminated for a brief second before a blade of white-hot electricity sliced cleanly down toward them. The others flinched. Cole was the only one who didn't look away, and as a second bolt jointed the first, he realized what the two were striking at.

Joss cried out as the beams lit up the top of the tower. "Joss!" Cole screamed.

He had assumed the magic of the circle would draw the lightning away from the most obvious target. Nature, it seemed, had other ideas.

"Joss!" he screamed again, shielding his eyes from the rain.

It took a moment, but Cole's eyes pierced through the light and rain. Joss had somehow gotten free. Part of his body was still tethered to the metal receiving tower, but his right arm had come loose. It almost looked as though Joss had torn free. The flesh covering it had peeled back, showing the obsidian and silver underneath. Joss was extending his hand, and in the blinding confusion, Cole thought he saw his lover grab the lightning bolt in his fingertips.

There was a flash of movement from Joss's arm, and the circle near Cole exploded. Electrical energy from the sky incinerated the space. Cole was thrown backward, and had to dig his feet into the tar of the roof and bury his fingers into the side to keep from going over. When he'd righted himself again, Cole thought he heard music. Something that sounded like familiar singing echoed off the raindrops.

Turning around, Cole felt his jaw drop as Claiomh Solais rose up out of the burned space that had been the magic circle.

The song was Faerie song, sung in a language Cole hadn't heard another soul use for over a mortal lifetime. The voices rang in his ears, causing something warm to swell inside his chest. His heartbeat thudded loudly in rhythm to the words. There was no need to think about what the words meant. He could feel their meaning as clearly as he could the blood rushing in his veins.

As though in a trance, Cole stepped forward.

The sword seemed to sense his presence and flashed in response. Cole was but a few steps away, his fingers extending outward to touch the blade's hilt, when something happened. A hand made of silver and light appeared. The fingers gripped Claiomh Solais, clutching it tightly for a moment, before whisking it away.

The heavens above roared with thunder as Joss's body tore free from the tower. Cole stepped back, half because of shock, but also to give his lover space to land. When Joss rose up from the crouch he'd fallen into, Cole saw that the eye patch Joss normally wore had burned away along with his shirt. The inspector's left eye was glowing like a tiny sun.

Claiomh Solais was clutched in his right hand.

Cole took a step or two forward, his whole body trembling now from disbelief. Joss seemed to register his approach and snagged Cole's forearm with his free hand once he was within reach. Cole felt himself being yanked forward, fell into Joss's arms, and met his lover's rough mouth. They crushed their lips together as the clouds praised their union with a clap of thunder.

When Joss finally pulled back, Cole turned toward where the others stood watching the scene unfold. Hansel was grimacing, while Robyn watched Hansel with an amused expression on her face. Gretel appeared just as bewildered by the turn of events as Cole.

Just barely, he heard Gretel speak. "Uh, was that supposed to happen?"

This seemed to shake Hansel out of his revulsion. "I don't think so," he answered his sister, backing up to the very edge of the roof. "We should probably get out of here."

Robyn shot him a glare. "You're leaving?"

"The sword's been reforged," Hansel said as his sister pulled out a metal hook with a rope attached to it. "Our job's officially done here."

Robyn didn't try to stop them. Cole reached for his guns, only to remember he didn't have them with him. Quickly, he turned to Joss, who remained perfectly still as the two vaulted over the side together.

"Joss," Cole said insistently.

"Next time," Joss replied, his voice sounding distant.

Cole watched as his boyfriend turned slowly toward him. "There's something else," he whispered. "Something else we're supposed to do right now."

Cole waited. "What?" he wondered impatiently when Joss didn't elaborate.

"I don't know," Joss replied, as if it were of no consequence. "I just know there's something else we need to be doing."

"There are probably several more of Naryssa's half-fey running around downstairs," Robyn suggested, calling out from the other side of the roof. "That could be it."

Cole frowned as he watched Robyn leap casually over the side of the building without a rope to aid her.

"What about her?" Cole asked.

Joss didn't answer, and Cole found himself staring down at the sword still clutched in his lover's grip.

"The sword will come to the aid of a great king," he recalled, remembering the words of Alice Tweedle's ghost. "Joss—"

Something buzzed, snapping both Cole and Joss out of their stupor. Joss dug into his pants pocket and pulled out his cell phone.

"I can't believe that thing still works," Cole said as Joss answered it.

Joss was only on the phone for a second. "He's right here," Cole watched him say before passing the phone over to him.

"It's your godson, David Bryne."

Cole took the phone, wondering what was wrong now. "Hello?" he said, just as a horrific crash resounded in the background.

"Cole!" David's panicked voice set every nerve ending in Cole's body on high alert. "I tried calling you on your phone, but you wouldn't answer. Cole, something's attacking my house!"

"We can be there in just a few minutes," Cole assured him, looking toward Joss for confirmation. Joss nodded once. "David, what's attacking you?"

"A house," it sounded like David said as another crash muddled his voice.

"What?" Cole wondered. "David, I couldn't hear—"

"It's a fucking house!" David's voice rang loud and clear now. "Cole, my home is being attacked by this big fucking house on chicken feet!"

Cole slowly lowered the phone from his ear and looked at Joss again. "You're not going to believe this one."

IT TOOK only a few minutes to gather everyone. Marcel, Rainette, Corhagen, and Staffelbach were already outside the building, searching through the crowd for Joss and Cole, when Joss rang their cell phones. Cole took the time to run downstairs, retrieve his weapons, and head to the locker room area for his pants. Once adequately covered, he rendezvoused with the other Section members outside. Joss hadn't bothered looking for a spare shirt. Everyone piled into a squad car and punched it.

There were sure to be questions when they returned, but this was an emergency. Plus, Cole already had a suspicion as to what, or rather who, was attacking David's castle estate at the moment.

David Bryne's home was on top of one of the larger buildings in the financial district. Several years ago, Cole's godson had paid to have a castle disassembled and shipped over to be his residence. The place would have been easy enough to find, but Rainette, who was at the wheel, didn't need a map. Before they got to the right building, sounds of a huge fight could be heard, coming from somewhere overhead.

"What the…?" Rainette blurted out, slamming on the brake.

Everyone winced in pain as the car skidded to a stop in the middle of the wet road. Marcel had taken the front seat, being that it was the only space big enough to hold him. He'd spent the whole drive with his feet turned sideways and curled up on the seat like a small human child might. The rest of them had crammed into the back as best they could. Staffelbach, being smaller, had rested on top of Cole, who was sandwiched between Joss and Corhagen. Despite the situation, he couldn't help but notice the symbolism.

"What is it?" Cole asked, having given up trying to see around Staffelbach.

Joss and Corhagen were already getting out of the car. "Here," Staffelbach said, climbing out of Cole's lap. "Sorry about that. See for yourself now."

Cole crawled out on Corhagen's side, since it was closer to David's building, and saw what Rainette meant. Something had dug huge, gaping holes into the side of the building. The shape reminded Cole of claw marks, except for an extra notch behind the horizontal row leading upward.

"It looks as though something scaled the side of the building," Marcel said.

"A house on chicken legs," said Joss. "I'm still having a hard time buying that, though."

"Baba Yaga," Rainette responded, looking over at Joss. "She was the inspiration for the crone witch to some people. Baba Yaga was said to have been a European witch figure who lived in a cottage that had big chicken feet, allowing it to move around on its own."

"And now Baba Yaga's house is attacking this guy," James said, clearly befuddled. "Any ideas on why?"

"Naryssa," Cole answered plainly. "Remember, one of her children mentioned a cabin after our battle at Bowling Green. They were going to the cabin. This must be what they were talking about."

Everyone's eyes widened. "Then," Staffelbach began, looking back up at the top of the skyscraper in the distance, "Naryssa is up there?"

"Let's move," Joss said, breaking into a run. "We have a chance to finish this. Let's not waste it by standing around in the rain."

No one argued. Once inside, they made a beeline for the elevator that would take them up to the top. Joss had been here before and was leading the charge with Claiomh Solais in his hand. Joss hadn't let go of the sword once since it was reforged.

Cole ignored that for the moment and looked around the large area. The place was empty as far as his senses could detect. David must have given the order for everyone to evacuate once the attack started.

The power inside the building was still working. Once everyone was crammed into the express elevator, Staffelbach punched for the top floor, closing the doors.

Music began playing as the chamber rose up the shaft.

"I always hated this song," Rainette grumbled, glaring up at the speaker above her that was spouting some sugar-coated candy-pop number.

"Would you have preferred 'Ride of the Valkyries' instead, my love?" Marcel joked, cracking his knuckles in anticipation.

"Anything is better than this," she declared.

"What about Queen's 'We Are the Champions'?" James offered as the elevator picked up speed.

Rainette grimaced in response. "I stand corrected."

The ride seemed to take forever. Finally, Cole felt them come to a stop, and the doors opened. Everyone filed out into a stairwell leading upward to the roof. Joss took point again, followed by Cole and the others. Before they got anywhere near the door, Cole could already hear the sounds of hell being unleashed.

Joss kicked the door open, knocking it off its hinges in the process. Outside, the grounds were lit up by flashes of lightning. Men were scattered everywhere, armed to the teeth, and dressed in some very familiar-looking uniforms. The armed men had positioned themselves around something big in the center of the courtyard. Even before the storm lit the area up again, Cole saw it for what it was.

It was a house on chicken legs.

Gigantic ones.

"Okay," Rainette said, coming up behind Cole. "Seeing it up close, that does look kind of silly."

The house resembled a storybook cottage, except for the enormous poultry feet holding it up. Everyone hung back as the soldiers opened fire on it. Doors swung open on both sides, allowing figures to spring forward through the darkness into the courtyard below. Cole recognized the iron-clawed scarecrows Naryssa had used months ago to trap them in a hospital. Alongside them were new creations, mobile suits of armor wielding heavy-looking axes.

"Ideas, commander?" Cole asked.

Joss gripped his sword and raised it high overhead. Lightning seemed to respond to the blade's presence, rolling across the cloudy sky. If Joss noticed, he gave no outward sign.

"Let the rent-a-cops handle Naryssa's goon squad," he ordered. "Take down the house. Then go for Naryssa."

"All in a day's work," Staffelbach said, clasping his palms together. "Let me at that armor."

"Be careful," Cole warned.

"Always," Joss said, saluting his lover with Claiomh Solais.

From there, the battle began. Cole spotted an easy solution almost immediately and charged forward into the fray under the line of gunfire aimed up at the moving cottage. Once in front of the Baba Yaga house, he drew out Aed Deigh's frost-covered blade and slammed it into the ground. Ice spread over the grass in front of the house's staggering feet, then moved forward toward them. The gunfire seemed to be doing a good enough job of keeping the cottage distracted, leaving Cole room to work.

Rainette saw what Cole was doing and summoned more falling water to the spot where the ice was forming.

"Pour it on," she told him, before calling out to the others. "Lure it this way. Maybe we can trip it up."

Something whizzed past the side of the cottage like an annoyed horsefly, but much larger. Cole tried to keep track and realized he was seeing Staffelbach. The officer had evidently snagged one of the armor suits and transmuted it into something of his own to play with.

Extensions rose out from his back, making a "thumping" noise like that of a helicopter.

"He's made a propeller pack for himself," Rainette noted, watching Staffelbach closely while Marcel charged into one of the cottage's legs like a linebacker. "How did he come up with that?"

"Ask him later," said Cole, turning his attention back to the task of freezing the ground.

Staffelbach buzzed out in front of the cottage's path, taunting it to come closer. Off in the distance, Cole spotted Joss plowing through the scarecrows and suits of armor. One quick slice cut two clean in half. The mystical blade shined against the darkness like it was made out of starlight. As another golem creation of Naryssa's fell, Cole thought he saw an apparition of some kind loom above his lover.

He almost called out, thinking it might be another one of Naryssa's tricks, but then the Baba Yaga house stepped onto the icy patch, which sent the chicken feet right out from under it.

The chicken feet kicked the air desperately as the house fell backward, crashing through the support structure of the roof and causing it to cave in slightly. The house sank halfway down, stopping before it could fall all the way through. Cracked ice and broken pieces of roof stuck upward as it fought in vain to free itself.

"Now what?" Rainette asked.

"Now Naryssa," Cole said. "She'll be out momentarily."

The front door of the cottage exploded upward as if in answer. "Or maybe sooner," Cole amended.

Naryssa flew up out of the cottage, supported by a whirling wind as the battle raged on around her. The other armed soldiers were keeping busy with what was left of the scarecrows and living armor. Naryssa didn't seem to notice any of them. Her eyes narrowed once she spotted Cole.

"You!" she screamed. "How could you? They were my children!"

Rainette shielded her face as wind whipped over it. "What's her problem?" she demanded. "She sent her kids to try and kill us in some fucked-up Trojan horse gambit."

"She's like that," Cole replied, yanking Aed Deigh out of the ground. "Don't try to reason with her. It'll just give you a headache."

"Thanks for the help."

The voice caught Cole off-guard. Turning around, he spotted David a few steps behind him, watching Naryssa closely.

Cole went very still as the chaos caused by Naryssa's Hand of Storms raged on. "It was you," he said, the truth dawning on him. "You were the one she was talking to."

David looked away from Naryssa momentarily to give Cole a very grave stare. "What else was I supposed to do?" he demanded, almost making it an accusation. "My mother is dying."

Cole was cut off from speaking as several whirlwinds surrounded the castle, tearing trees and shrubbery up out of the ground.

"We'll discuss this later, young man," he decided.

Cole started to walk toward Naryssa, but found himself distracted as Staffelbach careened down at them, completely out of control.

"Watch out!" he warned, just before a sharp wind cut sideways and threw him headlong into some nearby bushes that Naryssa's windstorm hadn't managed to uproot.

"See to him," Cole said as Marcel joined the party.

"Naryssa!"

Joss's voice sliced through the air like a hot knife. Cole looked down past the halfway sunken house to where his boyfriend was. Claiomh Solais was still glowing as bright as ever, casting a shadow for Joss that stretched out behind him.

"You," he declared, pointing the sword tip up at her. "And me."

Naryssa didn't seem to find him as impressive a figure as Cole or any of the others did. "Impudent little pretender," she hissed, raising both hands above her head. "I shall smite you until you are nothing but a black soot stain."

Naryssa Goodwynch loomed above them for a moment, her stringy hair whipping around her face by the wind she'd conjured. Her hands were gnarled and bore sharp claws. Cole knew from having seen it up close, though, that the skin covering those hands was impossibly soft. Naryssa was a creature of contradictions, a contrasting blend of youth and age.

Cole saw that Joss was holding the sword in his left hand. His right arm was glowing obsidian and silver, the flesh having peeled away again. Naryssa brought both hands down hard, calling lightning onto the spot where Joss stood. Cole ran out to meet him, knowing he would never get there in time, but Joss didn't move. The lightning struck the tip of the sword, sending sparks everywhere. The air popped and crackled as electricity jumped down to the ground around where Joss had planted his feet. The light from the sword was brilliant, illuminating the castle grounds like a football field.

The apparition Cole had seen moments before appeared again, standing just above and behind Joss. Now that he was closer, Cole thought the thing might have been guarding him. The creature was difficult to see, somehow, always shifting slightly whenever Cole's eyes locked onto it. Joss, meanwhile, brought Claiomh Solais down.

Joss held his right hand out toward Cole, who was still several steps away. Cole hesitated before walking up to take it. As he turned to stand at Joss's side, his eyes caught Corhagen across the gap, standing alongside the others. Their eyes met, but it was James who looked away first.

"Ready?" Joss asked, snapping Cole out of it.

Cole gave his lover's hand a squeeze. "Always," he said softly.

Both of Aed Deigh's blades sprung free as Cole brought his own weapon down to cross blades with the mystical sword of light.

Naryssa howled again, sending another lightning bolt their way. The bolt struck both weapons at the point where they crossed, sending more sparks everywhere. Keeping Joss's hand clutched tightly in his own, Cole pushed alongside his lover and sent the bolt back up through the air where Naryssa hovered.

Naryssa screamed as she dropped to the ground like a stone.

"Together?" Cole asked, letting go of Joss's hand.

"Together," Joss affirmed. "With me."

Cole did not see James as he rushed forward alongside Joss. The two surrounded Naryssa on either side as she stood.

"Naryssa Goodwynch," Joss declared. "I am placing you under arrest for the kidnapping of numerous children and the murders of their parents. You have the right to remain silent. Anything—"

"Silence, you fool," she snarled, swiping her very long nails toward him. "I have no time for your petty mortal guidelines."

"—you say will be used against you in a court of law," Joss resumed.

"My children are dead," she howled, still attacking. "You have no idea what that is like. My children are gone forever, and it's all his fault!"

Cole commended Joss for doing things by the book, but Naryssa wasn't about to listen. Holding his hand out cautiously, he summoned a burst of black flame out of his right hand. The effort caused the bones in his whole right arm to ache, revealing just how much magic he'd burned off earlier. Still, there was enough to handle this.

"Naryssa," Cole called out, as Joss prepared to counterattack.

The half-night-hag whirled around in a rage as Cole coiled the black fire around the firebrand of Aed Deigh.

"What?" she screamed.

Cole leveled his eyes at her before pointing the blade's tip at her heart. "Shut up," he said coldly, hurling the fire at her.

The blast from the blade's tip shot straight into Naryssa's chest, sticking out from there like a fiery arrow. Naryssa looked down at where the black fire was spreading, wearing a stunned look, like a mortal who'd just been shot.

Joss raised Claiomh Solais over his head behind her. "For all those you've murdered," he declared, his voice sounding different, more ominous. "Die, Naryssa."

The apparition behind Joss appeared and swung at the same time he did. A blade made of pure energy, but the size of a man's body, cut through Naryssa at the same time Joss did. The double blow split her clean open. Black fire exploded up out of her body as she screamed. The wind died at once, fading into the night like a forgotten dream. Both Cole and Joss leaped back out of the way as what remained of Naryssa's body was incinerated.

Neither of them moved as they watched the body burn together.

"It's over," Cole heard Joss say to himself. "It's finally over."

In answer, Cole turned to where David was standing with the others. James was there as well, taking point with Marcel. The two were guarding David, which meant Rainette had already told them.

"Almost," he told Joss sadly. "There's still one more detail to wrap up."

THE armed, uniformed soldiers were moving out. Helicopters had arrived to carry them back wherever they'd come from. None of them paid the house any attention, like it was just another day at the office for them.

"Those were the same guys that went with us into that paracosm last month," Rainette said, pointing after one as he walked past. "I mean, not the same group of people, but they have the same uniforms."

"They were soldiers under the employment of the Hermetic Order of the Golden Dawn," Marcel said, closely watching them leave. "Why did they come here?"

"Good question," Joss said. "I think we'd all like to have that answered."

David didn't flinch away from Joss's stare. "I would be happy to answer any questions the NYPD has about the incident," he said calmly. "So long as my lawyer can be present."

"Robyn is on your roster of employees," Cole said, keeping David in his sights. "She said that the person who hired her had given instructions for me not to be harmed."

No one spoke, but all eyes were on David. "I think you're gonna need that lawyer," Joss advised him. "Better give him a call now."

David's calm facade didn't falter. "I'll do that," he said. "In the meantime, I think all of you know the way out."

The comment stung Cole, yet he refused to give his godson the satisfaction of seeing just how much. Once David was out of earshot, Cole turned to face Corhagen and Joss, both of whom were looking at him expectantly.

"I didn't want to believe it," he said softly. "Maybe I should have been around him more when he was a child."

"You're not his father," Joss said reassuringly.

"He said something about his mom," Rainette started, before being cut off by Marcel's gentle hand on her shoulder.

"David's mother has Alzheimer's disease," Cole explained. "He must have thought the sword would cure her, or at least lead to a cure. I've heard he'd gotten desperate, but I didn't want to believe it was this bad."

"What do we do now?"

The question came from James, who seemed almost hopeful when Cole looked toward him. James's face fell as Cole looked from him to Joss, who smiled sadly at the grief on Cole's face.

"I really wish I knew," was all Cole had to say.

J.L. O'FAOLAIN was born the youngest, with four older sisters, in the backwoods of the Deep South. Those that have braved getting to know him have attributed this to being the root of his growing insanity. A teased bibliophile in his youth, O'Faolain spent his years prior to getting published as a cook, laundry man, delivery boy, grease monkey, and retail stocker. He has a plethora of skills and abilities, none of which would work well on a job application. In his spare time, O'Faolain enjoys weightlifting, philosophy, deconstruction, reading, writing, porn, and the Internet in general. Aside from becoming a successfully published author, he would very much like to pilot a giant robot while Two-Mix's "Rhythm Emotion" is playing in the background. Either that, or travel the world in a dirigible. In short, the general consensus by all, including himself, is that he is a mighty strange fellow.

Section 13 from J.L. O'FAOLAIN

http://www.dreamspinnerpress.com

Also from J.L. O'FAOLAIN

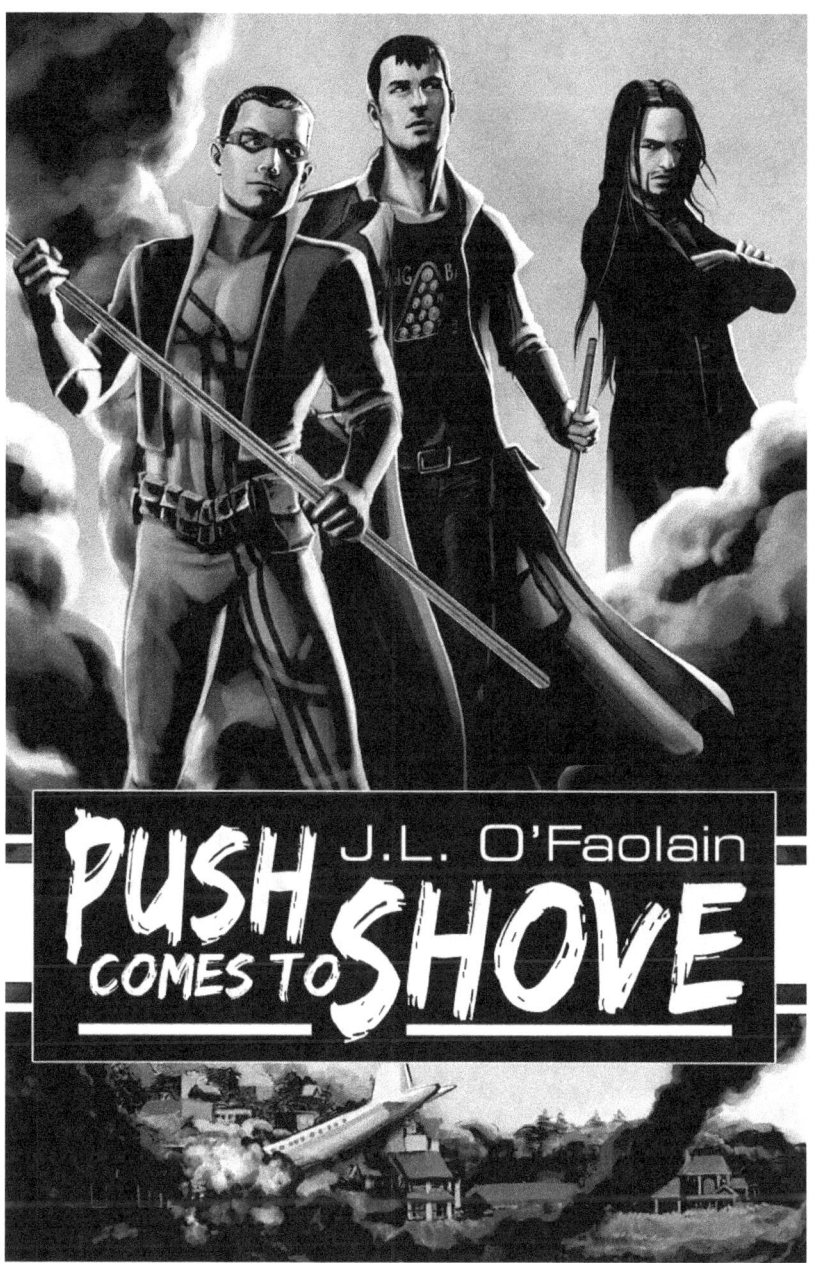

http://www.dreamspinnerpress.com

Also from J.L. O'FAOLAIN

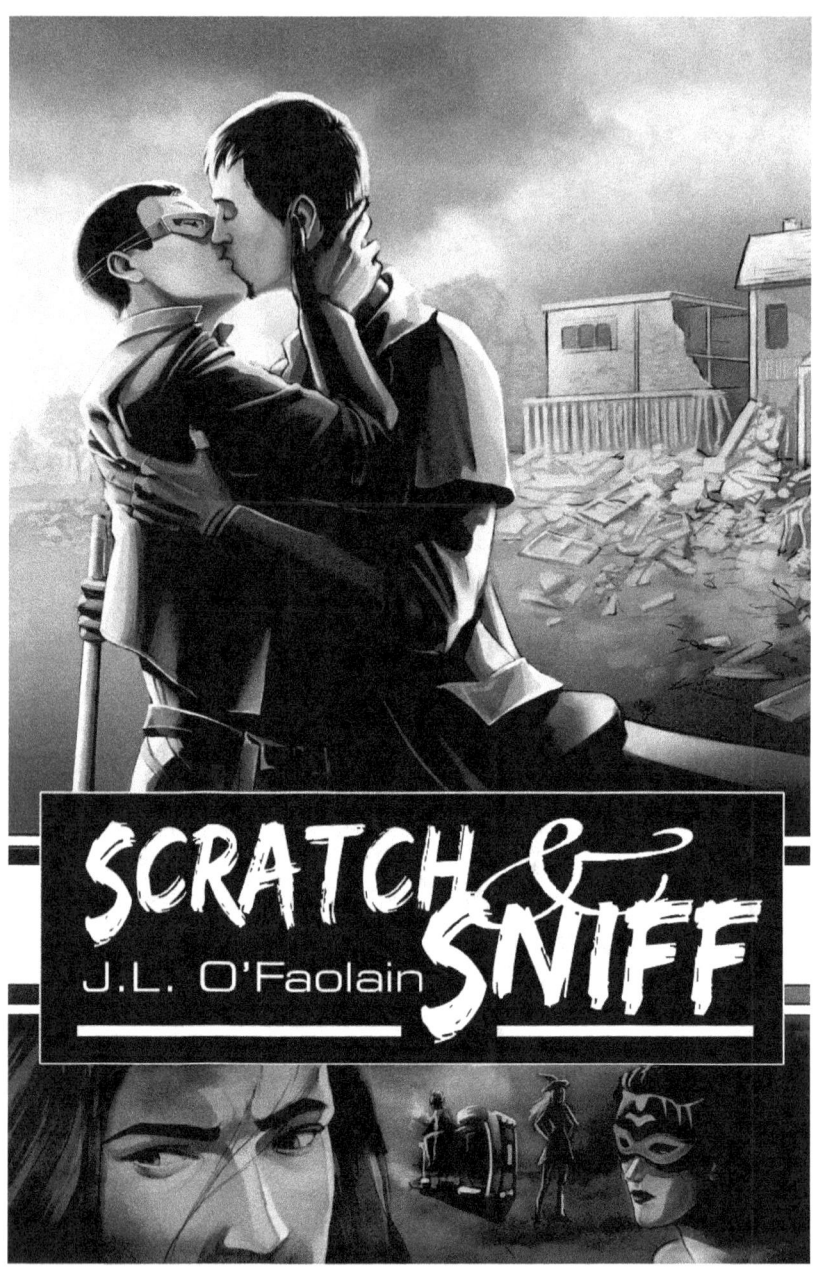

http://www.dreamspinnerpress.com

Also from DREAMSPINNER PRESS

http://www.dreamspinnerpress.com